A village is a hive of glass, w
served.

*Charles Spurgeon*

Sleepy quaint English villages are often admired and rightly so as most can be found in areas of outstanding natural beauty, but in some cases, they can hide a more sinister side, a side that is often better left well alone.

In 1932, the National Socialist German Workers' Party is gathering momentum and far reaching plans are being prepared by the fanatical members. Their success is threatened by the potential future involvement of the United States of America and Great Britain, and something must be put in place to prevent this.

In a seemingly unrelated event in England two years later, a farmer dies and the local village has something to hide. Frustrated by the lack of progress from the nearby Clitheroe Police and the tight-lipped villagers of Pendlewick who refuse to co-operate, the suspicious authorities decide to bring in a renowned Scottish detective to resolve the situation.

On further investigation, he reveals a plot with massive implications for World peace and a village not quite as quaint as it seems.

Thanks for the
support Linda!
Regds.

1

# *Prologue*

## February 1934

## Pendlewick, East Lancashire

The bitterly cold wind howled and whistled across the bleak fields and the tiny village of Pendlewick looked miserable in its Winter attire.

The driving rain and ominous dark clouds made it difficult to see clearly as Alf Davenport stood in the doorway of the *Sun Inn* looking out at the honey coloured stone houses on the opposite side of the lane.

He absentmindedly rubbed at his stiff leg. He was in two minds whether to stay or go home as he listened to the laughter and the cheerful plinking of the piano filtering out from the tap room into the early evening air. Looking up at the brooding sky he knew where he would rather go, and he considered going back in for another pint of ale but shook his head. His sister would have made his evening meal by now and he didn`t want to give her any excuses by him being late.

After looking briefly up and down the lane, he pulled up his jacket collar and leant into the storm as he made his way home from his local pub. The *Hen Harrier* ale had been good, better than good actually and helped dull the pain in his leg a little. It had never fully healed after being crushed up against the cow shed wall by a high-spirited heifer. He winced slightly as he kneaded his fingertips into his leg and finally confident that he had got the blood flowing a little, he braced himself against both the weather and the five pints of beer he had downed over the last couple of hours.

He was very familiar with the route home, after all, he had used it every evening for as long as he could remember, and although he knew every pothole and blemish in the surface of *Twitter Lane*, he was still cautious and kept his gaze downwards as he scanned for possible trip hazards. The sky suddenly lit up as sheet lightning flashed across the dark sky and peering ahead, he thought he saw a figure in dark clothes stood by the wooden gate further up the lane. As the low rumble of thunder rolled across the land, he scanned the lane ahead, but the figure was gone the next time lightning lit up the scene. He shrugged his shoulders, *must `ave bin a trick o` t` light*, he thought and approaching the five-bar gate that led up the back lane to his farm, he was thankful that the headlights of an approaching car lit the way, allowing him to see clearly and steady himself for the climb.

Gripping the slippery top bar of the wooden gate and placing his left foot on the bottom rung, he grunted at the pain in his leg as he stepped up and then cocked his right leg over the top. As he did so, another clap of thunder boomed overhead, and he felt a thump and an intense burning sensation in his back and chest. Tumbling over the gate he crashed into a muddy puddle below. Laying there for a moment, he thought he heard footsteps squelching in the mud beside him before gently closing his eyes as the dirty cold rainwater ran into his open mouth.

# Chapter 1.

## September 1939 – Pendlewick, East Lancashire

The brass clock on the wall chimed twelve as he stood at the window of the Smithy Cottage and as the rain began to fall, he contemplated the view towards Pendlewick Hall that sat across the narrow brook and the lane beyond that ran through the tiny village.

He smiled to himself. Everything had gone well, exceptionally well in fact. Yes there had been a few unfortunate occurrences, but nothing he hadn`t been able to deal with and he was proud of his achievements although the wait was now becoming interminable.

He continued to gaze thoughtfully out of the window and slowly tamping the fresh tobacco down in the end of his pipe, he clenched his teeth around the stem and walked over to the open log fire and bending down, he took out a small burning twig and offered the red ember to his burnished wood pipe bowl. A couple of deep draws soon had the pipe lit and a cloud of aromatic smoke filled the small room and swirled around the old oak beams in the ceiling.

He settled down in his leather armchair by the fire and reached for the *Daily Mail* newspaper on the small table beside him. It was Friday, and looking at the front-page headline, it wasn`t going to be a very good day.

### SUBMARINE SINKS LINER, 160 AMERICANS ABOARD

The British Liner the *Athenia* with fourteen hundred people on board had been torpedoed in the North Atlantic, four hundred miles off the Hebridean coast.

"We agreed no American targets," he whispered to himself as he shook his head slowly. But the plan could still work, it had to.

As he turned the page of his newspaper, he heard a knock at the door. He wasn`t expecting anyone so folding the newspaper neatly, he rose and after placing it on his chair, he walked over to a large oak cabinet and removed his pistol from the top drawer. Briefly checking the loaded chamber indicator, he held the gun cautiously in the inside of his jacket and opened the door a fraction of an inch.

"Yes, how can I help you?"

# Chapter 2.

## February 1934– Pendlewick, East Lancashire

Frederick Black slowly focused across the field and counted two police cars and four policemen as he peered through his field binoculars, the rain bouncing off the brim of his hat. *Quite a turnout,* he thought to himself.

As the rain lashed down, even the ever-present crows and magpies appeared to be staying away from the muddy ploughed meadows before him.

The body had been found at first light by the deceased`s sister, but it didn't matter, the farmer had enough enemies in the village and surrounding area to keep the police occupied for years and placing the binoculars back into the worn leather case, he gently sniffed and dabbed at his nose with a white handkerchief. *All will be well*, he thought to himself reassuringly, the people they needed to influence were paid handsomely and would remain silent.

Striding over to the black Morris Minor parked on the lane, he opened the door and slid into the dark brown leather seat and put the binocular case and his hat precisely in the centre of the seat beside him. He contemplated the scene he had just witnessed then he pressed the starter button and the engine chugged into life. Moving the ignition leaver slightly, he drove off down the narrow lane back to their cottage.

They had discussed at length the use of motor cars to travel around and would it bring unnecessary attention? Where there was a motor car involved, wealth was also mentioned in whispered conversations amongst locals, especially in these times of economic turmoil. Eventually, it was agreed that a modest motor car would be selected, and they would both share. They couldn`t afford the attention, not after the incidents in London and Manchester.

# Chapter 3.

## August 1932 - Two years earlier - Salford, Manchester, England

The two men sat either side of a small wooden table in the tiny apartment on the third floor of the tenement building by the docks. Manfred Swartz reached over and tamped out his cigarette then immediately lit another one.

"You now see the dangers we face Arnold," he said tilting his head back and blowing smoke into the air. Turning once more to the dark-haired Englishman before him, "we must find a location where our work is uninterrupted. London was far too dangerous, and it was only a matter of time before the British Security Service discovered us."

Manfred was of Swiss descent, being born in *Lausanne* but his father was German. His grandparents had emigrated to the North of England in the late 1890s and after the early death of his mother they had taken young Manfred under their wing whilst his father went about trying to rebuild the failing family business in Switzerland.

When he was sixteen, Manfred learned of his Father`s untimely death from *Tuberculosis* and determined to show the world that he wasn`t a failure, he opened a small-scale scrap steel collection and delivery service for the Manchester factories from the back of a rickety wooden wheelbarrow.

By the time he was twenty-four, he had built himself quite a reputation.

Since the end of the Great War, there was still resentment from the British population to anyone with a German sounding name, so Manfred referred to himself as Frederick Black in any dealings he made. He was enormously proud when had been able to secure the tenancy to a small warehouse in Salford, but his destiny changed in 1922 when he had been introduced by a close friend to an engineer from the ship builders *Ropner Ship Building & Repair Company* in Stockton near Middlesbrough.

Manfred had dressed to impress in his best plaid suit, *Homburg* hat and his polished *Cap Toe Oxfords.* Catching the early train from Manchester across the Pennines and up to Stockton, he had made his way through the throngs of grubby workmen to a smokey public house called the *Three Tuns* down by the River Tees. Taking a quick glance at the name plate above the entrance door, he walked in and ignoring the looks from the dock workers stood around who immediately stopped talking to each other, he walked up to the polished wooden bar. "Good evening Mister Nugent. I would like a *gill* of your best brown ale if you please."

The Landlord`s eyes narrowed under his thick bushy eyebrows as he looked at the new-comer suspiciously and putting down the empty pint glass he had held in his hand, he folded his arms defensively across his chest, "wi don`t surve strange`az in `ere, `specially ones that `az no biznus knowin` ma name like."

Manfred removed his hat and placed it on the bar, "then if that is the case, don`t put your name on the brass plate over the entrance to your public house. Now pour me a drink there`s a good chap."

The Landlord physically relaxed and smiled. "Ah, haal reet, see what ya-meen," and he began to pull a *gill* of dark brown ale from a hand pump on the bar. "There ya go, that al`be thruppence man."

Manfred placed a small brass coin on the bar then lifted the frothing glass of beer and took a sip. After wiping the pale foam from his top lip with the back of his hand he placed the glass back onto the bar. "I am here to see a Mister William Blacklock, could you please point him out to me."

The landlord pointed his finger towards the corner of the pub. "Sat ova at yon table, reet in tha cornaa," and raising his voice, "hey Billy, gotta visitaa fo`ya man."

Seeing nothing more of any interest, the men around the bar commenced chatting amongst themselves and Manfred nodded a thank you to the Landlord and picking up his glass and hat, he strode towards the man sat in the corner where he coughed gently into his hand to gain his attention and announce his arrival.

"Good evening, Mister Blacklock, my name is Frederick Black."

A man in his early forties looked up, revealing a thick dark moustache. "Sit yourself down lad, you are early."

Manfred pulled out a chair and sat down at the black circular wrought iron table opposite Blacklock. "My sincere apologies Sir, I wanted to make sure I wasn`t late as I know your time is important."

The man looked him in the eye and nodded thoughtfully. "Good, I like a punctual person," and he reached into the inside of his jacket pocket.

Manfred had removed his hat placing it on his knees and now sat bolt upright with his hands resting on the top of it as the older man began lighting up his burnished pipe. His friend's words echoed through his mind, *I`ve set up the meeting with a Mister William Blacklock for you Manfred, now it`s up to you.*

Blacklock held a match to the strands of tobacco and took a draw on his pipe and satisfied it was lit, he shook the match out and dropped it on the stone flag floor. Manfred could see the tobacco glow red in the dull light of the pub as the man took another draw on his pipe. "I have heard good things about you Mister Swartz, that is your real name isn`t it?"

Manfred`s face couldn`t hide the shock and the man smiled. "Don`t worry yourself young man, we are all friends here. Now, what brings a foreigner to these parts, not enough business in your own country?"

Manfred cleared his throat, "Ahem, well I have lived in England since I was a child Mister Blacklock, so whilst I agree my original name is of foreign origin, I like to think of myself as an Englishman and I am known as Frederick Black."

The man smiled and blew another cloud of smoke from his pipe. "You certainly speak well for a.....foreigner."

Manfred pulled up his chair as close as he could to the table. "Thank you Sir, and I believe you have some new business we may be able to agree upon."

"I have indeed, both professionally and personal, I hope."

Manfred frowned, "I don`t understand Mister Blacklock."

"Your friend explained your background to me....and the unfortunate loss of your mother. Tell me, what are your views of the current situation?"

"The current situation? I am at a loss Mister Blacklock."

"Well for instance, what are your thoughts on the declaration of Egyptian Independence back in February or how about France now accepting raw materials as repayment from Germany instead of actual currency?"

Manfred laughed nervously, "I am afraid you have caught me on the hop a little Sir. I thought I had come here to discu....."

Blacklock waved his hand in the air. "We have young man, we have, but first I want to know who I am dealing with," and gesturing with his hand to the Landlord, "Edward, two pints here if you please."

Three hours later and after in-depth and sometimes heated discussions around politics and world affairs, the two men teetered out of the *Three Tuns* and onto the street where Manfred hiccupped loudly and immediately put his hand to his mouth, "my apologies Sir."

Blacklock, slapped him on the back and laughed. "No need to apologise Manfr...Freddy. I think the night has been well spent and I look forward to dealing with you more in the future. I take it you have arranged lodgings?"

Manfred was beginning to feel very woozy and put his hand to his mouth, afraid that he was about to be sick. Calming himself with some deep breaths he carefully removed his pocket watch from his waistcoat and rotating the face towards the streetlamp he attempted to focus, "huh, yes, there is a small guest house nearby and I believe a Missus Bentley awaited my arrival.... about two hours ago."

Blacklock slapped him on the back again, which almost made Manfred retch. "She`ll be fine man, off you go, and I will be in contact with you, very soon."

Initially, business dealings with the shipyard were insignificant due to a combination of a severely depressed British economy and a lower requirement for new ships, but to his surprise, Manfred`s company *LauSteel*, began to receive significant orders through his contact Mister Blacklock with payment up front and ridiculously long delivery expectations, even though the ship building company Blacklock had seemingly worked for had gone into liquidation.

Initially a little suspicious, Manfred had been reassured that the orders were for special customers in other countries and as the ability to make money anywhere was extremely difficult, he trusted Blacklock and accepted the situation. The payments also allowed Manfred to build his network under the guise of these legitimate business deals and he at last felt he was doing something to make his mother and father proud. But he had never forgot how his mother had died and who was to blame, and this fact had been put to full use by William Blacklock who over the coming months, gradually introduced him into the fledgling spy network of the National Socialist German Workers' Party.

In 1926, Blacklock had requested Manfred to accompany him on a trip to Germany in order to meet his *Gauleiter*. "This is a great honour for you Manfred and you should treat it as such. We are on the brink of greatness and he will fully explain our plans for the future, plans that we must execute efficiently at all times."

They had met in a small innocuous looking second floor office in *Berlin* and on entering, a gaunt man with a slight overbite and greased back dark hair greeted them warmly, although Manfred noticed the warmth failed to reach the man`s eyes.

He turned his back on them and looked out of the window with his hands behind his back and gazed into the distance.

"Gentleman, we have prepared and are ready for greatness," Blacklock looked at Manfred and nodded knowingly. "Our grand plans are many and detailed and the German people`s dreams will come true." He turned slowly and faced the two men and his dark eyes bored into Manfred`s. "Are you ready to be part of our plans Manfred Swartz?"

Manfred froze momentarily under the man`s manic stare, but after a surreptitious nudge from Blacklock, he immediately stood up straight, "yes sir, I am!"

The man looked at him and narrowed his eyes slightly, his unreadable face a calm mask.... then he clapped his hands together and clicked his heels. "Excellent! I take it Mister Blacklock has already informed you of my name?"

Manfred swallowed nervously, "no Sir he has not."

The man held out his hand, "I am the regional leader of our party and my name is Goebbels, Paul Joseph Goebbels, but you can refer to me as Joseph."

Arnold Forsythe nodded thoughtfully and gently stroked

his tiny black moustache with his thumb and forefinger. "And here in Salford?"

Manfred again stubbed out his cigarette and moved in closer to the Englishman. "For the moment, yes we are safe, but our informers indicate we and others are being watched and it is only a matter of time before they decide this building is a reliable target. We need somewhere we can operate anonymously, somewhere out of the way yet close enough for us to maintain communications and supplies, but we must move swiftly."

The Englishman nodded again. "It is no secret that the Security Service are trying to intercept and read my post. The fact that the Home Secretary is reluctant to sign Home Office Warrants to enable them to do so will sooner or later stop as my influence in Parliament only goes so far. At the moment I am still seen as little threat, so I am able to go about my business with impunity."

He stood and calmly walked over to the window of the tenement block building and casually pulled the white net curtain to one side by a fraction of an inch. Peering out carefully, he saw below them a man nonchalantly leaning against a lamp post reading a newspaper.

Turning back to Manfred. "I have an acquaintance by the name of Lady Snook. Has a small estate with a cottage near Pendlewick," at which, Manfred raised a questioning eyebrow. "It's a small village in the countryside, just North of here," Forsythe continued, "beautiful place by all accounts and very quiet and she no longer has need of it. Old money you see but very few left of the family and has too many things going on in London I am told. It is located far enough from prying eyes yet close enough to give you what you need. Give my men until the end of the week to arrange the logistics and make sure she.... fully understands the importance of our plan."

Manfred nodded, "all right, and we will make sure there is no evidence left in this building, but please be aware, we have no time at all."

The Englishman stuck his chest out proudly and faced Manfred then raised his right arm in salute.

Manfred raised his own arm and stamping his foot, he returned the gesture.

# Chapter 4.

## February 1934 – Pendlewick, East Lancashire

The two black Wolsey Hornet police cars dipped and bobbed as they splashed through the puddles and pulled up by the side of the lane. The cars rocked slightly as two policemen got out of one car and one out of the other. The three constables then stood to attention and eventually the passenger door opened and an over-weight man in his mid-forties pulled himself out of the car.

Having joined the police straight after the Great War ended, Sergeant George Entwistle was a seasoned police officer of fifteen years and as such, he thought he knew far more than the others at the Clitheroe Police Station, including Sergeant Pilkington, and played on this fact.

He smoothed down his waterproof cape and donned his *county style* helmet and with a sniff of approval to himself, he walked over to the assembled constables who stood miserably in line as the seemingly never-ending downpour ran off their helmets and down their capes, dripping mournfully onto the ground below.

"Well, how do you three look then?" He said rhetorically walking up and down with his hands behind his back as though he was an army sergeant major inspecting a parade. He shook his head disapprovingly at the three young constables then barked. "Right then, we have an unfortunate case here that needs looking into. Constable Sanson, get yourself over to Mister Davenport`s body and let`s hear what you have to say for yourself!"

Sanson, a recent recruit, was a wiry but strong young man who had a slight stutter when he became nervous. He quickly turned and reaching up to hold his helmet in place, he scurried over to the prostrate figure led in the gateway and crouched down to examine the body, his boots squelching in the sodden mud.

"Well Sanson, what`s your deduction lad?"

The constable stood up and turned to his sergeant wiping his hands on his dark blue cape as he did so. "L...looks a bad business S...Sarge. L...looks to me like `e `ad too much to drink and must `ave fallen off this `ere gate an` drowned in that there big puddle of w...water."

Entwistle turned and harrumphed to the other two constables who nervously stood observing their hapless colleague examine the rain sodden body.

"S....so you s...say he drowned d.... did he young man?" He enquired mockingly. "You sure about that are you?"

Sanson began to blush profusely. "W...well, when I say drowned Sarge, I mean.... `e c.... could `ave drowned?"

"Excellent deduction. So did he drown before or after he shot himself?"

The young constable's eyes opened wide. "S...shot himself Sarge!"

"Aye shot himself lad. See the gun by his hand and the tear in the back of his jacket where the bullet came out? Now gather round the lot of you and you might learn something!"

The three constables shuffled into place in front of the Sergeant. "Right, which of you has seen a dead body before?"

They all looked at each other eager for one or the other to speak first.

"I seen a dead `orse once, in yon top five-acre field," offered Constable Jones. "It `ad all swollen up, must `ave been there a while an` it...."

"I meant a human dead body you bloody fool!" Thundered the Sergeant irritably.

Jones immediately looked at the ground and started scuffing his feet about on the spot. Donald Jones was a handsome, well-built young man and a bit of a favourite with the local girls, but he readily admitted that his mind did tend to wander at times. Having been with the Clitheroe police for over three years he liked to think he was a pretty decent policeman, but he was often capable of losing focus.

"I`ve seen a dead body before Sarge, it was my Grandmas."

"Well, well, we have an expert amongst us," and he theatrically gestured towards the body with his arm. "Constable Warburton, would you like to give us the benefit of your extensive knowledge on this subject by examining the victim and give us your thoughts on what happened here?"

James Warburton was in his early twenties and three years earlier, had represented the county in the sprinting and jumping events at the all-England athletics competition held in Worcestershire. His father ran one of the pubs in the nearby village of Pendlewick and he was a firm believer in law and order and on his twenty first birthday, James had been accepted into the police.

Warburton pulled back his shoulders and walked over but stopped short of the gate being careful not to disturb the water filled footprints in the mud by the now opened gate and he bent down at the knees. He carefully examined the footprints in the mud tracing the outline and depth with his finger and glancing at the shape of the boots on the dead body, and by way of comparison, he isolated the victim`s footprints from the many others in the immediate area. He looked inquisitively at the body and how it lay in the mud and every so often, he wiped the rainwater from his face as it dripped from his nose. Satisfied, he stood then sidled along by the left-hand gate post and approached the body from the field side and once again bent down, then looked up to Sergeant Entwistle.

"Am I all right to turn the body over Sarge?"

Entwistle spread his hands and shrugged. "Not sure why you would want to but if you think it will help you....."

Warburton gripped the saturated body by the jacket collar and trouser belt and with a grunt, heaved him over onto his back. The body splashed muddy water onto the constable`s uniform and face and the Sergeant smiled smugly to himself.

"And?"

The constable ignored the request and he leant over and began to examine the large wound in the man`s chest and then he gazed thoughtfully at the pistol laying partly submerged by the victim`s outstretched hand and the partly healed scratches to his face.

"I don`t think he shot himself Sarge. Looking at the footprints in the mud and the soles of his boots, he walked over and climbed the gate. I can tell because I could feel this footprint is deeper on this one as his weight shifted on to it when he climbed up. Then someone shot him in the back, and he fell into the muddy water and died from the wound. He didn`t drown or commit suicide....in my opinion Sarge."

Entwistle guffawed. "And there you have it boys. That`s why I`m a Sergeant and you three are mere constables. Shot in the back my arse, this has suicide written all over it. Now get back in the cars....." but out of the corner of his eye he spotted Constable Jones walking to the corpse. "Jones what the hell are you doing?"

"Sorry Sarge, I just never seen a body afore, at least not a dead one."

"Get away from there you fool and all of you, get yourselves to the station. I`ll wait here for the undertaker to take the body away."

"But Sarge....," protested Warburton.

"I said, back to the station, now!" Roared Entwistle.

The three constables walked forlornly back to the police car and after removing their capes and shaking off as much rainwater as they could, they got inside. Jones, who sat in the back of the police car, lent forward between the two front seats. "Ya shouldn't rile t`Sarge like that Jimmy, ya know we`ll pay fer it now."

Warburton looked in the small rear-view mirror. "No way on God`s Earth was that a suicide Jonesy. Even you can see that can`t yeh?"

Constable Jones shrugged his shoulders. "Well I never `eard nothin `bout folk solvin` crimes be lookin` at footprints before and t`Sarge does know a lot more about policin` things than us Jimmy, maybe ya just didn't see it reet," and he sighed, leant back in the seat and after wiping the condensation from the glass, looked out of the side window at Entwistle who was now standing with his hands on his hips glaring at the three of them. "Best get a move on Jimmy, Sarge looks like `e`s bout t`explode."

James quickly started the car and with a sharp salute towards the Sergeant, he drove off down *Twitter Lane* back towards the Police Station.

Sergeant Entwistle looked on as the black police car drove away. *Hope that lad`s not going to be trouble,…. for his own sake*, he thought. Entwistle was a man well past his prime but who still expected more than he was actually capable of. This had led to a bitterness creeping in, a bitterness that led to his head being easily turned and walking back towards the body of Alf Davenport he looked down at the soaking wet ashen grey face staring back at him and he shook his head slowly. "We survived the trenches and now look at you. Shouldn't have got greedy Alfie."

# Chapter 5.

## August 1932 - Security Service Headquarters, Broadway Buildings 54, London

The polished wood panelled office walls gleamed as Rear-Admiral Herbert Simpson stared across his desk at the man stood before him.

"Well, is everything in place Johnson?"

Cedric Johnson was a small bespectacled and balding man in his late forties. A somewhat successful career in the Royal Navy had meant he had crossed paths several times with his boss, and he had been persuaded to join the Security Service. Johnson hadn`t even taken offence when Simpson had declared, *you can be useful man, someone plain and boring like you blends in with the crowd.*

"Yes Sir, we move on Wednesday, at dawn."

"Excellent Johnson, we will catch them red-handed and string them up by their buster browns. If it`s not the blasted Communists causing a row it`s the blasted Irish!"

Johnson looked at his boss whose face was going redder by the minute and he knew from experience that it was just best to leave Simpson be until he had got his daily rant over and done with.

The Rear-Admiral stood and walked towards the window and looked out towards the nearby St James`s Park underground station. "You see Johnson, slippery characters the lot of them and I`ll not have them doing their dirty work on my watch, no Sir, indeed I won`t." He spun around sharply and walked to his desk and sat down, "which of them is it this time then?"

"We believe it to be the Communists Sir. Our contact *Johann De Graff* informed *Foley* in Berlin of the plot and eventually this led us to a building in Salford, Manchester. We have had it under surveillance for the last few weeks."

"Well what are you waiting for then Johnson, go and get them man! Can`t have these rascals upsetting the apple cart can we," and he proceeded to scribble something on a large notepad.

"No Sir we can`t," and Johnson stood motionless awaiting further instructions. Nothing came and in the end he relented. "Will that be all Sir?"

Simpson looked up from his desk. "What? Yes, off you go man," and waving him away he started to rifle through some papers oblivious to the other man`s presence.

Johnson closed the door softly behind him and looked up to the ceiling and sighed just as a friendly voice interrupted his thoughts.

"Going off on one of your exciting missions again are you Mister Johnson."

He smiled amiably at Simpson`s secretary. "Looks like it Doreen, no rest for the wicked eh."

"What`s it to be this time then?" She said playfully twirling her finger through her hair.

Johnson smiled at the attention from the voluptuous red head sat behind her polished desk. He was married but his wife took no interest in him. After leaving the Navy, she believed he now worked in a bank and frequently had to go on business so hardly saw him at all, and when she did, she nagged at him about all the things she had to do around the house.

"Well Doreen, you know how it is, top secret and all that," and he walked over and stood by her side idly toying with some of the papers on her desk.

"Ah Cedric, but you know I don`t mention anything I hear," she whispered as she slid her hand up the inside of his trouser leg. "Life can get a bit boring for a girl these days so any sort of stories I get to hear, well, they cheer me up no end."

Johnson wriggled on the spot, uncomfortable with his uncontrolled arousal. "When do you think me and you can get together, you know for real?" He asked in hope.

"Well, as I keep saying, once my Eric is out the way, maybe you can pop round."

"That would be very nice Doreen," he panted.

"Best get yourself on the other side of my desk Cedric, just in case anyone comes into the room."

Johnson coughed into his hand, "huh, yes quite right Doreen, quite right," and he walked back around to the front of her desk.

"So have you got any juicy stories to tell me then?"

Johnson smiled and looked both ways to make sure he couldn`t be overheard. Leaning down onto her desk he whispered, "can you keep a secret?"

"That`s hurtful Cedric, you know I can!"

"Well there are these chaps in Salford, that is a part of Manchester you know. Nasty and very dangerous, about seven of them, maybe more." Johnson thought a bit of theatrical license would add to the story and impress Doreen even more.

She took a deep breath and held her palm to her open mouth in shock. "Seven of them Cedric!"

Johnson stood and puffed out his tiny pigeon chest proudly. "Maybe even ten! We are going to catch them at dawn on Wednesday, the lot of them. It will be very dangerous, I mean I am probably risking my life on this mission as I will be leading the men into the building, from the front you know!"

Doreen tilted her head to one side and averted her gaze coyly. "Oh Cedric, you are so brave."

"Oh it`s nothing for a chap like me my dear, all in a day`s work. Now when do you think I can visit you?"

"Oh, I will let you know as soon as I can Cedric, honest I will."

Johnson smiled, then it slid from his face. "I will be off then, see you when I get back." He gave an exaggerated sigh, "if I get back at all that is."

She gave him a little wave goodbye. "Close the door on your way out please Cedric."

Johnson turned and strode to the door doing his level best to show what a man of action he was. He opened it briskly and then closed it behind him, his heart pounding with excitement.

As the ornate wooden door closed with a soft click, Doreen stood and walked over towards Simpson's office and placed her ear to his door. She could hear his muffled voice issuing another tirade of bad language at someone. Satisfied, she quickly walked back and sat at her desk, lifted the phone receiver and spun the dial with her finger.

"Operator, I would like Salford four three one please."

Cedric Johnson had travelled from London to Manchester Victoria station by train. Sitting in the plush first-class carriage due to a highly impressive bit of negotiation with the station master, he had stared out of the window at the countryside rushing passed him and found it difficult to concentrate on the mission ahead. His mind constantly wandered to Doreen`s face and to her... he shook his head as though to clear his mind. *Come on Johnson*, he chided himself, *get a grip man.*

After arriving at Manchester Victoria, he put his hat on and stepped off the train and took a deep breath just as the locomotive on the opposite platform whistled and with a huge plume of choking black smoke pulled away on its way to Glasgow. He coughed irritably and covered his mouth with his white handkerchief, then hustled off through the crowds towards the awaiting taxis.

"The *Weaste Hotel*, Salford please my good man and step lively," and he jumped unasked into the back of the taxi-cab.

"That`ll cost ya an extra shilling Sir, out my area it is."

"Nonsense my man. I travel this route all the time, now away with you, I have important business to attend to."

Realising his ruse would not work on a seasoned traveller, the taxi driver tutted to himself, stuck his right arm out of the taxi window and after waiting for a slow horse drawn wagon carrying bales of cotton to pass by, he joined the busy early evening traffic.

Knowing he had to be up before dawn, Johnson had a restless night at the hotel, and on rising and walking down into the bar area he was met by a not too pleased looking Landlord who stood behind the bar wiping the inside of a glass with an off-white cloth. The Landlord glared at him with undisguised anger at having to get up at such an hour. An anger that refused to subside when he then saw Johnson picking at his breakfast that he had just been served.

Having paid his bill for the stay and his breakfast, he bid the Landlord farewell who instantly locked the front door behind him without a word.

After meeting up at the end of *Ordsall Lane* near to the Salford Docks, he walked along the curved pavement at the end of the building and peered down the lane as the distant horns of departing and arriving boats echoed through the dawn mist.

"How is it looking Guv?" Asked one of the operatives.

Johnson moved back and turned to address his men. "Are we sure they are still in there Smith, I mean, I can`t see much activity in the street at all, never mind a hoard of Communists."

"Huh, it *is* dawn Guv," advised Smith cautiously. Johnson didn`t have a good reputation with any of the operatives. He was viewed as a small man trying to have a big man`s reputation and it carried no weight with the hardened service men who knew he had only got where he was because of his links with Simpson. It also irked the men who risked their lives on the street when Johnson had shown on numerous occasions that if there was the slightest sniff of danger, he kept himself well out of the way.

"I know it`s dawn damn you," snapped Johnson. "I mean, my trained eye sees no obvious danger."

"Ah alright, sorry, we ready to go in then Guv?"

"It would have been better to wait for the Police constable to arrive, but yes, prepare yourselves. I will stay here and make sure.... none of them slip by you."

"Right you are Guv," and Smith rolled his eyes at the others and beckoned them to follow him towards the building.

Johnson held up his hand. "How.... how many are we expecting of these vagabonds?"

Smith stopped and sighed then turned back towards his boss. "I would say no more than two or three Guv, should be an easy one.... unless they are carrying shooters."

"Then it`s even more critical that I stay here and observe the situation. You never know when we may need to call for more back up. Signal me when it`s saf.... secure to come in," and he ducked back and stood in the doorway of the end dwelling.

*Ordsall Lane* was more of a large street and the tenement buildings on either side housed many families, mainly dock workers. The pavements at the end curved in a semi-circle on either side of the straight cobbled thoroughfare and Smith and the two others edged their way along the curve until they reached the straight and the end block number twenty-nine. The building was huge and standing four stories high, the lane was anything but.

A short stocky man in faded checked trousers, white shirt and braces and a *newsboy cap* tapped Smith on the shoulder. "Is `e fer real Smithy?"

Smith knew exactly what Stan meant but it was imperative that he kept discipline within his team and slapping his cudgel into the palm of his hand, "keep it buttoned Stan and get ready fer some trouble."

Smith looked up at the chimney stacks that lined the roof of the four-floor building and did a mental calculation to see if he could see if there was any smoke coming from their target indicating if the residents were still asleep or not, but he sniffed and shook his head. *Inconclusive*, he thought. He wasn`t an educated man in the strict sense as he had been unable to get much schooling due to supporting his sick mother and alcoholic father, but he was as bright as a button and had made money and been able to put food on the family`s table by *acquiring* things from the nearby docks. His special skills were soon spotted and after being used by the local police as an informer for a bit of extra money, his full potential was soon realised, and he was taken on by the Security Services.

Smith scanned for anything that may help them and reduce any risks and he smiled when he saw that right outside the building was a lamp post with an angular glass top. He was close enough to be able to look at the reflection of the target building in the lamp, but again inconclusive. The glass wasn`t as clean as he hoped, and the reflection was too distorted to be of any use. *Nice idea though*, he thought.

He turned to the others and whispered, "okay boys, let`s go fer it."

They slowly made their way through the gap in the iron railings and tried the front door which opened easily, and then climbed the filthy stairway up two flights until they reached the third floor. The building smelt of stale people and old cabbage. Smith pointed and mouthed to the others which room it was. The crooked wooden floorboards of the corridor creaked as they walked towards the end room, so the three operatives tried to keep as close to the wall as possible to reduce the movement of the floor so as not to alert the occupants.

All three men stood cudgels in hand and took a deep breath, then Smith stepped back a pace and with a grunt he kicked the door in with a loud crash sending splintered wood imploding into the room.

"Security Service!" Screamed Smith as they charged in waving their weapons before them.

# Chapter 6.

## August 1932 – Pendlewick, East Lancashire

As the two men approached the cottage door they stopped and looked around at their new base. The entrance was slightly covered by a clematis growing around the door frame but was easily pushed aside and Manfred slid the key into the lock and opened the sage green wooden door.

The sunlight flooding in through the small front windows highlighted tiny dust particles in the air, the faint smell of an unknown perfume indicating the recent occupant.

He placed his battered suitcase down on the floor and looked around at the room. A large fireplace commanded the room, complete with a pile of roughly cut logs in a wicker basket in the hearth. A modest amount of furniture was dotted around and walking through into the dining room then the kitchen he nodded his approval.

"This will suffice Frank," he said turning to the man following him in carrying two more cases.

Frank heaved the two leather bags onto the dining table. "I hope the move does not delay us Frederick."

"Do not worry, we are on schedule." Manfred looked at him and smiled, "and I believe you will also be able to sample the beer in the local public house that is located just a short walk from this very premises."

Both men looked at each other knowingly. The public houses were the cornerstone of life for British men and this is where gossip and influence could be obtained easily after a couple of pints of the local ale. And they were confident that the *Sun Inn* in Pendlewick would be no different.

The cottage was on the outskirts of the small village in the Ribble Valley in Lancashire and looked perfect. Based at the bottom of Waddington Fell, it was close enough for the local amenities but far enough away that he and his colleagues could go about their business in secret, or at least without raising any suspicions.

It had been unfortunate that they had to leave the building near Salford docks. It was an ideal location especially for supplies and equipment from the many ships that visited every day from around the world and this generated masses of people which made blending in simple and their dubious activities raised no concerns.

What had been fortunate though was the phone call Manfred had received on the Monday morning. They had less than two days to collect their equipment and sanitise the room of anything incriminating. It had been a bit of a rush, but they had done it, and by Tuesday evening, the taxi carried both him and his accomplice to the train station at Victoria where they found the train they required did not leave until the morning.

"All is well Frank. We will stay the evening at a local hostelry and leave in the morning."

Frank was an Austrian but had studied at Cambridge University and spoke perfect English. For safety reasons he had also changed his name and was referred to as Frank Barlow rather than his real name Franz Bakalow, and he blended into the British way of life perfectly.

The next morning at seven-thirty on the dot, the two of them waited for their breakfast in the bar area of the public house where they had stayed for the night.

"There you go gents, two cups of tea and two breakfasts," and the Landlord placed two mismatching china cups by their plates of eggs and bacon.

"Excellent, thank you and apologies for the early start, but we have to catch a train."

The Landlord snorted, "Early start Sir! This is nothin`, some little fool `ad me up at the crack of dawn this morning then all `e did was pick at `is breakfast then left. Wouldn`t `ave minded if `e `ad ate it all up!"

# Chapter 7.

## August 1932 - Ordsall Lane, Salford, Manchester

The echo from the door smashing into the room subsided and Stan turned one way then the other as the three men scanned the empty room. "What do yeh think Smithy?"

"Check the back rooms Stan and be careful, looks like they scarpered but yeh never know. Billy, go and get the Guv."

A tall wolf-like man with a shaggy brown beard and straggly hair nodded and loped back out through the broken doorway onto the landing.

Moments later, Stan returned and shook his head. "Nothin` doin`, looks like we missed `em."

Smith moved over and started to idly run his finger along the wooden bureau and on seeing the telephone he raised an eyebrow, *must `ave some money to `ave `ad one o`these*, he thought to himself. He walked cautiously over to the two armchairs that stood either side of a walnut gramophone. Lifting the lid he tilted his head slightly and looking at the turntable, he slowly rotated the record so the writing on the label faced him and he smiled. *Some Day I will find you*, by Noel Coward. *Now there`s a co-incidence*, he thought but he was interrupted by Johnson walking into the room and he quickly closed the lid and turned to face the new arrival.

"Right what have we got then?" He said looking at the shattered door hanging off its hinges and then at the room were the operatives had assembled.

"Looks like we were right about this place Guv. Blokes `ad a telephone an` everythin` but they`ve left an` not in too much of a `urry `cus it looks a bit too tidy fer my likin` fer `em to `ave rushed out. Maybe they were warned or somethin`."

Johnson sniffed and started to remove his black leather gloves as he walked towards the window. "I`ll be the judge of that Smith," and he pulled the net curtain to the side and looked down onto the street below and the lamp post. "Have you searched the place yet?" He asked still peering out of the window.

"No Guv, we was waitin` fer you before we touched or did anythin`," lied Smith and he winked at Stan and Billy who smirked to each other. "We just made sure it were saf.... secure fer ya to come in Guv."

"Quite right too gentlemen," and releasing the net curtain, he turned away from the window. "Very well, this needs a trained eye if we are to find out what has gone on here," and he pulled out a small ornate brass magnifying glass from his coat pocket. Raising it to his mouth he breathed onto the glass and then polished it with his handkerchief then nodded. "Perfect," and he walked over and started to examine the broken door.

Smith tried to hide a smile. "Uh, that was us Guv..... in case ya were wonderin`."

Johnson glared at him angrily. "I know that damn you! I was merely checking for clues. You see, there are always clues. You just need to be a clever chap like me to find them." He suddenly raised his nose in the air. "Smell that? A fresh smell of cigarettes. I`ll be damned if they didn't leave only minutes before we arrived."

The three other men glanced at each other and Smith rolled his eyes again in dismay. "Right ya are Guv, do ya need us to `elp in any way?"

"No, watch and learn, watch and learn."

He walked over to the polished wooden bureau and pulled at the top drawer which slid out easily. Finding nothing he opened the drawer below and fished around inside with his fingers.

"Hah, you see! I knew it! A clue," and pulling out a worn train timetable he rotated it in his fingers as he needlessly squinted at it through his magnifier, "and circled in pencil is.... Glasgow! Not as clever as they thought they were. Looks like the blasted Communists have made their escape to Scotland then."

Smith cleared his throat gently. "Ahem, Sir. Could it be they left it there on purpose to make it look like they `ad scarpered up to Scotland......I mean, just a suggestion Guv."

Johnson pushed his glasses further up the bridge of his nose with his index finger and looked up slowly from the battered paper timetable, his face full of contempt. "You are not paid to suggest things Smith, you are paid to....." and he pointed to the doorway," smash doors in for me so I can carry out my important investigations."

Smith looked down at the floor. "Righto Guv, just thought I would throw in me two-penneth that`s all."

Johnson harrumphed and pointed his finger at the three men. "Know your place Smith, and that goes for you two as well." He carefully folded the train timetable and placed it into his coat pocket. "Now let me see what other incriminating evidence I can find," and he walked straight at the three men knowing full well, they would give way and allow him to pass. As he was about to enter the back room he paused. "Are you sure you have checked there are none of these ruffians still in the building?"

Stan removed his cloth cap and pushed it under his arm and stood to attention mockingly. "It`s all clear Guv, checked the rooms me-self, not two minutes ago."

"Excellent," nodded Johnson making his way into the back room. Moments later he reappeared. "Just as I thought, the cowards have left and in a hurry by the looks of it."

Smith raised his hand slightly and opened his mouth to say something then thought otherwise.

"Right, I have all the evidence I need, and your job is done here so off you go. I will return to London and file my report. I will leave it to Baxter and his men to organise catching these ner-do-wells in Glasgow." Johnson stared at the three men before him. "Well, what are you waiting for? Go, the lot of you!"

As they were about to leave, a young constable came bustling in through the wrecked doorway.

"Beggin` your pardon Sir," he said breathlessly, "got caught up wi` some mischief down be t`docks," and he saluted and removing his helmet, he tucked it under his arm.

"You missed the show young man, missed the show.

When they heard Cedric Johnson was onto them, they left in a mighty hurry, but worry not, I have all the evidence required," and pushing past the young constable he walked out into the corridor and was gone.

The constable blushed slightly and began to put his helmet back. "Sorry `bout that lads it`s just I got all suspicus, susp...I got all worried somethin` was about to `appen down be t`docks. Saw some folks lookin` to steal from t`goods yards so `ad to wait fer some back up."

Smith patted the young constable on the back as he walked past him. "Don`t worry lad, ya missed nothin`, but I`m pretty sure our Governor won`t report it like that."

# August 1932 - Oxford Street – London

Even though the evening sun still shone brightly, the bedroom was dim behind the hastily drawn curtains.

"Oh Cedric, Cedric, you are so good," panted Doreen as she rolled her eyes then glanced at the clock on her bedroom wall.

Now drenched in sweat, he rolled off her and reached for the bedside table to put his glasses on. What little hair he had was now pointing in all directions. "Am I Doreen, really?"

"Oh yes Cedric the best," and as he lit up a cigarette beside her she looked at his pale skinny body and little pot belly and had to try with all her will not to grimace.

Johnson had made his way across *Oxford Street* and had narrowly missed being hit by a red *General* bus as he concentrated on finding her address and had held his hand up in apology when the driver shook his fist at him as the bus trundled off down the street. Johnson`s heart pounded with the exertion from not only walking through the crowds in the muggy early evening Summer air, but also the thought of finally going to Doreen`s house and… he shook his head. He dare not hope for what he hoped he was in for. *Look for the vertical DOLCIS sign on the corner of the building, my apartment is on the top floor, number six it is*, she had told him. And find it he had and had been welcomed with open arms by Doreen.

Brought up in the slums of the East End of London and having watched her mother and father toil all their lives for nothing, she was determined not to end up like them.

All she had ever wanted was to live the high life and having worked hard to improve her lot and eventually lose her East End accent she now had no loyalties to anyone other than herself. As she awaited his arrival, she put on her lipstick and looked at herself in the hallway mirror of her apartment and smiled. Although she despised all men, she would do anything to achieve her goal.

He blew a jet of smoke into the air then leant over to his left and put his cigarette out in the ash tray by the bed and started to move over to her again.

"Oh you've worn me out Cedric Johnson, let`s just have a cuddle instead shall we."

Johnson tried to hide his disappointment and laid back on the bed where she snuggled up beside him. He glanced around the bedroom and remembering the exquisite décor in the hallway and living area, "this is a beautiful apartment Doreen, it must have cost a small fortune!"

Doreen shrugged, "my Grandmother died last year and left me quite a bit of money in her will, or so the solicitor said," and she put her finger to her mouth as if in thought. "I mean I don`t know much about complicated things like that Cedric."

He slowly nodded at her and the condescending look on his face irritated Doreen immediately but with years of experience, she was able to easily mask her feelings.

"She must have been very wealthy my dear."

Doreen suddenly leant up on her elbow excitedly. "Anyway, enough about my boring house Cedric, how did it go today with the Rear Admiral?"

Johnson pulled himself into a sitting position and after

fluffing the pillows to support himself he lit another cigarette and casually blew a cloud of smoke into the air.

"Well, it`s probably all boring stuff to you my dear, espionage and danger and all that."

"Oh please Cedric, tell me all about it. You know I don`t say a word to nobody," and slipping her hand under the bed covers, "I find it really exciting when you tell me how brave you have been Cedric."

He nearly bit the end off his cigarette as he felt her hand slide slowly down over his stomach.

"Well, I am only telling you this because I know it won`t pass your lips to anyone else."

"Oh I promise Cedric, I promise it won`t," she replied huskily.

"Well, I marched into Simpson`s office and blow me if he doesn`t stand right up and shake me by the hand,…. vigorously he did. Excellent work Johnson he announces, you are the talk of the bureau."

Doreen leant over and whispered in his ear, "and did you do brave things Cedric?"

"Brave things my dear! Well maybe brave to some but not to me, just part of the job you see. I led my men up the staircase then told them to stand back. Didn't want any of them getting hurt you see. Rather me than them what?"

"Then what happened Cedric?" And she slowly slid her hand further down.

Johnson`s eyes widened slightly in reaction to Doreen`s antics. "Well I ran at the door and kicked it in, smashed it right off the hinges then charged in without a care for my own safety.

She feigned shock. "Oh, and were there many of the horrible men inside?"

"Fortunately for them, no, they had all just left minutes before, but they had left clues behind you see."

Doreen ran her fingers expertly up and down, "and where do you think they went then Cedric, I mean they must have had to run a long way to get away from a man like you?"

Johnson gently closed his eyes and swallowed then opened them again and whispered, "this must not be told to anyone, understand?"

"Oh you can trust me Cedric, you know that," she replied glancing away with a hurt look on her face.

He put a comforting arm around her shoulder. "I know I can my dear, I know I can. They went to Glasgow,... that's in Scotland you know. They ran as far as they could when they knew Cedric Johnson was on their tails," and stubbing out his cigarette, he rolled over towards her again and started clumsily kissing the nape of her neck.

"Oh Cedric, Cedric, you are so good......"

# Chapter 8.

## August 1932 – Pendlewick, East Lancashire

The Summer heat in the cottage was becoming oppressive and as Manfred heaved the sash window up to allow some air in, Frank sat at the dining table studiously working on some reports whilst every so often, dabbing his sweating forehead with a handkerchief. As Manfred leant towards the open window in a vain attempt to locate a cooling breeze, the shiny black *Bakelite* telephone in the front room rang.

They both looked at each other but neither of them spoke. Manfred walked over and paused before the ringing phone. He flexed his fingers slightly then he lifted the receiver from its cradle and raised it to his mouth and ear. "Hello, Clitheroe one seven."

A shrill voice on the other end announced that she had a call for him.

"Thank you, you may connect the person please," Manfred said softly. There was a succession of small clicks then Frank looked on as his colleague listened intently.

"Yes this is Mister Black." He paused and turned slightly towards the wall then replied, "there are eight crows in the field today." Frank could hear a faint voice on the line but was unable to hear clearly what they were saying.

Manfred turned his back to Frank, "I see, yes…., perfect, thank you, an excellent piece of work," and he replaced the receiver back into its cradle.

Frank raised an eyebrow questioningly. "Any problems?"

Manfred smiled. "No problems, they think we are in Glasgow. We proceed as planned."

The following week, Frank made his first visit to the *Sun Inn*. He had already visited the small Post Office in the cobbled square and had met the Post Mistress, a Missus Porter, who had introduced herself and welcomed him to the village of Pendlewick.

"You workin` round here then Mister….?"

He held out his hand, "Frank Barlow, pleased to meet you Missus Porter, and yes, I am doing some survey work in the area,…. for the Government, agricultural surveys and things. See if we can`t improve output and all that."

"Ooh sounds interestin`. Is it another like that there *Stocks Reservoir* that opened last month? Prince George `imself came up to open it, all official like."

Frank made to answer. "No, we are…." but the post mistress didn`t give him the chance.

"Me and our Mavis watched it from the `ill. It was a shame for all them folk who lost their `omes and farms and suchlike, but it was nice `avin` all them workmen bobbin` in every now and then," and she winked at him mischievously. "Gone now though, `undreds there were and spent a pretty penny in Pendlewick on more than one occasion they did. You be `ere long then? I mean not that I`m being nosey or nothin`, I just like to know who people are and what they get up to?"

Frank gave an ironic smile, "it`s no issue at all Missus Porter...." But she interrupted him again.

"Oh do please call me Dorothy, everyone`s on first name terms in Pendlewick."

"Very well.... Dorothy, I`ll probably be here for a couple of years actually, we are checking a few things out here and there, soil samples through the seasons and all that sort of thing."

Realising that the new arrival wasn`t as exciting as she had hoped, she picked up some cream envelopes and started to stack them together. "Well you `ave a good day Frank," and she busied herself at the shelf behind her.

He left the Post Office and as he walked down by the metal railings alongside the brook towards the *Sun Inn* he heard a squeal of laughter and a young boy hurtled past him on an old bicycle, his legs peddling like fury.

"It`ll go like a racer now I`ve oiled that chain o`yours," shouted a smiling man dressed in dark blue overalls holding a long spouted red oil can.

Frank waved a greeting to the man standing outside the small service station tucked in beside the row of cottages leading up to West Bradford Road. The man waved back then wiping his hands on an old rag, he walked back into the garage shaking his head, a huge grin on his face.

Frank also smiled as he watched the boy disappear down the lane. *I wonder if his mother will be as happy when the lad turns up with old engine oil sprayed up the back of his trousers.*

The *Sun Inn* was quite an imposing stone building with a small farm attached to the side and dominated the centre of Pendlewick. There was even a rumour it was haunted by the ghost of a cow!

A small brook ran all the way through the village and three narrow lanes met in the middle forming a Y shape. Frank stood outside the Inn and looked around with his hands on his hips. Directly in front was the Old Smithy Cottage with its Willow tree gently dipping it`s branches into the flowing brook and behind that, Saint Augustine`s church with its sixteenth century tower casting a shadow over the nearby lane. To the right was a row of honey coloured terraced houses, *recently built by the look of them* mused Frank and overhead, Swallows wheeled and dived on the warm Summer thermals.

He took a slow deep breath of the sultry air, the scent wafting from the flowers that surrounded the Stone Cenotaph filling his lungs making him feel alive. *I`m going to enjoy living here for a while*, thought Frank.

A man in brown britches, a worn tweed jacket and brown leather boots walked up to him. "Come on lad, out the way, gotta a bloke `ere that needs a pint," and he pushed past him and walked into the pub.

"Think I will join you Sir", replied Frank eagerly and catching the door as it swung to, he followed the man into the Inn.

A fug of smokey air hung over the bar area and stood behind was a portly gentleman with his grey hair greased back over his forehead. He wore a white apron round his waist and was leant on the end of the bar talking to three customers. On seeing the man enter the bar closely followed by Frank, he said something to the customers then stood up and wiped his hands briskly on a cloth tucked into his apron.

"Now then Alf, how`s it goin fella?"

The man in the old tweed jacket smiled, "as well as can be expected, all considerin`, but nothin` that a pint won`t sort out."

The landlord chuckled, "a pint of the usual eh, and what can I get your friend here?"

The man turned around and looked at Frank, who in turn also spun around not realising he was the subject of the comment.

"Not met `im afore to be `onest, what`s yer name fella?"

"Huh, Frank, Frank Barlow, pleased to meet you. I`m new to the area."

"Well welcome to Pendlewick, let me get ya a drink. Two pints of best please Andrew, and one for ye`self."

The landlord pulled two pints of best bitter and put the two foaming glasses on to the bar. "There you go gents, that`ll be one and six Alf."

"Ah, I`ll pay at weekend eh," and turning to Frank, "so what brings yeh to these parts then?"

"Work, I`m doing some survey work for the Government, up on Waddington Fell," he replied pointing his thumb over his left shoulder.

The landlord leant over the bar, "now then, sounds like somethin` my son there would be interested in," and he pointed at a young man reading the newspaper at a small round table near the window.

"What do you say James, gentleman here`s doin` surveys. That`s like investigations. You could help him what with you bein` an important policeman and all that."

The young man sighed and shook the newspaper as he turned the next page irritably. Frank looked warily at the young man and tried not to show any reaction but the landlord hadn`t finished.

"Just in case you weren`t aware Frank, this `ere son of mine is the famous Constable James Warburton of the Clitheroe Police. He catches vicious criminals daily he does, or so my missus says. Caught some real bad criminals steelin` clothes pegs t`other day." The customers in the bar roared with laughter and Constable Warburton shimmied in his chair, embarrassed at the unwanted attention.

Frank walked over and introduced himself. "Hello Constable Warburton, it`s a pleasure to meet you, my name is Frank Barlow."

The young man stood and looking him straight in the eye he shook him by the hand," pleased to meet you as well Mister Barlow."

The Austrian was an excellent judge of character and he immediately sensed danger from the young man before him. "I am sure our paths will cross at some point Constable Warburton."

The policeman maintained his grip on the other man`s hand, "I am sure they will Mister Barlow," and after a few tense moments, he released his hand and they parted ways.

# Chapter 9.

## February 1934 – Pendlewick, East Lancashire

The air was cold, damp and misty and two jet black crows squawked angrily at each other as they sat on top of an old tilted gravestone nearby. A fitting scenario for the funeral of Alfred Davenport some would say.

It was a small family affair. A few of the regulars stood outside the *Sun Inn* and had bowed their heads and removed their flat caps as the horse drawn hearse made its way to Saint Augustine`s Church yard but other than that, few people were saddened by the demise of the local farmer.

Constable James Warburton stood beside the grave with Davenport`s sister Sheila and after a curt nod from Father Swarbrick, the grave digger began to shovel the loose soil onto the coffin.

Sheila Davenport was dressed all in black with a matching veil that came down to the end of her pointed nose. She took one last glance at the coffin of her brother then turned on her heel and walked away seemingly unaffected by the whole proceedings.

Warburton also turned and started to follow her then thought better of it and instead walked out of the church yard and after climbing onto his bicycle and tucking the bottoms of his trouser legs into his socks, he set off to ride back to the Station in Clitheroe, but stopped immediately. "Bugger!" He exclaimed as he looked down at his flat rear tyre. James leant the bicycle against the church wall and bent down and after examining the whole tyre he concentrated on the valve. Eventually he stood up and slowly looked around the emptying graveyard. No puncture. Someone had opened the valve and let the air out.

"Where've you been lad?" Demanded an angry Sergeant Entwistle later that morning as he stood arms folded behind the station countertop.

"Sorry Sarge, I`ve been to pay my respect to the Davenport family, it was the funeral this morning and got a puncture on the way back."

"A likely tale and how many times do I need to tell you Warburton, the Davenport case has nothing to do with you so if I catch you harassing that poor family again, I will put you on record, understand!"

Warburton looked down at the floor, "yes Sarge, understood."

"You look me in the eye boy when you say you understand me!" Snarled Entwistle.

The young constable raised his head and looked the Sergeant straight in the eyes and after pausing for what seemed an age, "I said understood Sarge."

Entwistle stared back intensely and eventually he sighed. "Don't you go causing me any bother lad. You have the makings of a good policeman. Don`t go spoiling it by poking your nose in where it don`t belong. Now you stick to catching them fowl-stealers and poachers, there`s a good lad."

But constable Warburton couldn`t let it go. He had impeccable morals and when he knew something wasn't right, he had to deal with it, or it ate at him like a gnawing animal.

Having finished his shift, he quickly checked his tyres were inflated and jumped onto his bicycle and set off for Top Field Farm on the outskirts of Pendlewick. He panted slightly as he cycled up the steep track to the farmhouse and on reaching the top of the hill, he leant his bicycle against the wall by the outer gate to the farmyard. Confirming that the two snarling sheep dogs were secured to their kennels, he opened the gate and glancing nervously at the two dogs as they rushed out to meet him straining at their clinking lengths of chain he skirted the outside perimeter of the yard. Walking towards the farmhouse and after smoothing down his uniform and removing his helmet, he tapped smartly on the door.

He could hear a woman`s muffled voice cursing and another dog barking from within the house and he instinctively stepped back a couple of feet from the door.

The door creaked opened and a woman, bending down and holding a brown and white collie by the scruff of its neck, looked up at him. Before he could say a word she cursed, "oh bugger off, I`m sick o`you lot comin` round `ere!"

Warburton quickly gathered his thoughts. "I`m sorry Miss Davenport, I just want to ask a few questions about your brother that`s all."

"Questions! I answered all them questions that Sergeant

Entwistle asked me an` I`m not about to answer no more, now bugger off and leave me in peace!" And she slammed the door in his face.

Warburton grimaced as the door shook in the door frame. *That could `ave gone a bit better*, he thought. He motioned to knock on the door again, but he could hear Sheila Davenport screaming obscenities in the house, so he immediately put his clenched fist back by his side and walked towards his bicycle.

The ride back was more downhill than up, and he revelled in the wind rushing past him as he free wheeled down the sloping lane, the barking of the farm dogs disappearing in the distance. *If the Sarge `ad asked lots of questions, then they would be on file at the station,* and he set off back to Clitheroe.

It was getting late and opening the police station front door with his key he stepped inside and closed it behind him. "Evening Sergeant Pilkington," and he nodded to the night Sergeant who was completing some paperwork by lamplight at the wooden counter.

"Evenin` lad, what brings you back `ere?"

"Oh, I just want to check on the paperwork I did on the two poachers we caught in West Bradford last week. I want to make sure it`s all correct for tomorrow's hearing," and he lifted the hinged counter and walked through to the back of the station.

"It was a good job you lads did on them two nasty bastards. You don`t do things by `alf do you young Warburton," smiled the night Sergeant.

"I try not to Sarge," he replied over his shoulder as he ran his finger along the filing cabinets looking for the letter D.

Pulling open the drawer revealed neat rows of cardboard folders, all beginning with the letter D.

Warburton started at the front of the cabinet and tracing an imaginary line backwards he silently mouthed the file names to himself, *Dacre, Dalton, Darcey, Davenport...*

Pulling out the Davenport file, he placed it on the desk and after dragging a chair over he sat down, opened the file and began to read the contents, slowly absorbing the report.

*Name: Davenport, Alfred Albert*

*DOB: 10$^{TH}$ September 1890*

*Address: Top Field Farm, Pendlewick*

*Died: 18$^{th}$ February 1934, Twitter Lane, Pendlewick, confirmed cause, suicide by single gunshot to the chest.*

*Case Closed.*

Sergeant William Entwistle - 18$^{th}$ February 1934.

*That`s all! No details, nothin`* and James stared at the file incredulously. *Where were the notes on the questions he `ad asked Sheila Davenport and `ow could `e close the case on the very day `e `ad died?* He pondered his own questions just as he heard the front door open.

"Evenin` Bill, well I never known it as busy as it is tonight, what with young Warburton and now you."

James momentarily froze on hearing the conversation then quickly grabbed the Davenport file and thrust it back into the open drawer. Closing it as quietly as possible he slid down to the other end and opened the W cabinet just as Sergeant Entwistle walked in.

The Sergeant stared at him with undisguised anger, his

hands firmly pressed to his hips. "And what the hell are you doing in here at this time of night Warburton?"

The young constable whose fingers had already grasped the West Bradford file, held it up, "I... I came to double check my report Sarge, for tomorrow, make sure it's all correct."

Entwistle paused, then walked over and snatched the file out of his hand. Turning his back on Warburton he opened the file and sifted through the documents then slowly turned again and handed it back gazing at him suspiciously. "Right you are then lad," and folding his arms across his chest, "might be as well I just hang around then, in case you need to ask a more experienced policeman any questions."

Warburton swallowed nervously and then nodded, "thank you Sergeant Entwistle, that would be very helpful."

# Chapter 10.

## August 1932 - Security Service Headquarters, Broadway Buildings 54, London

Rear Admiral Simpson slammed his fist down and stood up from behind his desk, his face furious. "Damn and blast man, what do you mean they got away!"

Cedric Johnson stood with his head slightly bowed. "They escaped to Scotland Sir before we arrived...they must have realised we were on to them."

Simpson picked up a bulging brown folder and thumped it down angrily on the desk, dog eared pieces of paper spilling out from one end. "On to them you say, and how did they blasted-well know we were on to them?"

Johnson glanced nervously at the papers strewn over his boss`s desk then took a deep breath and held his head high. "I think someone warned them Sir."

Simpson peered at him suspiciously. "You think.... or you know?"

"I.... I know Sir. I have had my suspicions for some time now and the pattern is there. His name is Albert Smith. I checked into his background before he joined the service and the man is not to be trusted. I`ll wager he would do anything if someone slipped him a shilling. The man even tried to jeopardise my investigation when I was looking around the rooms in Salford. Tried to cover up the fact they had escaped to Glasgow even though the evidence was plain to see Sir."

The Rear Admiral closed one eye slightly. "You are sure of this Smith fellow are you?"

"Oh certainly Sir, the man`s a ruffian but thinks he is clever chap. I have had to put him in his place on a number of occasions in order to make sure we get our job done. I will bring him in and interrogate him further, as way of proof."

Simpson sat down his eyes staring at the papers on his desk thoughtfully. "No you won`t Johnson."

"But Sir....."

"I said no you won`t damn you! I am seeing too many of these instances for my liking and I want to know how deep this treachery goes. Catch the big fish Johnson, that`s what we need to do."

Johnson`s shoulders sagged slightly, and he looked down disappointedly.

Simpson guffawed loudly, "chin up man, plenty more adventures for you to be getting your teeth into. I`ve read your report from the Salford incident. Damn good show on your part. Leading from the front and all that, damn good show indeed. Knew you were the right man when we took you on. How`s the shoulder doing?"

Johnson lifted his head and smiled. "Oh, my shoulder is fine Sir, takes more than a wooden door to stop me and thank you Sir, I always try to set the example, even when I am confronted by people like Smith and his accomplices."

Simpson started collecting the papers from his desk and

slotting them back into the folder. "You leave this Smith fellow to me. Now, pick up your next assignment from Doreen on the way out. I believe there is a new chap in Germany causing some problems. Sounds a bit of a rabble rouser and we don`t want that spreading here do we Johnson?"

"No Sir, we don`t," and he turned on his heel and left the office.

# Chapter 11.

## April 1933 – Pendlewick, East Lancashire

The small room at the back of the cottage was in darkness as the modified *Koenig & Bauer* printing press clicked away rhythmically as the sun slowly set over *Longridge Fell*.

Manfred walked in and after flicking a switch on the wall he lifted a printed sheet and looked at both sides carefully with his magnifying glass, paying particular interest in the signatures and colours. He gave a satisfied nod of approval, turned off the machine then called to Frank who was busy reading reports in the other room. "Come and take a look, I think it is time we carried out a test."

Frank joined him by the press, and he repeated the process with Manfred`s magnifier. Holding a sheet up to the light bulb of a nearby lamp, he twisted the sheet of paper one way, then the other and after comparing them with a genuine note in his hand he smiled. "They are excellent Frederick. Where are you thinking?"

They had carried out initial tests on formal documents and the like and now that they were happy the process was sound and repeatable, they had moved on to their true goal.

"Well, I think it is time for a pint of beer so I would say the

*Sun Inn* is as good a place as any to start."

After carefully cutting the printed sheet up, they put on their coats and hats and set off walking to the local public house. As they approached they could hear laughter and see the welcoming light streaming out of the windows onto the lane. They were now both regular visitors to the *Sun Inn* and were trusted by the locals.

The two men walked in and rubbed their hands together to warm them then walked over to the bar where as usual, the landlord was chatting to his customers.

"Good evening landlord, two pints of Stout please and two small whiskeys, there is still a nip of Winter in the air by the feel of it."

"Right you are gents," and the landlord started to pour the drinks, first placing two small glasses of whiskey on the bar, then reaching for the pump handle and drawing the dark Stout into pint glasses. "What you two been up to today then, still doin` them there surveys?"

Manfred tipped the whiskey into his mouth and after a satisfying sigh, "yes we are, it is a long job so you will have to put up with us for a while longer I`m afraid."

"Ah don`t you worry yourselves about that Mister Black, I like you comin` in `ere, `specially when you both pays yer bills on time," and he glanced over and rolled his eyes at Alf Davenport who stood talking to another man at the end of the bar. He turned back and smiled, "that`ll be two and six gents."

Manfred took out his wallet and offered a pound note to the landlord who took it from him and held it up to the light. "Blimey, we are well-off today aren`t we," and he winked at the two men. "An` looks brand new an` all, you been printin` these yerselves?"

"He was joking wasn`t he," whispered Frank as the two men sat down out of ear shot at a small wooden table by the roaring log fire.

Manfred took a sip of his beer and carefully placed his glass on the table in front of him. "Of course he was Frank, it is British humour!" He hissed. "You should know this by now, you have lived here for long enough!" He leant in towards him, "and *never* react the way you just did ever again. The look on your face would have raised suspicions in other situations. I am a reasonable man, but others who are working for our cause …. are not as lenient as I am."

His colleague looked at Manfred`s fanatical glare in a new light and nervously picked up his glass to take a drink. "My apologies Frederick, it will not happen again."

Manfred stood and picked up his coat. "No it will not. I shall return to the cottage whereas you will engage with Mister Davenport over there." He smiled but it got nowhere near his eyes. "I sense a weakness in this man that we can exploit," and bidding farewell to the landlord, he left the pub.

Frank picked up his glass and walked over to join Davenport at the bar. "Evening Alf, how are you?"

Davenport turned and wobbled back slightly on his heels, "well if it isn`t me best mate Frankie Barlow."

Frank smiled and looked at Davenport`s bleary eyes and how his mouth was drooping slightly at the corner. "Might be time for you to be going home Alf don`t you think."

"Rubbish lad, time fer one more at least," and he staggered back against the bar.

"You`ve `ad enough Alfred Davenport, and you`ll be getting` no more drinks in `ere tonight. Now pay yer bill and get on yer way!"

Frank glanced to his left to see where the commanding voice had come from and his heart missed a beat. A young woman with her brunette her tied in a bun stood with one hand on the bar and the other held out gesturing for payment. *She is beautiful*, thought Frank.

Davenport shook his head slowly and started to fumble in his jacket pockets. "I.... I must `ave left me money at `ome," he slurred.

She glanced disapprovingly at the landlord who looked down and carried on wiping the glass with an old cloth. "A likely tale and one you use a lot by the sounds of it. You`ll come in `ere tomorrow and settle yer debt or ye`re no longer welcome at this Inn Alfred Davenport, now get yerself home and sober up!"

Davenport made to put his half-finished drink back on the bar but missed by several inches and the glass smashed on the stone floor. He then staggered towards the exit and after bumping into either side of the door frame on his way out, he wandered off into the night.

"This isn`t a bloody alms-house yer know. These people need to pay up, we`re not a charity!" And she stomped back behind the bar.

Frank gazed at her in admiration, his mouth drooping open slightly. *How had he not seen her before?*

"Well! What are you gawping at?" she demanded.

Frank quickly gathered himself together and coughed into his hand, "sorry Miss, I wasn`t gawping Miss. My apologies if it did look like I was.... gawping."

She harrumphed then turned her back as she went towards the cellar door.

Laughter erupted around the bar at Frank`s expense and one of the locals shouted across, "don`t you try tacklin` this one Frankie, Isabelle will turn yeh inside out she will!"

Frank stared at her as she disappeared through the cellar door. "Who...who is she?"

The landlord leant over. "She`s my daughter, so you keep yerself to yerself Mister Barlow."

Frank stood up straight, "oh I certainly will Mister Warburton, I certainly will, no need to worry on that account."

The older man looked at him warily." Good an` make sure ya keeps it that way."

As Frank finished his pint his mind began to clear, and he remembered the task he had been given. "How much does Alf owe you Mister Warburton?"

The landlord stopped in his tracks. "What do ya mean?"

Frank took out his wallet, "what does he owe you for his drinks? I would like to pay his bill, merely as a good will gesture. He helped me recently with some gardening work."

"Ah `e did, did `e, all right then," and he walked over to the till, which opened with a soft *ching* and he removed a small slip of crumpled paper. Reaching to a shelf below the bar he pulled out a black leather case and removing his glasses he perched them on the end of his nose and sniffed slightly. "Ee`s not paid fer weeks ya know," he said warily.

Barlow nodded approvingly, "that is fine Mister Warburton."

"Well all right, that`ll be.... fourteen shillin`s an` sixpence."

Frank opened his wallet and took out a pound note and handed it to the landlord. "Please accept this as full payment and round it up to fifteen shillings for the trouble he has put you to."

The man beamed. "Thank ya kindly Sir, that's a grand gesture ye`ave made, and I probably appreciate it more than Davenport ever will."

As Frank was leaving, Isabelle returned from the cellar and he gave her his best smile, but she was oblivious, and she began talking to her father. But he didn`t care and walking home he had a spring in his step just thinking about her.

The following morning was bright, but a chill breeze blew down the valley as Frank drove up the lane to the Top Field Farm. Pulling up by the gate he got out of the car and after lifting the latch, he started to walk across the yard to Alf Davenport`s farmhouse. No sooner had he entered the farmyard, two snarling dogs ran out of their kennels and launched themselves at his throat. Frank looked on in horror and raised his hands to his face to shield himself from the inevitable vicious onslaught but just as they were about to strike him, they yelped and were suddenly jerked back by the long chains tied around their necks. Frank lowered his hands and with his heart pounding he started to take deep breaths to calm himself down.

"They`re `armless pups Frankie, barks worse than their bite it is. Now get yerself in and I`ll get our Sheila to make us a cup o`tea."

Frank turned and could see Alf Davenport leant against the farmhouse door frame with his arms folded, a mischievous grin on his face.

"If they are harmless pups Alf, I wouldn't want to meet their parents!"

Inside the farmhouse Frank looked around at the clutter everywhere. There was a sickly smell of old cooked food, wet dogs and cow manure and Frank moved his hand to his nose pretending to scratch it in a vain attempt to block the foul-smelling odour until his senses became familiar with it.

Davenport walked over to one of the two armchairs either side of the crackling fire and after sitting down with a slight grunt of pain, he turned towards the kitchen and barked, "Sheila! Two cups o`tea and be sharp about it woman!" He laughed, "useless woman, that`s all she`s fit fer."

Frank walked over to the other old armchair by the fire and made to sit down but was met by another dog who lifted its head from the chair arm and silently bared its teeth at him.

Davenport leant over and slapped the dog on its flank. "Go on, get down Jess, gentleman needs a seat! Now then, so what brings yeh `ere then Mister Barlow?"

As the dog sidled off the chair with its ears down and its tail between its legs, Frank made himself as comfortable as he could.

"You may not be aware yet Alf, but I noticed you were," and looking around the dishevelled room, "are, having some financial problems. So, after you had left the *Sun Inn* last night, I settled your debt with the landlord."

Davenport leant forward and picked up a small log and threw it onto the dying fire sending a shower of tiny orange sparks crackling and dancing in the air. "Did yeh now, and why would yeh be wantin` to do that Frankie? Yeh don`t owe me nothin` so what ya after?"

Frank coughed gently into his hand as he leant forward. "Myself and my colleague have frequent need of supplies, deliveries and the like and we are far too busy with our work to deliver and collect them ourselves. Now the problem is, our work for the Government could be seen as contentious by some of the locals so we need someone who can be trusted to work for us but keep the details of our work secret."

Davenport looked at him and smirking he waved his hand around the room. "As ya can see, I`m a little bit down on me luck at the moment, what with the current e-co-nomic situation, so I could be open to some other kinda work…. well paid other kinda work y`understand," and he winked and tapped the side of his nose with his finger.

A woman wearing a stained floral dress walked in carrying two cups of steaming tea and she placed the cups on a small side table.

Davenport looked at her and he snarled, "an` don`t spill any, I just cleaned that rug!"

The woman averted her gaze and scurried back into the small kitchen at the rear.

Frank looked down at the filthy rug in front of the fire and wondered how much time had elapsed since Alf had *just cleaned* it. "We will pay well for your services," and removing two crisp pound notes from his wallet, he handed them towards a surprised Davenport. "But you need to understand that once you accept, you become an employee of the British Government and therefore you must sign the *Official Secrets Act*," and he raised an eyebrow. "Can you keep a secret Alf?"

Davenport frowned momentarily as if to show he was thinking about the offer seriously, then a smile spread across his face and he snatched the money from him. "Course I can, where do I sign up Frankie?"

Two weeks later, Manfred returned from Germany and sat at the dining room table of the cottage pondering the situation. "Sit down Frank, I wish to discuss my trip with you."

Frank joined him at the table and leant with his elbows on the table eagerly awaiting an update.

"My meeting with Joseph went very well. He and Mister Blacklock are pleased with our progress but they demand more. Our leaders have set ground-breaking targets for the new regime but have also had the foresight to evaluate and identify who our enemies are and more importantly, are likely to be."

Frank licked his lips as he listened intently.

"We are on the brink of greatness and we must do everything in our power to thwart our foes. Nothing must stand in our way, nothing is more important than our task. Do you understand!"

"Yes Frederick, I understand. Who is the man we are to target?"

His colleague looked at him, his eyes glittering. "Our enemy is not a man. Our enemy is two-fold and we are tasked to bring them down and we have only five years in which to do it."

"Frank`s eyes widened. "Five years! But that is an eternity Frederick!"

"Not for the task we have. We are infiltrators Frank and infiltration takes time. Our task when completed will be monumental for the German people, but we must build to its completion in a methodical and logical manner, and this will take time. Our leaders understand this, and therefore they have given us the time to plan and succeed."

Frank leant back in his chair. "We can achieve anything in five years, I don`t see a problem."

"Maybe you will reflect on that statement when I am able to share what the task is," and he looked him straight in the eyes. "Be aware Frank, failure will not be tolerated."

Three days earlier, Manfred had sat with Blacklock and Joseph Goebbels in a small suburb of Berlin. Goebbels had asked him and Blacklock directly. "Do you have the men you require for the task?"

Manfred straightened his back as he sat up in his chair. "Yes Joseph, Frank is a good friend and......"

Goebbels slammed his fist on the table. "I care not for who is a friend! Do you have the men who can complete the task? Friendship is nothing to the Reich. Loyalty to our leader and results are the only things that matter!"

Manfred swallowed and shifted nervously in his chair. "Yes Joseph, I have the man I require. He is loyal to our cause and we will build our network to achieve the tasks you have set."

Goebbels paused as he stared at the two men. "Five years may seem a long-time gentlemen, but this task is pivotal to our success. We are not reactionaries. We have planned meticulously, and the *Third Reich* will come to be." He stood and with his hands behind his back, he walked to the small office window and looked out into the distance as though he was looking into the future. "Our enemies' gentlemen are concentrating their efforts in other directions and this is to our advantage. Whilst they fumble around chasing false stories and intelligence about the *Bolsheviks*, we plan their downfall."

As the aeroplane bumped and jerked around on its final approach to Croydon Airport, Manfred had looked out of the window. He had once again been inspired by the rhetoric from Goebbels and thoughts of his mother and revenge flitted through his mind, *but could Frank be trusted? I will need to test him. We cannot fail*, he thought.

He tapped his fingers lightly on the dining table. "You say the Davenport farm looks to be in difficulties?"

"The place is a mess. There appears to have been no work done for some time. This I feel, is why Davenport has taken to drink."

Manfred steepled his fingers in thought. "Drink leads to a loose tongue. Are you sure he can be trusted?"

"I have had friendly conversations with other locals and

Davenport`s drinking to excess has only been evident for the last few months. He is far from being well-liked, but he is respected in the village and it would appear that he hit financial problems, and this led to him visiting the *Sun Inn* on a more frequent basis."

"Good, a desperate man is easily manipulated. We will test him with a piece of non-critical information and monitor the result. Our cause grows in strength and we *will* deliver on our promises."

# Chapter 12
## May 1934 – Clitheroe, Lancashire

Constable James Warburton sat on the old stone wall below the Castle and gazed across the park at the cherry trees laden with their pink blossom. The sight eased his tormented mind a little as it heralded the coming of his favourite time of year. He sighed at their beauty which seemed to be even more extravagant in the morning sun.

The smile left his face as he looked intently at the brown envelope in his hands. He had thrown it in his bedroom drawer and slammed it shut more times than he could remember but each time, he had reluctantly taken it out again and this time, was the closest he had ever been to taking it to the post office and actually sending it.

There was too much information that didn`t add up. He had carried out some unofficial investigating into Alf Davenport`s death and had tried to get some answers from the villagers in Pendlewick but he was always met with what looked like fear or outright aggression whenever he asked too many questions. Eventually, Sergeant Entwistle had literally pushed him up against the wall outside of the police station and warned him to keep his nose out.

But it still burned into him each night as he lay in bed with seemingly unlinked information churning through his head.

*The entry and exit of the bullet was all wrong for it to be a suicide. The scratches to Davenports face were not from an animal, `ad he merely `ad an argument with `is sister Sheila and ended up in a sibling scuffle where she `ad clawed at `is face? It was well known in the village that Davenport treated `er badly. Could the brother and sister rivalry be at such a point where she might kill `im?*

He had shook his head, *this was too big for an inexperienced policeman and who could `e go to for `elp?* He felt trapped. *Sergeant Pilkington seemed trustworthy but `e and Sergeant Entwistle `ad gone to school together and were like brothers. `Is Dad was the landlord at the Sun Inn and although `armless, was probably the biggest gossip and rumour monger in the whole village. Tired of the inane chat with the bar flies, `e would love nothing more than a juicy bit of intrigue.*

Warburton lay motionless for a moment and a chill ran down his spine at the thought. *An` would I potentially be putting my family in danger?* The warning had been scribbled on a folded piece of paper and nailed to his front door.

On returning home a little later than usual one evening, he had removed it from the door and after taking a look around to see if anyone was watching, he went inside and read the contents.

# ceep yer noze out if you no wots gud fer ya

James had deduced the perpetrator was probably not the most literate person in Clitheroe, but then you didn't need to be intelligent to cause someone harm and to be on the cautious side, he had told nobody about the note.

So once again, he sought solace in sleep and closed his eyes.

The following morning as he sat on the wall below the castle looking down the street towards the marketplace, he heard the snorting and whinnying of a horse and as he turned to his left, Harold Wolstenholme was carefully guiding his tired black and white horse up the sloping road.

"Morning Constable, nice day for it."

Warburton smiled and waved. "Certainly is Harold," although he was a little unsure what *it* he was referring to.

Harold Wolstenholme looked like an overgrown chimney sweep but actually made his living from delivering coal around the local area. Warburton smiled and tried to remember if he had ever seen the man not covered in black dust from head to foot. Although only in his early forties, he walked with a permanent stoop from heaving the heavy bags of coal onto his back which made him look much older than he was.

"Glad to `ear you got them there poachers t`other month, vicious swines them lot are. If an they`d tried pinching my coal, they`d a got more punishment from me than you gave `em Constable."

"Well it's the law Harold, and we all abide by the law`s decision don`t we."

"Well there`s some us do and some us don`t, and them us don`t, gets what`s comin to `em," and he flicked the rein across the horse`s back and they rattled off down the cobbled street.

Warburton heaved a sigh and he slid the envelope back into the inside pocket of his jacket and leaning over he put his head in his hands. *The `ead of the secret service.* He had read a newspaper article some time ago about a gentleman in London called Herbert Simpson. The article was mostly propaganda for his department and to keep any ner-do-wells on their toes, but it was certainly impressive daring do stuff and had been the talk of the station amongst the young constables for weeks. *What am I thinkin` of sending a letter to the `ead of the Secret Service? Never mind reportin` that I suspect murder, police corruption or worse! I`m just a Constable for heaven's sake!*

"You all reet Mister Warburton?"

He looked up into the worried eyes of young Tommy Moffatt who sat astride his shiny black and gold Butchers delivery bicycle. "Mornin` Tommy, yes I am very well thank you, just tryin` to decide if I should do somethin` or not that`s all."

Tommy leant forward and placed his arms on the laden wicker basket in front of the handlebars, his ill-fitting flat cap tipped back at an angle. "Well Mister Alpe always says to me, Tommy, if it`s the reet thing ta do, then tha should do it."

Warburton paused then grinned and patted the lad gently on the head. "You know what Tommy, that`s the best piece of advice I have `eard all week, thank you."

The young lad smiled, proud that he could help a grown up, a grown-up policeman at that! "It's all reet Mister Warburton, I always likes to `elp I does and Mister Alpe `s normally reet in these things," and he gave a cheeky grin. "`Cept when I thought it was the reet thing to do pinching some apples from old Missus Walker`s orchard last year. Got a reet leatherin` off me dad for that I did," and he rode off down Castle Street whistling cheerfully.

Warburton watched as the young lad disappeared. Children very often cut through the complexities of life and his mind began to finally focus. He stood up defiantly, reached into his pocket and removed the envelope from his jacket and took one final look at it. *This is it James, no going back now,* and he set off towards the post office, hopefully to set the wheels of British justice in motion.

# Chapter 13

## May 1934 – The White`s Club, 37 St James`s Street - London

There was a gentle hum of quiet conversation from the other room and a fug of cigar smoke hung in the air as Rear Admiral Simpson chalked the tip of his billiard cue and addressed the table before him. He winced as he leant over the billiard table to take his shot, but the white ball ricocheted around the table without the desired result and he stood and rubbed at the discomfort in his lower chest.

"Not on your game today Herbert," smiled the bearded man stood by the wall holding his own billiard cue.

"Things on my mind old chap, things on my mind."

William Cooper was the Chief of the Imperial General Staff and Simpson trusted him implicitly, hence the reason they were playing billiards together that evening.

"How do you mean?"

"Blasted Bolsheviks are kicking up a fuss. Ruined their own country and now they are sticking their noses into our business. I`ll not have it William, I`ll be damned if I will."

Cooper nodded and nonchalantly potted a ball with his first shot. "What`s your view on this new chap causing a stir in Germany? I think he is one we should be keeping a watch on. A troublemaker by all accounts."

"Nonsense man. Had the intelligence in only last week, hates the Bolsheviks as much as we do. Our Airforce chaps reckon we should sign a joint alliance with Germany and unite against them! There are even rumours the Bolshies are financing the Irish Republicans! Encouraging blasted revolution on our shores!" He shook his head determinedly, "shan`t be having that William."

Cooper leant over to take another shot. "Sounds like normal Secret Service stuff to me Herbert, what`s so different now?"

Simpson looked around the Billiard room then walked to the doorway and peered left and right before walking back to his friend.

"Got ourselves an informer," he whispered. "Thought it might be an isolated case at first but no, too many instances William, too many for my liking at least. No sooner are we on to these people, they get away. Got to be someone warning them. Looks to have been going on for years!"

Cooper showed concern on his face. "Have you any ideas who it might be, I mean if it is only one person that is."

Simpson`s eyes widened slightly at the thought of more than one mole in his department. "I`ll be buggered if I know truth be told. My man Johnson tipped one of our operatives by the name of Smith up in Salford, told me he was a favourite to be our man. Turns out he is a diamond. Had him followed all over the North of England. Excellent operative and a chap you wouldn`t mind getting into a spot of bother with. Johnson got hauled over the coals for that I can tell you! No, I`ll be damned if I know who is giving away our information but it`s spreading. Hearing strange things that normally wouldn`t come my way. Something is brewing William, something big and I can`t put my finger on it."

Cooper gave him a friendly pat on the back. "I`m sure you will get your man Herbert."

The next day Simpson sat at his desk perusing the morning`s post. A handwritten plain brown envelope caught his eye as it was addressed to him personally and he turned it over and sliding his paper knife along the edge he opened it and began to read.

May 15th 1934

Dear Mister Simpson,

I wouldn`t normally think to bother a gentleman of your stature but as a loyal police Con stable, I feel I have nowhere else to turn but to your good self Sir.

My name is James Warburton and I am a Constable in the Clitheroe police in Lancashire. I have reason to believe that there is some suspicious goings on in my area and I have also reason to believe that my superiors are involved in some way so I cannot report this to them for fear of reprisals.

There has been strange things happening around the countryside and a death recently that was officially recorded as a suicide on the same day, but it is my strong belief Sir that it was a murder, and the villagers and certain police officers seem to have something to hide.

I would be grateful if you could offer some help Sir as I do not know which way to turn as I no longer trust my colleagues or the villagers.

My address is 12 Duck Street, Clitheroe Sir and I would appreciate any correspondence is sent here and not the station.

Yours Sincerely,

PC James Warburton

Simpson stared at the letter then his eyes narrowed in thought for a moment. Standing up he walked over to a map on the office wall and began tracing his finger over the North of England.

"Clitheroe you say, not that far from Salford. Right, I know what to do," he whispered.

# *Chapter 14*

## January 1934 – Blairgowrie, Perthshire, Scotland

A flurry of sleet gusted down *Allan Street* in the centre of Blairgowrie and Inspector Robert Anderson pulled his coat collar up against the chill as he peered through the shop window of gunsmiths *James Crockart & Son.*

Spotting his target, he quickly moved back beside one of the stone columns that stood either side of the entrance and waited with his back to the shop door. On hearing the faint *ding ding* as the door opened then closed again, he tensed and as the man scurried past him, he stepped forward and smashed the brown paper parcel out of the surprised man`s arms.

"Ye`ll no be needing that McNally."

Alistair McNally, a wiry red-haired man in his thirties, initially looked shocked but quickly gathered himself together, looked at the gun still wrapped in brown paper, cursed, then ran off down the street towards the river.

Anderson was far from being an athletic man, he liked his food too much and had long ago given up on the thought of chasing criminals and as in this case, there was no need to. No sooner had McNally made to run off down the street, the Inspector reached for his whistle and blew twice and instantly two uniformed policemen darted out of the doorway opposite the gun shop in pursuit.

By the time Inspector Anderson had reached the bridge, the drama was unfolding below and as he caught his breath, he looked over the balustrade at the two policemen as they inched their way along the ledge of the old stone bridge determined to catch their quarry.

"I`ll jump, I swear I will," screamed the man looking left then right along the ledge.

Anderson tucked the brown paper package under his arm and leant over to look at the ledge below. "It`s over McNally, just come quiet, ya canny get away from us, not now laddie."

The fugitive looked at the two constables and the two others inching their way determinedly along the ledge from the other bank and then down at the freezing cold *River Ericht* rushing through below him.

"I`d rather die than let ye catch me, ye bastards," and he launched himself into the raging torrent below and disappeared beneath the bridge and was gone.

Anderson looked down in horror as McNally disappeared in the churning river and turning to the young constable beside him, "quick Connelly, run tae the other side and see what ye can see."

The Constable ran across to the other side of the bridge and watched helplessly as the fugitive's arms waved about in the water in a desperate attempt to keep afloat, but it was no use and he slowly went under and out of sight.

As the group of policemen congregated on the bridge,

the Inspector gathered them together. "I want the body found. This is nay over `til I see `is body. Do ye all understand me?" The Constables all nodded in agreement

One week later, the battered and swollen body of suspected murderer Alistair McNally was found downstream of *Blairgowrie* wedged between rocks near *Kitty Swanson`s Bridge* and yet another case was closed for the highly successful Inspector Robert Anderson of the Perth and Kinross police.

# Chapter 15

## June 1933 – Pendlewick, East Lancashire

As he walked down the bone-dry track to the farmhouse, Alf Davenport took a deep breath of the warm Summer air, the scent of newly cut grass drifted across him from the nearby fields as the farm hands toiled in the heat.

As the Great War had ended in 1919, Davenport had taken over the family farm when his elderly father had finally succumbed to a long illness. He and his sister Sheila felt little sadness at the death of their bullying father and although the farm was profitable, Davenport showed no real flair for farming and it soon began to struggle. For many years he had watched the nearby Billington farm and envied their prosperity and unjustly the view that Henry Billington constantly looked down his nose at him.

But now, in his mind, the tide had turned. The Billington farm was in difficulties, another victim of the recent recession and Henry was doing everything he could to make ends meet.

Davenport looked back across the field where the tall grass was being cut and smirked, *tryin` to get a `ead start and `opin` to get two or three lots of `ay are yeh? It won`t do you no good Billington.* He chuckled to himself as he walked up the path to the neighbouring farm to his own and banged loudly on the front door. A petite blonde-haired woman opened it but failed to smile a greeting to Davenport. "What do you want?" She snapped.

Davenport casually leant against the frame of the door with one hand. "Ah Maureen, such a sight fer sore eyes," and he leered at her chest.

The terrified woman immediately put her arms defensively across herself. "Get away from `ere, now!"

He smirked at her. "I`ll have me way with yeh, you just watch if I don`t. I`m the richest man in this valley and I`ll get what I want," and he threw a pound note at her feet, laughed in her face then turned and left.

Two hours later an exhausted Henry Billington returned to his farmhouse for his mid-day meal. Taking off his shabby boots at the door, he smartened himself up as much as possible and wiped the beads of sweat from his brow with an old rag he had in his pocket. Satisfied he would look much more presentable for his wife, he entered the small tiled hallway. "Maureen luv, I`m home."

There was no answer, so he went into the kitchen and found his wife sat at the large wooden table. "Now where is my beautiful wife," and he trotted over and tickled her playfully under her arms, but she turned, and he saw her eyes were red and tears still ran down her cheeks.

He gripped her in his arms and gently laid his palm against the back of her head. "Maureen, what`s the matter?"

"Davenport `as been round again throwin` `is money at me. Telling me how `e is goin` to `ave me."

Henry`s face was like thunder and he released his embrace and stood up, his fists clenching, relaxing and clenching again. "I`ll show that bastard once an` for all," and he reached up and snatched his shotgun down from the kitchen wall.

Maureen jumped up and grabbed her husband by the arm. "No Henry no! If you do owt daft they're gonna hang ya fer it! Go an` speak tut police again, ask fer help."

By now Henry was seething and almost frothing at the mouth with anger. "What an` get the same condescendin` answer I got from Entwistle. Do you want me to be the laughin` stock of the whole county Maureen? Besides that bugger will be worth swingin` fer." He broke the shotgun and took a cartridge out of the top drawer, slotted it into the gun, snapped the barrel back into place and put two more shotgun cartridges into his pocket. "It ends `ere Maureen!" And he strode out of the farmhouse.


"Well well, if it aint the tough Mister Henry Billington come to shoot me to death on me own doorstep."

Henry Billington stood shaking with a mixture of fear and anger outside Alf Davenport`s farmhouse. His mind swirled with all the implications of what he thought he was about to do. The embarrassment of not doing what he was about to do, and the sound of the farm dogs incessant barking made his head hurt.

Davenport laughed at him. "You aint got the nerve Billington!"

Henry stood and looked Davenport straight in the eye and lifted the shotgun and pointed at his face. His hands trembled and sweat ran down his back. He could feel his throat tightening with nerves. "I.... I `ave you bastard," he managed to say unconvincingly.

"Well, are ya goin` to shoot me or stand there like the coward ya are? No wonder ya wife would rather `ave a real man like me!"

Henry felt his finger tighten against the trigger and momentarily saw the fear in Davenport`s eyes, but as soon as his finger tightened he released it again and pointed the gun to the floor. He felt his shoulders slump and heard the roar of mocking laughter from Davenport. He looked up at the face of his tormentor and there and then he would have given anything for the courage to shoot him dead. But he couldn`t. He wasn`t that kind of man and Davenport knew it.

"Knew you couldn`t do it Billington. Let me know when I can come round an` sort yer wife out for yeh."

Henry turned to leave but Davenport called to him. "Hey Billington, take this, you need it more than I do," and he turned and went back into the farmhouse, his laughter echoing from the hallway.

Billington looked down at the dirty farmyard and there fluttering in the breeze were some pound notes. Davenport was right. He did need it, desperately, but he was determined to leave with at least some of his pride intact. He looked at the money, his torment weighing him down, but he proudly shook his head and he left it where it was then trudged back to his farm and to a wife he could no longer support or protect.

# Chapter 16
## May 1934 – Police Station –
## City of Perth, Scotland

Chief Constable Charles Stephen leant around the doorway of his office and after quickly scanning the room, he spotted Inspector Anderson sat at his desk.

"Robert, gentlemen from London on the phone for you," and without waiting for an answer he walked back into his office.

Anderson stood up and stretched his arms and flexed his back then made his way into the Chief Constable`s office. Here he found the phone receiver sat on the desk and as he picked it up, the Chief Constable nodded to him and politely left the room.

"Anderson `ere, `ow may I be of `elp?"

"Anderson my man, it`s Herbert Simpson, still up to your sleuthing are you?"

Robert Anderson and been in the Naval Intelligence with Hugh Simpson during the Great War and in 1919, they had parted ways as great friends and admirers of each other. Anderson joined the Scottish police whilst Simpson remained in the Navy. Both were very intelligent men and had soon risen through the ranks of their respected disciplines where their integrity meant they could be trusted implicitly.

"It`s been a wee while Simpson, and aye, I`m still sleuthing as ye put it."

"Excellent man, just what I was hoping. Tell me, are you alone, can`t be overheard and all that?"

Anderson, placed the receiver on the desk, walked over and closed the office door then walked back and picked up the phone again, "Aye, I`m alone, what`s this about Simpson?"

"Got myself a bit of a problem you know. Blasted Bolsheviks on one hand, *Sinn Fein* on the other and now rumblings of some corruption in our local police. Wouldn`t normally get involved with the local bobbies Anderson but this one is a bit too close to home for my liking you know."

"Ye suspect corruption in the London police!"

"No, no Anderson, let me explain myself. I suspect we have a mole in my department, maybe more than one you know and I`ll be damned if I know who it is. Then two days ago, a letter turns up from a Constable up in Lancashire asking for my help as he suspects a covered-up murder and untrustworthy local officers. Now as I say Anderson, wouldn't normally give it two ticks of my time, but the location is too close to a recent operation in Salford where the blighters got tipped off and made a run for it before we got there. I don`t like coincidences Anderson as well you know, so just to give me peace of mind, I would like you to take a look and let me know what you think. Tick it off the old list if you know what I mean. Already cleared it with your superiors Anderson so no problems there. You up for it man, would be like the old days?"

Inspector Anderson thought about it for a moment, *things are getting a wee bit tedious around `ere*, he thought. "Aye Simpson, ye can count on me. When do ye want me tae start?"

"Right away man, right away, no time to waste! You still riding that death trap of a motorcycle?"

"Aye, she`s a real beauty, black and silver Triumph 6/1 with….."

"Yes, yes Anderson I`m sure she is a beauty, now get yourself down to Lancashire straight away and meet up with this Constable Warburton fellow. I have sent him a warrant for both of you, so you have the full power of the Government behind you, but word of warning Anderson, trust nobody, not even this Warburton chap until you are sure of him."

Inspector Anderson picked up a pencil and pulled a scrap of paper across the desk, "Gimme the address of this constable will ye."

After giving the location details, they bid each other farewell and Simpson replaced the phone receiver and leant back in his chair with his hands behind his head and sighed with relief.

*I will be damned if I know who to trust but if there is one person who I can trust to get the job done, it`s Anderson,* and he smiled to himself, *just hope they have lots of food in Clitheroe, they are going to need it!*

# Chapter 17

## May 1934 – Blairgowrie, Perthshire, Scotland

Inspector Anderson stood by his neatly made bed and after briefly scratching the back of his head in thought, he carefully folded some extra underwear and socks, two more shirts and two extra pairs of brown trousers into his battered leather bag.

"Should be enough," he confirmed to himself confidently and closed the bag, fastened the leather strap and buckle securely and after heaving it onto his shoulder went into the small living room to bid farewell to his mother.

He looked into her watery eyes unsure if they were damp from age or because she was sad he had to leave again. "Right Ma, I`ll be away then," and he bent down and kissed the top of her grey-haired head.

She looked at her son and dabbed at her nose with a tiny lace handkerchief. "Ah wee Bobby, do ye hav` tae go? I mean, there`s plenty o`work fer ye here laddie," and she turned her head away a tad and sniffed dramatically into her handkerchief.

Anderson looked on, it was the same every time. "Ah ma wee hen, I`ll be back before ye know it. Besides, I canny go too far from ye homemade oat cakes canna? Gimme two weeks at most and I`ll be home, no lyin` Ma."

"All right but mind ye be careful on that big motorcycle machine o`yours wee Bobby," and she shook her head disapprovingly. "I dunnay know why ye canny use the train like anyone else."

Anderson smiled and kissed her on the cheek then walked to the front door of their small cottage where he half turned. "I`ll be careful Ma, don`t you worri`none."

He stepped outside and proudly approached his magnificent motorcycle parked outside their home and once again carefully appraised the lines and intricate features of the design. It never failed to make his heart skip a beat and he chuckled to himself as he tied his bag to the back of the saddle.

The previous year on a bright spring morning, he had been summoned to Blair Atholl Castle by the Eighth Duke. At first a little apprehensive, Anderson had accepted the invitation and after unsuccessfully trying to commandeer a police car he had made the torturous thirty-mile journey from their home in Blairgowrie by hitching lifts from farmers and delivery wagons along the way.

As he walked up the long drive to the foreboding white castle walls, he stopped and combed his greying dark hair with his hands, pushing his long fringe to the side in a futile attempt at making himself look a little more presentable. Finally pleased with himself and resigned to the fact that his large hulking frame was never going to be aesthetically pleasing to everyone, he approached the arched front door, took a deep breath and pulled the worn metal ring by the side.

He heard a muffled tinkling sound and as he stepped back,

he once again attempted to improve his appearance by quickly brushing his coat down and hand combing his hair again.

Within seconds of the bell ringing, the door creaked open and an ageing butler stood before him. The old man sniffed and looked Anderson up and down slowly. "You are Inspector Anderson I presume."

"Aye, that I am laddie," and he handed the crumpled-up invitation to the butler who looked at it as though someone had just spat into his hand. After opening up the piece of paper he perched his glasses on the end of his nose and Anderson saw the butler`s eyes scanning the details. Eventually, he looked up. "This way Sir."

Anderson was surprised to be led away from the castle and not actually through the front door. As they crunched along the shingle driveway, it crossed his mind that he had probably gone against etiquette by approaching the front door and should have used the tradesman`s entrance, which was probably in the direction they were now walking.

As they turned the corner, they were met by an elderly man in his early sixties, his grey moustache neatly trimmed, who looked sternly at them as they approached.

The butler nodded politely to the man and duly introduced Inspector Anderson who in turn bobbed his head politely in the Duke`s direction. At this point, Anderson wondered what the hell he was doing here and suddenly decided the long trip may not have been wise.

"That will be all Murdoch," and the Duke dismissed the butler with a wave of his hand.

As the butler made his way back, the Duke turned to Anderson and smiled broadly. "Now then Inspector, how are we today?"

Anderson relaxed a little at the sudden lack of formality. "I`m well thank ye Sir...Duke... ah mean ......."

The Duke roared with laughter at his discomfort. "Ah leave it be Inspector, you can call me by my nickname, *Bardie*, we won`t be standing on ceremony today," and he patted him warmly on the back.

"Thank you.... Bardie. May I ask why I`m here Sir?"

"Certainly my good man. You are here at my invitation so I can thank you in person for catching the rogue who stole some of my property which, was thankfully returned without damage. Meant a lot to the family you know."

The Inspector looked down at his feet. "Ah it was nothin` Sir.... Bardie. Just part of ma job."

"Nonsense man," and he guided Anderson towards a large wooden shed with a sloping roof. "Heard you were very brave and had quite a tussle with the chap."

The Inspector smiled, "well, not exactly true. As ye can see I`m a big lad, gotta say it was a wee bit one sided if I`m tae be perfectly `onest."

"One sided or not Inspector, I very much appreciate it," and sliding a small key into a rusting padlock he wrenched open the large shed doors and pointed at a gleaming black and silver motorcycle. "What do you think of that?"

Anderson stared at the *Triumph* motorcycle and his mouth opened but no words came out and his eyes widened as he walked towards the exquisite machine parked in the shed, the black paint and chrome work glinting as the sunlight flooded in through the doorway.

"It`s a real beauty Sir, you`re a lucky man to own such a thing," and he walked around reverently running his fingers along the fuel tank and across the leather saddle in admiration.

The Duke walked over and joined him. "I heard from a little bird that you appreciate this kind of machine Inspector."

"Oh aye Sir, ye can say that again. Is it a 6/1 be any chance? I thought they had nay released these tae the public fer sale yet."

"Quite correct, you certainly know your stuff, and no they are not on sale as yet, but I have my contacts you know," and he winked at the Inspector mischievously. "Trouble is, I`m getting a bit long in the tooth to ride it you know, so I am on the lookout for a new owner. Do you happen to know of anyone who may be interested in it?"

Anderson didn`t lift his appreciative gaze as he looked at his distorted reflection in the chrome headlight bezel. "Och, there would be plenty o`men interested in owning this motorcycle Sir."

"And how about you Inspector? Would you like to own it?"

Anderson suddenly snapped back into the real world and his cheeks flushed a little with embarrassment. "I`m afraid not Sir, as much as I`d like tae…..it`s just that ma police wage…. I mean… no Sir it's a wee bit outa ma price range, if ye take my meanin`."

The Duke stepped forward and once again gave him a friendly pat on the back. "Fully understand Inspector, no need to be embarrassed about it. I realise the cost of these things and the money that you are paid means it is way out of your reach, which is why I am giving it to you. By way of a thank you."

Anderson turned to the Duke, his mouth and eyes competing for which could open the widest. "What did ye say Sir?" He gasped in disbelief.

"It`s yours man, that`s what I am saying. Take it as my way of thanking a brave policeman for doing a sterling job."

It had been the happiest day of his life and standing outside looking at it again was no different to the first time he had set his eyes on it with the Duke. He grinned again at the thought and after double checking his bag was secure, he stretched his leather helmet into place and as he straddled the bike, he took a last look at the tiny white walled cottage he shared with his mother. The beautifully kept wooden picket fence with the spring daffodils still poking through and as he tilted his head back slightly, he caught the faint smell of wood smoke from the chimney on the roof top. "I`ll be back soon enough Ma," he whispered, and he roared off down the lane. Passing the *Meikleour hedge* and over the narrow bridge that spanned the mighty *River Tay*, he headed South for England with the wind rushing in his face and the rhythmic throbbing of his motorcycle engine reverberating from the narrow lanes and hedgerows.

Anderson had estimated eight hours to complete the two-hundred-and-fifty-mile trip to Clitheroe and he was looking forward to the final section through the stunning *Trough of Bowland* and into Clitheroe. He revelled in the twisting bends as the scenery flashed by him and the rush of cool air blowing into his face made him feel alive.

Eventually he reached the centre of Clitheroe and as he slowly rode up the main street towards the imposing castle, he turned right at the top as he looked for Warburton`s address. He was soon joined by a throng of young children happily laughing and shouting as they ran beside him, pointing excitedly at the newcomer and his splendid motorcycle.

Eventually he pulled up and turning the engine off he beckoned to a young couple on the nearby pavement walking in the other direction.

"`Scuse me, can ye tell me `ow I can find a place be the name of Duck Street?"

The couple looked a little wary at the huge figure sat astride a motorcycle and speaking in a strange accent, but then the man stepped forward a little and pointed down the hill.

"Yes Sir," he deemed this to be the best way to address anyone who could afford a motorcycle and he pointed his finger down the hill. "Follow the street down then turn right onto Wellgate then go almost to the bottom and Duck Street is on your left."

Anderson tipped his hand to his head, "Thank ye kindly," and starting the engine again, he made his way to Warburton's house.

He scanned the house numbers as he pottered down Duck Street, his motorcycle engine thumping away at idle and he pulled up at a small dwelling with a windowless black front door. He assumed that number twelve was here even though it had no number on it. There was a small hole where the number had been held on by a nail at some point. It didn`t need a genius to work out that the odd numbers were on one side of the street and the even numbers on the other, nor the fact that the house with no number was sat between fourteen and ten.

Anderson turned off the engine and hauled the motorcycle on to its stand, stretched his arms in the air then removed his leather helmet. His hair was plastered to his head with sweat in an almost exact copy of the helmet shape and he ruffled it up a bit to make it look decent. Content that his appearance reflected a policeman of his stature, he stepped up to the house and smartly rapped on the door.

"Not be home for another `alf hour he won`t."

Anderson looked across the street at the source of the information and there, on her hands and knees was an old lady rubbing her front step with a worn pale-yellow coloured stone gripped firmly in her hand. He smiled as he observed how her head and backside counterbalanced each other as she scrubbed from side to side on the step.

"Then I`m `appy tae wait fer him. Thank ye kindly."

The old lady paused on hearing his peculiar accent and she looked up at the man, shook her head and carried on as though he wasn't there.

It was actually more like forty-five minutes when Warburton came home, but Anderson didn`t mind. He had been on his motorcycle for most of the day and although the trip was thoroughly enjoyable, his back and legs were ready for a good stretch, so he had spent the intervening time walking around the local area looking for somewhere to get a bite to eat. He eventually stumbled on a small shop selling fresh food and the like and had purchased six warm meat pies.

"Expect the family will be looking forward to you gettin` `ome with them," smiled the shop owner as Anderson placed some coins on the countertop. The Inspector looked at the man non-plussed. "Family? Nay laddie, these ar` all fer me," and he immediately bit into one, revelling in the crunch of the crispy golden pastry and succulent tangy melted jelly that ran down his fingers. Anderson sighed with pleasure as he ran his tongue over his fingers to lap up the liquid, "an I may be back a wee bit later fer more I might add," and he winked at the bemused shop keeper.

James Warburton had finished work for the day and as he turned onto Duck Street he noticed a group of local children crowded around listening to a huge man sat on something by his house. As he got closer he could hear their excited chatter as they bobbed up and down with excitement in a bid to get the man`s attention.

"And so ye see, that, is how I got ma motorcycle."

Warburton walked up and stood behind the children and put his hands on his hips, "now then what`s all this?"

The man raised his head and smiled. "Och, nothin` to be worryin` about young man. These bairns where just keepin` me company until ye came `ome that`s all."

Warburton clapped his hands together briskly, "come on you lot, have you no homes to go to," and they squealed with laughter as he shooed them off with his hands. He smiled as he watched them run off down the street pushing and shoving each other but his smile faded as he turned to the stranger. "Can I be of any help to you Sir?"

Inspector Anderson heaved himself upright from the motorcycle and towering over the young Constable before him, he looked him up and down thoughtfully stroking his chin with his fingers. "I dunno, can ye be of any `elp tae me?"

Warburton quickly felt uneasy and stepped back a little towards his front door, but the man stepped forward as well, so he gained nothing.

The man looked at him and he raised his eyebrow. "Would ye be a Constable Warburton now?"

The young constable swallowed nervously, and his mind started to race. *Was this giant some relative of the poachers I just brought to justice, `ad he come to wreak vengeance on their captor? You're a policeman Warburton, pull yerself together man.*

"I am Sir, and what is that to you, may I ask?"

The man smiled, "A` think this is better discussed inside laddie," and he walked over and stood expectantly beside the front door of Warburton's house.

The Constable paused for a moment then nodded his consent. He would have to find out what this was all about at some point so why not now and after opening the door with his key, he held his hand out and gestured for the man to go first, just to be on the safe side.

He watched as the man crouched over and squeezed in through the tiny front door of the terraced house and as he followed him into the front room, he wondered if he was actually going to fit into his house! But he did, and he slumped down onto one of the mismatched chairs by the fireplace which creaked under his weight.

Warburton remained standing. "Now Sir would you like to tell me why you are here? I mean I don`t even know your name."

The man looked him in the eye. "Ma name is Anderson, Robert Anderson and I believe ye tae have a wee problem."

The idea of revenge from the poachers suddenly flashed through Warburtons mind again and he shifted defensively towards the lobby door. They were well known for carrying out violence against anyone who dared challenge them and challenge them he had. Head on!

Tansy McNeil and Denny Wild were the poaching ring leaders and James, plus constables Jones and Sanson had been extremely proud when they caught both of the men red handed and had cornered them in Jackson`s farmyard just outside West Bradford. After putting up a struggle, the two poachers realised they were no match for the three powerful young Constables and they had both felt the full weight of the law, not enough to satisfy the likes of Harold Wolstenholme who would have strung them up from a nearby tree, but sufficient to say that they wouldn`t be carrying out any poaching or violence towards others for a long time. Although pleased with the result, Warburton had seen a side of Constable Jones that concerned him and had been surprised that he had to pull him off one of the poachers during the scuffle in the farmyard to prevent him beating Tansy McNeil to a pulp.

"Am I tae take it that ye problem is ye canny close ye mouth or speak laddie?"

Not realising his mouth had started to droop open, Warburton snapped out of his thoughts of poachers and violence and addressed the man. "It would depend on the problem Sir. As a Police Constable, there are always problems that need my attention."

"Aye, and ` ow would ye go about that then? Would ye sort things ye self or would ye go thinkin` o` writin` a wee letter to someone?"

Warburton froze and he stared intently at Anderson. "If it was a big problem Sir, I would probably have to write to someone, someone who I could trust Sir."

"And would that be someone in London be any chance?"

He could now feel his adrenalin start to pump through his veins, a mixture of excitement and trepidation at what the outcome would be when he uttered his next words. "Yes Sir, it would be Sir, if I needed to trust someone, that is where I would write Sir."

Anderson leant back in the chair which gave another creak in protest and as he reached inside his coat, Warburton physically tensed up. The Inspector smiled. "Calm ye self down," and from his coat pocket he produced his warrant card, "Inspector Robert Anderson, at ye service."

# Chapter 18

## June 1933 – Pendlewick, East Lancashire

Frank Barlow leant against the bar in the *Sun Inn* waiting to be served. He hoped it would be Isabelle who served him and not her Father. In fact he really hoped it was Isabelle that served him.

He had become smitten, and the fact that she had put up some resistance to his advances made it all the more satisfying. She had shyly ignored him on a number of occasions, but as time passed, once or twice she had looked over her shoulder and smiled as she walked past him.

The landlord finished handing over a drink to one of the locals then he walked over wiping his hands clean on a cloth tucked into his apron. "Now then Frankie what can I get ya, the usual?" As Frank was about to speak, Isabelle came around the corner and almost pushed her father out of the way.

"It`s okay Dad, I`ll serve Frank, you can sort the cellar, the stout is gettin` low again and we need a new barrel puttin` on fer tonight."

One of the regulars stood at the bar and laughed. "Yeh come on Andrew, get some work done man. It`s about time ya did a bit round here, place is goin` tut dogs."

The landlord muttered an expletive under his breath but

reluctantly complied with his daughter`s request and disappeared down into the cellar leaving the men stood around the bar to their conversations.

Isabelle smiled and reached for the pump handle of the *Hen Harrier* Ale but didn`t pull it. "Usual is it Mister Barlow?"

Frank gave her his best smile, "yes please, but just a *gill* today, I have some important work I need to do later so need a clear head."

"Right you are," and she reached for a small glass and tilting it on its side, she filled it with frothing ale and as she handed it to Frank, she paused so that she gained his attention, then ran her tongue slowly once around her lips. "Looks lovely that beer does. Makin` me thirsty for somethin` nice myself."

Frank`s mouth opened but nothing came out and he gazed at her.

"That`s not a very flatterin` look you know Mister Barlow, makes you look like you `ave a slate loose."

He quickly regained his senses, "what, yes, sorry Isabelle, it`s just that, I have never, erm, you see I have never met a woman as, as....."

"As what Mister Barlow?" And she leant on the bar towards him revealing her cleavage as she did so.

Frank gulped and tried with all his might to drag his eyes away from the sight before him, but it was no good and his transfixed stare was only interrupted when Old Walter walked past, slapped him on the back and cackled, "what you been told about gawping young fella?"

Later that evening Frank lay in bed, the thought of Isabelle dominating everything else in his mind, including the conversation he had just had with Frederick as he had been about to climb the narrow staircase to his bedroom. She seemed to be toying with him, right in front of him, close enough to touch, but seemingly out of reach. *Dare I*, he thought, *should I make my move. Make a move, you don`t know any moves! You haven`t even kissed a girl, never mind a beautiful woman like Isabelle.* He frustratingly shook his head and turned his face into the pillow as if to hide from the conundrum, the words from the pub ringing in his ears. *Don`t you try tackling this one Frankie, Isabelle will turn you inside out she will! Was she just mocking me and after I had left were all the regulars laughing and joking about me?* He rolled onto his back and inhaled deeply then slowly released it. "There is only one way to find out," he whispered and closed his eyes.

Two weeks later Manfred angrily paced up and down by the side of the kitchen table where Frank sat with his head bowed.

Stopping beside Franks left shoulder, "can you explain why the tasks I gave you are not complete!"

Frank took a deep breath, "the tasks were more difficult than I first thought Frederick, but I was afraid to tell you as you would get angry," and he raised his head and looked at his friend. "You have been getting angry at the smallest details lately and I thought….."

Manfred thrust his face into Frank`s and his voice hissed like escaping air, "you thought me a fool Franz, that is what you thought! Your tasks are not completed because your mind is elsewhere. You have been concentrating on the wrong things Franz. Did we not agree that nothing,

nothing is more important than our cause! Well did we?"

"Yes Frederick we did," replied Frank forlornly.

Manfred slammed his fist down on to the table. "Yet you spend your time with some local harlot whilst our plans fall by the wayside and you think I don`t know these things!" Spittle was now flying from his mouth as he raged around the room. He strode over and knocked Frank`s breakfast plate off the table and it smashed onto the floor. Frank didn`t dare turn to look but shifted his eyes slightly and could see the food dripping down the nearby chair leg and he waited for the tirade to continue hoping in vain that there would be a pause where he could try and make amends.

Manfred walked over to the kitchen window and sighed, his shoulders sagging slightly as he did so. "You see Franz, we cannot fail, and we will not fail, but I must be able to fully rely on my colleagues."

Frank saw this as his chance. "I know you do Frederick and that is why you can be assured I am fully behind our cause, I really am. Please," he begged, "let me make things right, I am you friend Freder.... Manfred, we have been friends for years, you can trust me, you know you can!"

Manfred placed his hand into his pocket and pulled out his black leather gloves and slipped them on, paused, and after reaching into his pocket once more, he smiled and walked over putting his arm around Frank`s shoulder. "Yes Franz, we are friends, good friends, which makes this all the harder" and he suddenly thrust a capsule into Frank`s mouth and clamped his hand under his jaw to prevent him spitting it out. Frank shook his head to and fro and grappled frantically at Manfred`s hand but within moments the struggle ended, and Manfred allowed the body to slump to the cold stone flagged kitchen floor. He looked down with contempt. "Failure will not be tolerated. Nothing is more important than the cause, not even you my friend."

# Chapter 19

## July 1933 – Pendlewick, East Lancashire

Constable Warburton leant his elbow on the bar of the *Sun Inn,* "well `e must `ave gone somewhere Issy, maybe `e went back to London?"

Isabelle had a pensive look on her face. "Do you think so Jimmy, I mean, `e just said goodbye that night and no mention of going off anywhere. That isn`t like Frank, `e always told me of `is whereabouts."

"Oh stop worryin`, `e`ll probably come walkin` in `ere tomorrow and explain it `imself, these government gents are busy people, "and he chuckled mischievously. "You know `e can`t be wastin` `is time with bar maids when there`s important things to be attendin` to in London."

Isabelle reached over and slapped her brother on the shoulder, "I`m worried Jimmy, worried sick somethin` `as `appened to `im. `E might be trapped in a ditch somewhere with nobody to `elp him," and with the corner of her apron, she dabbed at a tear forming in her eye.

Warburton stood up shaking his head slowly and inhaled deeply. "Blimey Issy, talk about thinkin` o` the worst."

Just then they heard the door swing open and in walked Mister Black. He paused and removing a packet of cigarettes from his pocket, he tapped the end to his mouth and gripped one with his lips. Lighting it up he blew a jet of smoke into the air and walked casually over to the bar.

Warburton turned to him and once again reverted to what he hoped was his professional sounding voice. "Now then, just the man we wanted to see."

Manfred gave an amiable smile "and why would that be Constable?"

"Well then, my sister here has got herself all worried about your friend Mister Barlow. Says she hasn't seen hide nor hair of him for a week, which I`m told is unusual in this here establishment, and she has taken to thinking something bad has happened to the gentleman."

Manfred looked straight ahead and took a deep draw on his cigarette and as he exhaled he spoke through the exiting smoke. "The answer is a simple one. Mister Barlow has had to return to London, he has been reassigned, permanently. Now may I have a small whiskey please."

Isabelle glared at him but eventually spun and picking up a small glass, she splashed a shot of whiskey into the bottom. Handing it to her customer she held on to it as Manfred also reached over and gripped the glass. They both stared intently at each other for a moment then Isabelle spoke. "Can you provide me with his address, I would like to write to him," and she let go of the glass.

Manfred raised the glass to his lips and drained the amber liquid in one then returned the glass to the bar with a satisfying sigh. "I am afraid that is not possible my dear, his whereabouts are not for public knowledge," and after placing a coin on the bar, he tipped his head to them, and walked out of the pub.

Warburton looked at his sister and did his best to put on a sympathetic face, "yeh see, busy gents Issy, as I said they were. Now I need to be off, I `ave a report to write, and it `as to be ready for tomorrow or I`m in trouble wit` Sarge."

Isabelle looked on as her brother left the pub and she frowned. *I can spot trouble a mile off an` somethin` fishy is goin` on `ere, something very fishy*, she thought.

Alf Davenport carefully twisted the brass doorknob of the farmhouse door and as carefully as he could, he pushed the door open and stepped in. He could see Maureen Billington stood at the old wood kitchen table preparing some food, probably for her husband`s dinner later that day. He licked his lips as he looked at how her tight cotton dress clung to her figure and arousal came upon him.

Three days later, as the sun was setting in a fiery red sky, Henry Billington stretched his tired back and after packing away the tools in the shed he walked over to the barn to close the doors for the night. *I`ll sharpen them scythes in the morning*, he thought. The Summer days were long and tiring but that was the nature of farming and he never complained. He smiled at the thought of sitting down and eating his evening meal with his wife. Reaching for the barn door he pulled it towards him and as he glanced inside, he froze. His stomach lurched and as he sprinted into the barn he let out a primal scream as tears flooded down his cheeks.

# Chapter 20

## July 1933 – Pendlewick – Lancashire

Isabelle ushered the last customer out of the door and watched hands on hips as he walked off down the lane. Shaking her head irritably, she walked back into the pub, "you do know `e nursed that same pint all night don`t yeh. We`ll not mek no money sellin` one pint a night!"

The landlord of the *Sun Inn* bobbed his head up from behind the bar where he was neatly stacking some freshly cleaned glasses. "Lives on `is own an` `as nowt an` nobody. We`re `is only company so don`t get all harsh wi `im lass."

Isabelle looked at her father and smiled, "yer a soft bugger you are."

He smiled back, "aye but I`m your soft bugger aren't I."

"Aye y`are an` I`ll remind ya of it when we`re broke."

Isabelle, slipped on her jacket and after tying her scarf loosely around her neck, "I`ll just go an` check on Grandma afore I turn in. I`ll lock up when I get back"

"Right an` mind yeh mek sure her doors` shut an` all, she`s fer ever leavin` it open."

As she stepped out into balmy evening, she scurried towards the *Buck i`th Vine* public house opposite the post office and the smell from the warmth of the trees that had baked all day in the hot Summer sun wafted over her. Turning right, she suddenly halted and spun around. She sensed someone was following her, but the lane was empty, the night still and silent.

She peered towards the shadows by the post office. "Who`s there?" She swallowed nervously, "I know someone's there, come out an` show yerself!" The silence was now deafening, and she could feel her heart pounding in her chest and her mind was screaming, *run Isabelle run!*

Just as she was about to run to her Grandma`s house, she felt the grip of a hand on her shoulder and she shrieked and swivelled round

"What you doin` out `ere on yer own missy?"

Isabelle sighed with relief at the sight of Old Walter who was out taking his dog for a late-night stroll. "Oh Walter it`s you, I think someone`s followin` me," and she pointed a shaking finger towards the side street by the Post Office.

"Followin` yeh are they, well you get yerself off `ome lass, leave this to me."

Although Walter was nicknamed *Old Walter*, at fifty-four years old and an ex-Army boxing champion, he was far from being *old*. He had a son who was also called Walter, and it had seemed perfectly logical to the villagers that they would identify one as old and one as young to prevent any unnecessary confusion.

As Isabelle set off up the lane she glanced nervously over her shoulder and saw Walter marching towards the post office, his black and tan Staffordshire Bull Terrier snarling and straining at the leash.

Walter`s voice echoed down the lane. "It`s all right missy, nobody `ere."

She relaxed slightly at the news, just as a gloved hand wrapped around her mouth and she was unceremoniously dragged into the nearby ginnel.


The following day, Sergeant Pilkington was carrying out the morning alphabetical roll call in the station yard.

"Balmforth?"

"Here Sarge"

He eventually got to S for Salter.

"Here Sarge."

"Sanson?" On hearing nothing the Sergeant scanned his eyes along the line of constables. "Where`s Sanson, anybody seen him?"

Constable Jones stepped forward and saluted. "Gave me a message Sarge, `e won`t be on duty today, `urt his leg `e `as Sarge."

"Right-o," and looking at his list again, "Thomas?"

"Here Sarge."

"Warburton?...... Warburton?" The Sergeant looked towards the end of the line. "Warburton! Wake up constable!"

James jolted out of his thoughts. "Sorry Sarge, I was just thinking about Constable Sanson. I pass his house on my rounds so if it's all right, I will nip in and see how he is."

"That's fine Warburton but make sure you don`t end up nattering away an hour or two with him. Bad enough losing one of you never mind two constables!"

# Chapter 21

## May 1934 – Clitheroe – Lancashire

The two men had sat for hours in the small front room of Warburton`s house where Anderson had grilled him on his letter and the reasoning behind him sending it to Herbert Simpson.

"Murda` ye say? That`s a bold statement I`ll have ye know," and placing his cup of tea on the table beside the chair he looked Warburton straight in the eye. "Would ye care to explain yerself laddie."

Warburton shifted nervously in the chair opposite, took a deep breath and began. "The bullet `ole... hole wound was hall...all wrong for it to be a suicide Sir." He realised he was getting himself in a twist and he tried to calm himself, *come on get yerself together Jimmy.*

Already sensing the young man`s predicament, the Inspector sat calmly, "take ye time laddie, we`re in no `urry."

James paused momentarily then began again. "I have studied this type of thing in my spare time and although I admit I am no expert in the matter, the logic I used when I examined the body seemed reasonable in that the exit wound is always larger than the entry wound. In the case of Mister Davenport, the wound in the chest was larger than the wound in the back, meaning he had been shot from behind, which points to there being someone else who killed him," and he looked at the Inspector for some form of affirmation, but he was disappointed when the man just sniffed and said, "aye, an` would ye be lookin` tae add anythin` else then."

The young Constable`s hands started to tremble and wondering if he had made a colossal mistake, the words of Constable Jones came unbidden into his mind, *t`Sarge does know a lot more about policin` things than us Jimmy, maybe ya just didn't see it reet.* He clenched his fists to prevent them from shaking and once again he started to explain as the Inspector`s gaze bore relentlessly into him.

"You…. you see Inspector, when I checked the files at the Station, there was nothing about any interviews that had taken place with Mister Davenport`s Sister Sheila, not one Sir even though I know full well some took place. There was only a brief one-page report showing the basic details and that it was suicide with a gunshot to the chest and it was signed the same day as the death. That was all Sir, I mean you would expect more wouldn`t you Sir?" He asked desperately, "and whenever I mentioned the case or looked into it, I was warned off by Sergeant Entwistle who had signed the report, he even pushed me against a wall and threatened me he did Sir!" Frantically trying to think of some more information to back up his story the abduction of his sister Isabelle and the note pinned to his front door suddenly sprung into his mind. "Oh and this Sir," and he reached for the note in his pocket. "This was left nailed to my front door and….and someone followed my sister last year and tried to kidnap her!"

The man merely leant back and looked momentarily towards the ceiling. "So, let me see if I canny understand this then," and leaning forward to look at Warburton, "ye thought to write a wee letter to an important man such as Rear Admiral Herbert Simpson on the pretext of a bullet wound, a report ye deemed tae be too brief," and pointing to the note in the Constable`s hand, "and a poorly written warning note eh?"

Warburton`s heart sank, and he began to feel foolish, *what `ave I done*, he thought and putting his head down slowly, "yes Sir, as well as the attempted abduction of my...." But his voice tapered out to silence. "I am extremely sorry to have wasted your time Sir."

The Inspector slapped his hand on his knee. "Nonsense young man, this `as me more than a wee bit intrigued an` Mister Simpson did ask me tae make sure everythin` was above board and proper, so that is what we will do laddie," and the chair gave one final objection as he stood up and stretched his arms.

Warburton raised his head, "you believe me Sir!" He exclaimed.

"Aye, but I wanted tae check you an` yer story fer ma self. Need tae know I can trust ye, if ye take ma meanin`."

The Constable immediately jumped up and saluted him, "oh you can trust me Sir, certainly you can trust me. I`m very trustworthy Sir."

The Inspector paused as he looked at the eager young policeman before him then smiled, "calm down laddie, don`t go over boilin` the egg now," and putting on his jacket he turned to Warburton. "I believe ye are in possession of a letter sent tae me at this very address."

"Ah yes Sir, it`s right here," and he quickly reached for

a brown envelope from behind the broken clock on the mantlepiece.

The Inspector ripped it open and removing the contents, he quickly scanned the document mouthing words silently as he did so. Stuffing the letter into his pocket he clapped his hands together, "and how would ye sister be fairing as we speak?"

"She is fine thank you Sir. One of the locals had been in the area and she was able to escape."

Isabelle had indeed been able to escape but only because of the actions of Old Walter who had decided to make sure the young lady got to her destination safely.

As she was hauled into the narrow alleyway, she had heard the animal like grunting and had felt powerful arms and a hand tugging at her clothing. With his hand firmly clamped over her mouth, she was unable to scream but with all her might she kicked and struggled as hard as she could. Unexpectedly, and as she started to weaken and her hopes began to fade, she heard a voice and a low menacing growl.

"Hey, get yer hands off her yeh bastard!"

Isabelle felt the man release his hold on her, and she fell to the floor pulling her clothing across herself to hide her modesty.

"Get after `im lad, go on Jacky, go on lad!"

Walter`s snarling Staffy, hurtled after the man who had run down the ginnel and as he made to escape by jumping up on to the wooden fence at the end, it bravely launched itself grabbing his trailing leg with its vicious jaws.

Isabelle heard a mixture of snarling and yelping and

could see the man frantically kicking the dog in the face with his other foot. Walter ran down to help but as Jacky momentarily opened his mouth to get a better grip, the man fell backwards over the fence and was gone leaving a shaken Isabelle to be comforted by old Walter.

On hearing of the event the following morning, Warburton went to see how his sister was and after telling him the story he had set off for work assuring his sister that the man would be caught.

His mind had reeled when he heard at roll call that Constable Sanson had hurt his leg. Surely it couldn`t have been Billy! There was only one way to find out and that was to see if his story was true and to examine his leg.

Warburton had parked his bike against the wall near to Sanson`s house that he shared with his Mother and Father and he paced up and down nervously before finally knocking on the front door. His mouth went dry as he heard the door unlocking and it swung open.

"Mornin` James, how are yeh today?"

"Good morning Missus Sanson, I`m very well thank yeh very much."

"Come in then lad, have yeh time fer a cuppa` tea?"

James followed her down the hallway, "not today thanks. I just said I`d call in and see `ow Billy was doin`. `Urt `is leg I believe."

His mother glanced over her shoulder, "yeh silly bugger went out last night wi` no torch and came in all hobbling` about the place. Told him to watch it goin` out at night like that, but oh no `e knows better than `is Mam."

She led James into the front room where Constable Sanson sat with his right leg resting on a strategically placed cushion on top of a wonky looking stool.

On seeing Warburton enter the room he immediately shimmied up in the chair. "M…. mornin` J…. Jimmy, wasn`t expectin` to see yeh t…. today I w…wasn`t."

James sensed the nervousness, he always stammered more when he was nervous. "Mornin` Billy. Sarge just asked me to `ave a quick check on yer injury, just so `e can record it on file that`s all. Nothin` to worry `bout."

Sanson subconsciously slid his hand down towards his lower leg as if to hide it.

"Well I`ll leave yeh to it then," and his mother went to the kitchen singing softly to herself.

James took a deep breath. His next actions depended on what he found, and he could already feel anger rising within him. *How could his friend have done this to his sister?*

"Roll yeh trouser leg up Billy, I needs to look at the wound."

"Oh it`s not a wound Jimmy, I just went over on me ankle that`s all."

James stared intensely at his former friend and snarled. "I said roll yer trouser leg up Sanson, now!"

Billy lurched forward, "a…. all right Jimmy, what`s the m…. matter with ya?" And he rolled up his trouser leg.

James looked down, at Billy`s swollen ankle. Leaning towards his leg he carefully looked for any bite marks. He had heard that dog and cat bites could quickly cause swelling so it might not just be inflamed because of a sprained ankle, but he found no signs of bites or scratches.

He sighed thankfully. "Sorry Billy, it`s just that Issy got attacked last night an` only escaped because of Old Walter an` `is dog. The bloke who did it got badly bitten on `is lower leg as `e tried escapin` over a fence. I `ad to make sure when I heard about...., well yeh know."

Sanson looked hurt that his friend didn`t trust him, but eventually he smiled, "don`t worry `bout it Jimmy. How is she doin`, she all right?"

"Aye Issy`s as well as can be expected. Will affect her fer a bit yet though. Anyway, best be on me way Billy and sorry again."

As James closed the front door behind him he felt a mixture of anger and embarrassment at the situation. He had let his emotions get in the way of policing but as he cocked his leg over his bicycle, his blood suddenly ran cold. *I didn`t check `is other leg! `E could have sprained `is ankle falling off the fence and the bites on the other leg!*

With a mixture of renewed anger yet also pleased that his detective skills had drawn this conclusion he marched straight back into the house without knocking and found Billy hobbling towards the kitchen.

"Billy wait, I needs to check one more thing. Roll yer other trouser leg up fer me."

Billy now looked angry, "w.... what? D.... don`t ya t.... trust me Jimmy?"

"Aye I trust ya all right, now show me yer other leg Billy."

Hearing the heated discussion in the hallway, Billy`s mother came marching from the kitchen a floured rolling pin in her hand. "What`s goin` on `ere James Warburton, can`t ya see my Billy`s hurtin`?"

"I can Missus Sanson, but I needs to be sure, now roll yer trouser leg up Billy!"

Billy sighed and with his stare never leaving James`s face, he bent down and rolled his trouser leg up to the knee.

James looked down at the pale calf and ankle. Not a wound of any kind in sight.

He had left the house with Missus Sanson`s sharp tongue lashing him. "Yer not welcome no more in this `ouse James Warburton so don`t you go tryin`." He could still hear her ranting as he cycled down the lane. I `ad to find out, but could I have done it a different way? He shook his head to clear his mind. It was done now and more importantly, if it wasn`t Billy, who had done it?

The Inspector had pondered for a moment. "Do ye feel there may be a link tae all this and ye sister?"

"To be honest Sir, I don`t even know where to start."

"Right laddie, well I do, so let`s away to the Police Station, we have some work tae do."

The last of the falling cherry blossom swirled around in the breeze and collected like pink snow drifts against the pavement edges as the two men walked purposely towards the police station, but both had different thoughts and feelings running through their minds.

One had the benefit of years of experience in dealing with all matter's criminal. The confidence of a man who had been exposed to violence and had dealt with investigations at all levels.

The other, a young man whose only experience was chasing poachers or trying to apprehend bicycle thieves and his stomach was now doing somersaults with nerves and doubts.

As they reached the front door the larger man turned, "alright laddie, let me do the talkin`," and Inspector Anderson pushed the heavy blue wooden door open and stepped into the station, closely followed by Constable Warburton.

Sergeant Entwistle looked up from the reception counter as the door opened and placing his pen down beside an open file, he welcomed the man before him. "Morning Sir, how can I be of help?" He grimaced slightly when he saw Warburton easing himself around the huge figure standing in front of him. "You`re late Constable, where have you been?"

"He`s been with me Sergeant, been havin` a wee chat we have," and he pulled out his warrant card and offered it towards the bemused Sergeant who looked at it for a moment then pulled his shoulders back and saluted. "Welcome to Clitheroe Police Station Inspector. I`m Sergeant Entwistle. May I ask what brings you to these parts, if you don`t mind me asking that is Sir."

Anderson appraised the man before him then after a short pause, "don`t mind ye askin` at all. I`m here as part of separate investigation and I just want tae make sure there are no loose ends. Can`t be doin` with no loose ends when it comes tae investigatin`, if you take ma meanin` Sergeant. I would also care tae mention that I will be relieving Constable Warburton of his current duties at this station in order fer him tae aid me in ma work."

The Sergeants' face blushed, "with all due respect Sir, you cannot just take Constable Warburton, he has important work to do. For something like this you need the help of an experienced policeman," and he waved his hand dismissively towards Warburton, "not someone who is still wet behind the ears."

Anderson nodded then turned to the Constable. "Aye and would ye care tae explain what this important work is at the moment. I mean, what does it entail exactly?"

Warburton coughed gently into his hand, "I am currently investigating and looking for the perpetrator who stole a gentleman's bicycle from *Woone Lane* Sir."

The inspector returned his gaze to the Sergeant and he raised an eyebrow. "Important work ye say?"

The Sergeant stood his ground. "It is critical these young policemen learn the basics Sir. An investigation is an investigation in my book, be at stolen bicycle or something more serious, the process is the same, and they need to practice and learn the art of examining evidence in order to solve the crime."

"Aye well be that as it may, I`ll still be takin` young Warburton under ma wing and he`ll be workin` with me until further notice, do ye understand Sergeant?"

Just then Chief Constable Burke walked in from the back room, his unlit pipe clenched between his teeth as he read a report in his hand. On seeing the three men he stopped and removed his pipe, "and what have we here gentlemen?"

Sergeant Entwistle saw his chance and before anyone could react, "afternoon Sir, I was just explaining to the Inspector here that he can`t just come in and commandeer our Constables."

Burke looked pensive. "Is this true, Inspector....?"

"Inspector Anderson is the name Sir and I ˋave a Government warrant that gives me approval fer any activity I see fit," and much to the chagrin of Sergeant Entwistle, he handed the letter over to the Chief Constable.

He read the contents carefully then nodded his approval and handed the letter back to Anderson, "seems perfectly in order Inspector. Am I to believe you will only require the services of one of our Constables?"

Entwistle went bright red in the face and blustered, "but Chief Constable, begginˋ your pardon Sir, but you are new to this station, we donˋt do things like this round here, Sir."

Burke looked at the Sergeant then once again turned to the two other men. "As I was just saying, am I to believe you will only require the services of one of our Constables?"

"Aye Sir, fer the time beinˋ. Been told some fine things about the laddie so Iˋll be happy fer him tae be ma assistant."

Constable Warburton straightened his back and stuck his chest out with pride. *The Inspector ˋad been told fine things about me! But by who......oh it doesn't matter yeh fool,* he thought, and he looked across at Sergeant Entwistle who was trying his best to stifle his resentment.

The Chief Constable rubbed his hands together, "excellent, you two gentlemen may use my office as your base if you like," and turning to the Sergeant, "and Entwistle, would you care to take a short walk with me please. I would like to discuss a couple of matters with you in private," at which point Warburton thought the Sergeant`s head was going to explode.

The morning after Sergeant Entwistle tapped at the front door of the cottage in Pendlewick. After a short wait, the door opened, and Manfred urgently gestured him inside where he followed him down the narrow hallway and into the kitchen. "Well Sergeant, what is the reason for your visit?"

Entwistle pulled out a chair and as he did so, he peered through into the front room. "Is Mister Barlow out and about then Sir?"

Manfred looked at him, his gaze unwavering. "Mister Barlow has been assigned to another project, you will not meet him again. Now why are you here, you know the system we put in place," and he turned and started to make a cup of tea by the stove.

"Looks like we might have trouble Sir."

The soft tinkling of the spoon slowly stirring Manfred`s pot of freshly brewed tea stopped. "Trouble? In what way?"

"Well there is this new Inspector shown up at the Station yesterday, says he is investigating something that might be linked to something else."

Manfred slowly closed his eyes then opened them again. "What an eloquent explanation Sergeant, would it be possible for you to expand on this with a little more detail please," and he started to stir the tea pot once more.

"What I meant to say Sir was that he has a special warrant from down London that gives him anything he wants so he must be important to get one of them, or he has friends who are important."

Manfred still had his back to Entwistle, so it was impossible to judge his demeanour. "Tell me Sergeant, is it you or someone else I pay handsomely to deal with small matters such as these?"

The Sergeant became cautious. He wasn't a fearful person, but he had seen how Mister Black could turn from amiable and courteous to a furious raging maniac in seconds. "I just thought I would let you know Sir, what with your work being important and secret and all that. Just wanted to make sure you was in the picture Sir."

Manfred spun round. "Very well, I am now in the *picture* Sergeant, so you may go," and he pointed to the front door. Taking the hint, the Sergeant stood and as he was about to leave Manfred put his hand gently on the other man`s shoulder. "I do not want this to become a problem Sergeant so it would be worth your while making sure it does not become a problem," and he closed the door leaving Entwistle on the doorstep to contemplate the situation.


After opening the wooden gate, Inspector Anderson and Constable Warburton turned off *Twitter Lane* and drove up to Top Field Farm.

They had commandeered one of the Police Wolsey`s and as Constable Warburton proudly drove the vehicle up the farm track, he tried not to smile. He just wished more people could see him. He was finally doing proper police work not chasing bicycle thieves or being sent to tell kids not to make too much noise outside Missus Glossop's house.

The car brakes squeaked slightly, and the tyres crunched on the gravel as they pulled up by the farmyard gate. Inspector Anderson looked thoughtfully through the windscreen towards the farmhouse. "So ye say the lady was less than welcomin` the last time ye visited eh."

James nodded his head, "yes Sir, told me to bugger off, if you pardon my language Sir."

Anderson grinned and he reached for the car door handle, "ah well, let`s away and see what kinda` mood she`s in today shall we."

Making their way through the gate and across the yard James suddenly remembered the dogs. "Oh Sir, I forgot to tell you…" but it was too late, and the two sheepdogs came rushing out of their kennels towards them.

To Warburton`s dismay, the Inspector just stood his ground as the snarling animals rushed towards him. He looked on as the Inspector confidently stood with his hands on his hips, the dogs snapping and snarling no more than a foot away from him. "Sir, how did you…."

"Ah they`re just playin` laddie, besides, I knew the chains would stop `em so don`t ye worri` none." Seeing the Constables perplexed look he turned to him. "Look at the yard floor Constable an` tell me what ye see."

James looked around paying attention to the kennel positions and the chains. "Did you somehow work out the lengths of the chains beforehand Sir?"

"Aye, and how do ye think I did that then?"

The Constable started to feel uncomfortable. He had no idea how and had just guessed about the lengths of the chains. "I must admit Sir I don`t know, I just made a guess."

"Good, I like an `onest man. Now then," and pointing at the yard floor, "ye see how the yard is a wee bit more worn in an arc along here from the gate tae the doorway. Now unless someone has lengthened these chains recently, I knew I was nay gonna get a tickle from the puppies so long as I kept ma self on the worn area of the yard."

And as Warburton followed the Inspector towards the door he ran his eyes along the barely decipherable path and nodded. "Sorry Sir, I never thought of that."

"Not to worri` laddie, ye learn these things as ye go along in life. Ye should always be on the lookout fer things that are outta place. Now a straight pathway would have been normal not a curved one wouldn't ye say," and on reaching the worn farmhouse front door, he reached into his jacket and pulled out his warrant card then knocked on the door.

The muffled sound of a dog barking and a woman`s voice cursing could be heard getting louder and the sound of a metal bolt being slid across announced the imminent opening of the door.

A middle-aged woman held a sheepdog by the scruff of its neck, and she glared at the two men. "Yes!" She snapped.

Anderson held out his warrant card. "Ma name is Inspect...." but before he could get his words out, Sheila Davenport slammed the door.....on to the Inspector`s boot that he had quickly wedged in the doorway. He smiled, "Now, as I was about tae say Miss Davenport, ma name is Inspector Anderson, and I have a few questions I would like answerin` be ye good self."

The woman looked angrily at them but relented and

opened the door again. "I`ve answered to you lot before and I don`t intend to answer no more of your bloody questions."

The Inspector gestured for her to go inside and he stepped in closely followed by Constable Warburton. "Well, ye`ll no have answered any questions from me, so let`s get ourselves in and have a wee chat over a cup of tea eh."

As the three of them sat at the kitchen table, the Constable stared at Sheila's throat where her dress failed to cover her neck. On noticing, she positioned the palm of her hand across herself. "Right I `aven`t got all day, what do you want?"

The Inspector went to speak but James unexpectedly spoke first. "Would you mind explaining how you got the scars on your throat please Miss Davenport."


As the two policemen drove off down the back lane from the farm, the Inspector turned to the James. "Would ye care tae explain ye thinkin` about the lady`s throat now Constable."

James kept his eye on the road ahead. "It just came to me Inspector. It`s the first time I have been that close to Miss Davenport. The scars on her throat look remarkably like the ones on Maureen Billington`s throat, according to the Coroner`s report.

"Aye, and Maureen Billington would be...."

"She was the wife of Henry Billington, a local farmer, committed suicide in their barn last July she did. Sergeant Entwistle said the poor lady must have had second thoughts and frantically scrawled at her throat and buttocks with her nails. At least he said that`s what the Coroner told him."

The Inspector carried on looking at the young Policeman as the car bumped around on the rough lane from the farmhouse. "So am I correct tae believe yer thinkin` there may be a link?"

Warburton pulled up with a squeal of brakes, yanked the handbrake on and opened the car door, "not sure yet Inspector," and he got out to open the five-bar gate at the bottom of the lane. The car rocked slightly as he got back inside, "but I think I know where we should look next, if that`s all right with you Sir."

Anderson chuckled to himself, "why certainly it`s all right, lead the way laddie."

They drove back to Clitheroe in companionable silence, the Inspector taking in the beautiful Ribble Valley countryside as it flited passed the side window and soon, they pulled up outside the General Registry Office. As they got out of the car, James spotted some of the local children running around in circles chasing each other, their laughter and playful screams echoing off the walls of the terraced buildings. "Hey, you lot, keep your noise down or I`ll have to move you on."

The children stopped immediately and one of the older children tilted his head down, "sorry Constable Warburton, promise we`ll behave."

"Aye well make sure you do then," and the two men walked into the Registry Office where they were met by a lady sat at a mahogany reception desk, its surface polished to a mirror finish. "Good morning Constable Warburton, what brings you here today?"

James walked over and took off his helmet, "morning

Missus Clacton, I am here on official police business," and turning to the man beside him," and this is Inspector Robert Anderson."

Anderson nodded politely in her direction, "pleased tae meet ye Missus Clacton."

James continued, "we are working on a case and we require access to the files from an inquest from last July, for a Missus Maureen Billington. Would you be so kind to locate the information please."

The lady pushed her chair back and walked over to row of filing cabinets, "I remember that inquest Constable, sad state of affairs that was, poor lady," and she pulled out a cardboard folder and passed it to the two men. "I will need you to just sign here on this line gents, to show that you have had access, it`s the rules you know," and she slid a piece of paper across her desk to them.

After signing, they sat themselves down at a nearby table and left Missus Clacton to her work. They kept their voices low as they discussed the contents. "This looks to be the information I was looking for Sir," and James passed one of the folder documents to the Inspector. "It`s the part where the Coroner has made notes about the injuries to Missus Billington`s throat and buttocks." The notes were brief, but critically, they failed to say that she may have had second thoughts and inflicted the wounds herself as Sergeant Entwistle had purported. They merely recognised the wounds were present and stated that they appeared to be approximately two to three days old.

The Inspector leant back in his chair thoughtfully rubbing his chin with his thumb and finger. "This Sergeant of yours intrigues me laddie. Think we may need tae have a wee chat with the man, and sooner rather than later I might add."

James pulled his chair right up to the table and leant forward towards the Inspector excitedly. "This is what I meant Inspector, no real notes on Alf Davenport`s file, no record of his interviews with Missus Davenport and now, he twists the story of Missus Billington`s wounds."

The Inspector picked up the papers and turning them on their ends, he tapped them into line then slipped them back into the folder. "Intriguing Constable, very intriguing indeed."

Later that afternoon, Warburton rested his elbows on the roof of the police car and as he peered through the sight glasses he rotated the small wheel of the binoculars to bring everything into focus.

"Can ye see anythin` Constable?"

"No Sir, the washing is on the line, but nothing is showing." He took the binoculars away from his face, "can we not just go in and search the farmhouse Sir?"

"No Constable, we need tae keep this covert fer now. I dunnay want tae set no hares runnin` be showin` our `and too soon. Lady appears tae do her washin` each day, let`s away and come back again tomorrow afternoon."

The following day, James once again focused across the field and right on time, Sheila Davenport came out of the side door of the farmhouse with a wicker basket resting on her hip. Placing it down by the washing line she proceeded to hang the day`s washing out to dry in the late Spring breeze.

The Inspector raised his hand to his brow and shielded

his eyes against the sun as he squinted across the field, but all he could make out was a small figure intermittently bending down and reaching up again. "How does it look Constable?"

Warburton maintained his gaze through the binoculars, "nothing yet Sir, but she is only halfway along the line. Mainly dresses and pinnies so far as I can see."

Anderson looked across the field and rubbed his chin slowly. "Give it time laddie, give it time." Suddenly Warburton`s body stiffened slightly. "What `ave ye seen Constable?"

James repositioned his elbows on the car roof. "Got it Sir! I can see the old blood stains on the underwear. They are vertical, just like the ones reported on Missus Billington`s body."

# Chapter 22

## August 1934 – Sacred Heart Catholic Church – Whalley – Lancashire

The man walked into the church and crossed himself, his head bowed. Looking up, he gazed down the aisle looking for the confession box. Finally seeing the location he walked solemnly forward nodding graciously to an older lady coming the other way.

Taking a deep calming breath he pulled the curtain to one side and stepped into the confessional box where he sat down and faced the ornate grill in the wall.

After only moments, he heard the sliding of wood on wood and he could just make out someone on the other side.

After making the sign of the cross once more he began. "Bless me Father, for I have sinned…."

After listening intently, the other man grimaced to himself then gathered his thoughts and finally spoke. "You are right to confess your sins my son, but am I correct in believing you are not one of my flock?"

"That is correct Father."

"Then why did you choose to come to me with your confession my son?" He asked calmy.

There was a moment of silence then the confessor replied simply, "I had need of spiritual help Father that cannot be obtained locally."

There was a creak as the other man adjusted his sitting position and he leant towards the grill and whispered, "would it not have been wise to go to your local Priest and make this confession?"

There was no reply.

"My son, are you still there?"

"I am here Father."

"Then answer the question my son."

There was another moment of silence, then he answered. "I *am* the local Priest Father."

# Chapter 23

## February 1934 – Pendlewick, East Lancashire

It was a cold afternoon and the sun, with its last vestiges of watery light, slowly sank behind the silhouetted Fell beyond.

Alf Davenport tapped on the cottage door and without waiting, he opened the door and walked in.

Manfred heard the door and immediately put down the papers in his hand and stepped into the hallway, closing the door behind him. He masked his anger at the impudent man before him.

"Evenin` Mister Black, `ow are things, still printing all that money are we?"

Manfred ignored the question and did his best to remain calm. He despised the man and it had been a mistake, a huge mistake to involve him in their cause, but it was too late now. "What are you doing here Mister Davenport? He asked nonchalantly. "The arrangement was that you pick up the papers for delivery tomorrow."

To his annoyance, Davenport walked straight past him and into the front room where after slumping down in an armchair, he lifted his leg and placed his booted foot onto the fireplace then winked at Manfred. "Takes the ache in me leg away it does Mister Black."

"I will ask again Mister Davenport, what is the reason for your visit?"

Davenport sniffed and held his chin with his thumb and index finger. "Well ya`see, I got to thinkin` t`other day and I said to me self, Alf, these `ere gentlemen is making lots of money but you don`t seem to be gettin` yer fair share, specially what with all the risks you is takin`. So ya see Mister Black, me wage demands `as suddenly gone and tripled," and he looked straight at Manfred, "that's if ya still want me to be all secretive an` that."

Manfred stiffened slightly but his face remained neutral, then he smiled. "You are quite correct Mister Davenport, it would appear that we have not kept your renumeration up to date considering.... the importance of your tasks, so we will look to increase it."

Davenport looked puzzled and his eyes narrowed slightly, "that`s all well an` good, but what about me wages?"

Manfred looked at the man before him, *how could I have been so stupid to allow this lout to become involved in our affairs*, "yes Mister Davenport, we will also look at your wages at the same time. Now make sure you are on time tomorrow," and he pointed towards the door.


Sergeant Entwistle cycled through Pendlewick each morning on his way to the Police Station and each morning he saluted the Cenotaph by the brook as he passed by, but this morning was different. The small wooden cross was upside down in the flower bed that sat under the large stone monument. Pulling up to a halt, he leant his bicycle against the railings and carefully put the cross in the correct position, saluted again then cycled off towards Clitheroe, but instead of carrying straight on towards the town, he turned right into *Katy Lane*. Ten minutes later he tapped on the cottage door.

The Sergeant sat opposite Manfred at the kitchen table and once again, he found that the expression on his face was hard to read. "I got the sign Mister Black, what is it you want to see me about?"

Manfred leant forward on the table and steepled his fingers. "I had the pleasure of a visit from Mister Davenport yesterday Sergeant and it would appear that he is far from happy with his current.....contract and he is demanding more."

Entwistle gently bit the corner of his bottom lip, "he is, is he, well there`s a turn up for the books."

"So with that in mind Sergeant, we need to resolve this problem with Mister Davenport, once and for all."

Entwistle stood and picked up his helmet from the table, "right you are Mister Black, consider it done," and as he went to salute him, Manfred held up his hand.

"One moment please Sergeant. I am about go on a trip, and I will be away for approximately three weeks. I would like this problem to have gone away by the time I return, is that understood?"

Entwistle put his helmet on and pulled the chin strap into place, "understood Mister Black," and as he was about to leave, "by the way, may I ask where you will be going on your trip Sir?"

Manfred looked at him with contempt, "no you may not Sergeant."

# Chapter 24

## February 1934 – Hotel Edison 228 West 47th street in Midtown Manhattan - USA

Manfred stood on the pavement amongst the bustling crowds and as steam billowed from a grate in the street beside him, he looked skyward at the word *EDISON* written vertically in enormous illuminated letters on the hotel roof.

It had opened three years earlier to a huge fanfare as Thomas Edison switched on the hotel lights remotely from his nearby home. Manfred found it a little distasteful, but it served his purpose.

The top-hatted Concierge stepped forward to greet him and as he did so, he tipped his hat in one smooth movement, "welcome once again Lord Turner-Hope, how was your trip Sir?

Manfred gave a curt smile, "as well as can be expected Duffy," and he surreptitiously slipped a five-dollar bill into the man`s hand as he passed him by.

The Concierge quickly glanced at the contents of his palm and his eyes widened in shock. "I.... I will deal with your luggage straight away Sir, same room as usual is it Sir?"

Manfred ignored the man and walked into the hotel and over to the reception desk where he was given a gushing welcome by the immaculately dressed man behind the desk. "Good evening Lord Turner-Hope, what a pleasure it is to have you here again."

Manfred flashed a smile that vanished as quickly as it had appeared and picking up the ornate pen from the holder, he dipped it into a small brass inkwell by the side of the guest register, and duly signed in.

The following morning, there was a quiet knock at the door to his twenty-sixth-floor suite and dabbing each corner of his mouth with a pristine white napkin, he pushed his chair back and walked towards the door. Putting his ear to the centre panel, he tapped twice and waited. Moments later he heard two knocks, then a further three in quick succession. Satisfied, he opened the door and let the visitor into the room where Manfred returned to his seat and commenced eating his breakfast again.

The man removed his hat and trench coat and placed them neatly on a chair by the window but remained holding his leather briefcase. "Apologies Sir, I would have come a little later had I known you were still eating breakfast."

Manfred waved his finger in the air as he finished chewing on some food, "it is not a problem Mister Ventnor," and placing his silver knife and fork down he once again dabbed his mouth with the napkin. "I have other matters to deal with in Washington, so it is in my interest that we conclude our business in a timely manner." He stood and motioned for Ventnor to join him in the sitting room adjoining the dining area of the suite.

Isaac Ventnor was a descendant of German immigrants, who after passing through *Ellis Island*, had made their way over the years to eventually settle near Boston where they started a shoe repair business. Isaac had taken over the business some time ago, but he had his eyes and ambitions set on larger ventures, larger ventures that required lots of money and this had been amply supplied by Manfred, but there was a catch. In return for his businesses being financed, he had to gain the trust and then influence selected American politicians.

Manfred took a cigarette out of a slim metal case and offered one to the other man who leant over and nodded his thanks. "So Mister Ventnor, now to business," and after flicking the flint roller on the cigarette lighter and lighting his own, he casually threw the lighter in a gentle arc to Ventnor. "During our last discussions, you told me you had decided upon the Senators who could be persuaded to aid our cause. Would you please update me on progress."

Ventnor reached down and Manfred heard an imperceptible click as he opened his briefcase and removed a sheet of cream coloured paper. " These are the men in question Sir and I have meticulously recorded the dates and all the details of my conversations with them and as you can see Sir," and holding the paper towards Manfred, he ran his finger along the neat lines of times, dates and words, "they are all in order, as you asked me to do Sir."

Manfred briefly ran his eye over the information and smiled, there was no need to check, it would be accurate to the second.

Ventnor bit his bottom lip slightly, "I am afraid I have maybe overstepped the mark with regards to the brief you gave me Sir."

Manfred looked up, "how so?"

"During my.....investigations, I was introduced to two men from quite diverse backgrounds. One a Texan oil baron and the other a union leader.

Manfred raised an eyebrow, "yes go on please."

It transpired Sir that the oil baron is a sympathiser for our cause and the union leader holds a large degree of power within the transportation systems of the United States and was open to shall we say, some extra income. Therefore, I have identified four accomplices, not the original two as directed by yourself."

Manfred paused as he looked straight at Ventnor then, "you do realise this is doubling our risk?"

"Yes Sir, in theory it does, but I have been through our plans and the rewards far outweigh the risk in this instance and if you disagree with my proposal, the men in question have been given no details so we can simply pull out.

Manfred looked at the man and smiled confidently. He had chosen well and was pleased with what he saw and heard. "Excellent work Mister Ventnor, I want you to proceed as planned. Keep me informed at all times by telegram"

# Chapter 25

## May 1934 - Oxford Street – London

The room was silent, and only the muffled clip clop of a passing cart in the street below and the drone of a faraway bus engine disturbed the scene. Cedric Johnson leant on his elbow and admired the woman led beside him. Even when she was asleep, she was the most beautiful woman he had ever seen. *I could stare at her all day and night,* he thought.

It appeared as though she sensed him watching her and she gave a little snort and sniff and opened her eyes. Smiling at him, she sat up and stretched her arms in the air as she yawned sleepily. "What…. what time is it?"

He twisted round and picked his pocket watch up off the bedside table and tried to read the time without his glasses.

Doreen looked on and she couldn`t help thinking he looked like a surfacing mole coming out of the ground into the sunlight.

Moving the watch back and forth he tried to get some sort of focus on it then finally resorted to closing one eye and he peered at the blurred fingers. "It`s only about six o`clock…. I think. Now go back to sleep Doreen, unless you want to stay awake for a while that is," and he cheekily tickled her ear.

She turned onto her side with her back facing him. "You had best be off and get yourself ready for work. I expect you will have some important reports to hand in to Mister Simpson, especially with all them things you have been doing lately. Couldn't believe my own ears when you said you were too busy to come round and see me Cedric Johnson. I was most upset you know!"

He snuggled up beside her, "I know you miss me when I don`t come round as much as you would like my dear but, I have a very important job to do and sometimes, well sometimes I can`t put that off, as much as I would like to of course."

Doreen rolled her eyes in dismay, then turned to face him, "do you really mean that Cedric, truly?"

Johnson swelled with confidence at the attention. "Of course I mean it my dear. Ordinarily, I would be round here like a shot, but I`m on a big case at the moment and it`s taking all my ti...my skills to try and sort it out you know."

"Crikey Cedric we are so lucky to have you at the Security Service. Is it something to do with the brown envelope Mister Simpson asked me to give you a few weeks ago?"

Johnson looked pensive, "can`t say much my dear but yes, we believe the Bolshies are messing around with our currency. Can`t say anything more than that, top secret this you know," and he tapped the side of his nose with his finger.

# Chapter 26

## May 1934 – Pendlewick – East Lancashire

Manfred was carefully reading a telegram from Isaac Ventnor when the telephone beside him suddenly rang making him twitch involuntarily. Out of habit, he placed the communication face down on the table and lifted the receiver, "hello, Clitheroe one seven."

"Call for you Sir came the woman`s voice, would you like me to connect you?"

Manfred quickly reached for a scrap of paper and his pen and inkwell. "Yes put the caller through please."

After a succession of clicks the connection was made. "Hello, how may I help you?"

There was a click then a crackle, "Mister Black?"

"Speaking."

"It`s Hilda from Wilkinson`s tailors, your suit is ready. Would you like us to deliver it….. or shall Sir be collecting it?"

Manfred frowned at her petulant tone then took out his pocket watch, flicked open the cover and glanced at the time. "What time do you close today?"

"We shut at five o`clock, prompt."

"Excellent, I have some errands I wish to carry out so I

will collect my suit in thirty-five minutes. Please ensure you have it packaged and ready for my arrival," and he put the receiver back in its cradle.

Hilda went to speak then realised the line was dead. She looked at the receiver then across at the other shop assistant. "Ooh harken `im, `ave it ready and packaged for my arrival, bloody cheek. Them rich folks are all alike. I`ve a good mind to tell `im it`s not ready when `e gets `ere."

"When who gets here?" Asked a balding man as he emerged from a back room. He was dressed in a crisp white cotton shirt, perfectly fitted dark blue trousers and matching waistcoat. A tape measure hung around his shoulders and he walked towards one of the bay windows at the front of the shop.

Hilda blushed profusely. "Ahem, sorry Mister Wilkinson, just `avin` a little joke with Edna `ere `bout Mister Black`s suit being ready for `im to pick up."

The tailor stopped in his tracks and looked at her, his face serious. "We are a premier purveyor of discerning gentlemen's attire." He sniffed pompously as he regarded one then the other. "They pay your wages, never forget that," and he walked over and climbed into the shop window and began adjusting the jacket on one of the mannequins.

At four thirty, Manfred returned home and after placing the brown paper parcel on the kitchen table he removed his hat and coat and put the kettle on the stove top. As he did so, the phone rang. No doubt the insolent Tailor`s assistant calling me to apologise, he thought indignantly as he lifted the receiver.

"Call for you Sir came a woman`s voice, would you like me to connect you?"

"Yes put the caller through please."

After a succession of clicks the connection was made. "Hello, how may I help you?"

"Mister Black?"

"Speaking."

There was the slightest of pauses then, "what colour are the women`s scarves?"

"The women`s scarves are white and have a red stripe down the middle," Manfred replied confidently.

"Thank you Mister Black. I have just received information that the Secret Service believe someone is interfering with the British currency. I apologise for the lack of detail, but I have been unable to find out anymore, but it can only be your work he was referring to."

Manfred`s heart palpitated slightly but he rapidly regained his composure. "We will close down the printing operations immediately. There is sufficient currency now in circulation to cause the problems we aimed for. Would you please arrange for the advertisement to be placed in the *The Times* newspaper immediately," and he placed the telephone receiver back in its cradle.

In London, Doreen Thomas heard the click as the line went dead and after putting the receiver down, she opened the drawer in her desk and removed an envelope pre-addressed to *The Times*. Slipping it into her handbag she walked over to the coat stand and put on her fur edged jacket then tapped on Rear Admiral Simpson`s door and walked in. He was on the phone but paused irritably and put his hand over the mouthpiece, "what is it Missus Thomas?"

"I'm just off to the stationary shop Sir, I will be back in fifteen minutes."

Simpson shook his head and waved her away, "now then, in Belfast you say....."

Doreen shut the door behind her and quickly trotted down the staircase and out of the double front doors and onto the busy street. They had contacts at the newspaper, but she felt it prudent to use a go between by the name of Sandy Blanchard who owned the nearby stationary shop.

By the following evening`s print, the advertisement was out and in an agreed position within the newspaper, where the people in the know, would get the message to cease operations immediately, destroy any evidence they could and move to their new locations.


The two policemen sat in the Chief Constable`s office poring over documents laid out on the table.

"Ye say the weapon was a wee revolver now?"

James licked his thumb and forefinger and flicked a sheet of paper off the desk then handed it to the Inspector. "Yes Sir, a *Webley Mark Four.* Mister Davenport served in the *East Lancashire Regiment* in the Great War Sir, he must have sneaked it home with him when the conflict ended.

The Inspector pondered the information for a moment. "Ye`ll no be havin` the bullet will ye?"

"I don`t imagine we do Sir, I mean not that I know of. Is that something that would normally be collected in matters like this?"

The Inspector sighed, "it would be in my line o`work laddie. If ye `ave the bullet and the gun, ye can examine them under magnification and see if they match each other. This would tell us if the Webley was used or if another weapon was involved. I`m discountin` the notion of being able to check fer any fingerprints as too much time `as passed, an` I`m in no doubt, quite a few people have `andled the weapon in that time."

Warburton looked down. He felt embarrassed at his lack of knowledge of what seemed to be basic policework to the Inspector.

"Look at me laddie!" And Warburton immediately looked up." Ye canny know what nobody teaches ye. De`ye think I was born knowin` this kind o`thing? Aye ye need an inquisitive mind for police work, but ye also need someone willin` tae show ye the ways. Ye can nae do it be yerself Constable Warburton," and standing up he gave the young man a friendly slap on the back. "Come on laddie, there`s a wee pie shop not far from `ere, an` I`ve a mind tae sample their wares once more."

As they walked up the street, Warburton stepped into the gutter to allow a lady to pass by them then he quickly re-joined the Inspector who kept up a surprising turn of speed for such a large man. "I have just had a thought Sir," he panted as he drew level with him, "when I said we didn`t have the bullet, maybe the Coroner has? I know he does these autro.... hawto, I know he sometimes cuts up bodies Sir."

The Inspector stopped, "ye mean an autopsy Constable."

"That's it Sir, maybe it would be worth us checking if he did one this time."

"It would indeed, but first I `ave a wee appointment with a couple`o those delicious pies."

No sooner had he finished wiping his fingers clean with his handkerchief the Inspector gave a satisfied sigh then nodded towards the door to the Coroner`s building and they stepped inside.

"Back again are we gents," and the clerk started walking to the filing cabinet. "Forgot something about poor Missus Billington have you?"

James removed his helmet. "Hello Missus Clacton, and no, we are here to see the Coroner on another matter. Do you know if he is in?"

The lady stopped, "I see, please wait here and I will ask Mister Mitchell if he is free," and she disappeared down a corridor at the back of the room.

Inspector Anderson walked around with his hands behind his back examining and admiring the ornate dark wooden panels on the walls. "Beautiful place isn`t it Constable."

James was about to answer but Missus Clacton returned and announced that the Coroner was free to see them.

The Coroner sat behind a large desk in front of a stained-glass window and peered at them over his tiny round spectacles as they sat down and explained the reason for their visit.

"So ye see Mister Mitchell, it would be of real benefit tae our investigation if ye `ad removed the bullet and kept it in a safe place ye know."

The Coroner nodded then steepled his fingers in thought. "I remember this very well gentlemen and I will tell you why shall I? In sad cases like this, I would normally just carry out a cursory examination and discuss the events with the investigating policeman. Everything seemed in perfect order but the Sergeant who provided me with the details, appeared to be, shall we say a little over enthusiastic regarding the evidence he provided, more so than in other similar cases I have dealt with. So, with this in mind, I decided just for my own information, I would examine the body of Mister Davenport more closely."

The Inspector leant forward in his chair at this new revelation. "And ye ` ave the bullet?"

The Coroner nodded, "you will be pleased to know that I removed the bullet.... but not from the body," and he smiled smugly when he saw the reaction on the policemen`s faces. "No gentlemen, I took it from the nearby tree trunk. You see, I always fancied myself as a bit of a *Sherlock Holmes*, so after my discussion with the Sergeant, I went to the location and had a look around and lo and behold, I found the bullet lodged in the tree trunk, complete with traces of blood and remnants of body tissue. Having cleaned it up, I placed it safely in my cabinet over there," and he pointed to a roll top cabinet in the corner of the room.

James let out a sigh of relief. "We would like to take the bullet for further investigation Mister Mitchell, and we would be happy to sign it out of your possession if that is what you would require."

The Coroner waved his hand dismissively in the air. "Nonsense Constable please take it. It`s always rewarding to find that after one makes a professional judgment, it is later confirmed that it was the right decision to make." Standing up he rubbed his hands together. "Now, what do you say to my sleuthing skills Inspector?"

Anderson stood and shook him by the hand, "an excellent piece o`work Mister Mitchell, couldn`t `ave done it better ma self, if ye take ma meanin`. Now whilst we are `ere Sir, may I ask if ye recollect the Maureen Billington case?"

The Coroner twisted his mouth to the side slightly and looked up towards the ceiling. "Ah, yes another suicide Inspector," and smiling politely, "I expect you think this kind of thing goes on all the time, but it doesn`t." His face turned solemn. "We haven`t had this happen in the twenty-two years I`ve been in the post, then we go and get two within eight months of each other! Damned bad luck I say."

"Aye, be that as it may Sir but do ye `appen to know if a statement is available from Missus Billington`s husband, I`m assuming that the lady `ad a `usband o`course."

"Yes, yes Inspector, a Mister Henry Billington. Lovely chap, or he was before the incident. He was so upset, had to be physically held up at the funeral. Then," and he paused for thought, "in fact it was around about the time of Mister Davenport's suicide, totally lost his mind. Man was a shaking wreck, looked like someone fresh from the trenches if I didn`t know any different. Two weeks later he was committed."

The Inspector raised an eyebrow questioningly. "Committed ye say?"

The Coroner slowly shook his head sadly. "Yes Inspector, committed to the Calderstones Hospital near Mitton, the man had gone quite mad. Looked like the grief had finally caught up with him."

As the two men bustled off back down the street to the

Station, James chatted excitedly to the Inspector. "That was a bit of luck Sir wasn`t it," and he threw the bullet up in the air catching it deftly in his right hand. "Who would have thought the Coroner was such a good detective."

The Inspector stopped and turned to James. "Would ye take a wee while tae think about what the man said Constable and let me `ave ye view on recent events."

Warburton`s stomach immediately lurched. *You've missed somethin` `ere Jimmy, now think an` think clearly afore yeh answer the Inspector.* He paused and chewed his bottom lip lightly in thought.

The Inspector smiled and sat down on a nearby wall by the butcher`s shop. "Well done Constable, ye did nae just blurt out the first thing that came into ye `ead. Shows ye`r learnin` young man. Now take ye time laddie, take ye time."

James thought hard and the recent conversation with the Coroner ran over and over in his mind. At one point he made to speak but at the last moment he stopped and paced up and down the pavement again. Eventually he stopped and turned to the Inspector. "First of all Sir, I am afraid that I should have....."

The Inspector held his hand up immediately. "Never be afraid Constable, now tell me ye view if ye`d be so kind."

James composed himself. "Well Sir, the Coroner said he found the bullet in the tree trunk. The only tree within one hundred yards of the gate on Twitter Lane is the one in the field about, I would say, five paces into the field."

"Aye go on Constable."

"This means that the bullet must have come from behind

Mister Davenport and not from the front, so this confirms it can't be suicide and someone else fired the weapon. It also confirms that the Coroner missed this fact as he still recorded a verdict of suicide, Sir."

Anderson stood up and stretched. "Excellent and I suppose this also tells us Mister Mitchell is no as good as 'e thinks 'e is Constable Warburton." He chuckled to himself, "maybe 'e should stick tae his story books eh? Now let's be away to this 'ospital. I'd like tae have a wee word with Mister Billington."

The hospital was a *Dual Pavilion* design and consisting of over thirty red brick buildings, it covered a huge area of the countryside and as the police car crunched to a halt on the shingle driveway beside a shiny white grocer's van, the two men got out and looked at the foreboding building before them.

As they looked on, James glanced at the delivery van with ornate lettering painted on the side, *Joe Fielding's Grocers, Dukes Brow, Blackburn.*

Just as he was turning back he noticed a young girl sat in the passenger seat of the cab nervously twirling her finger through her blonde curls. Walking over he tapped on the window and mouthed, "you all right missy?"

She nodded slowly but did nothing to make Warburton feel any less concerned, so he gently opened the van door and smiled. "I am a policeman young lady, is everything all right?"

The child glanced nervously at the hospital and pointed. "Me Dad's in there deliverin' food an' the like. I don't like it 'ere Mister Policeman, it scares me it does and me

Dad always slows down and points at the strange folk as we pass `em on the driveway."

James smiled reassuringly and patted her gently on top of the head, "well there`s nothing to worry about luv, your Dad will be back soon enough, and you can be on your way again."

Still unconvinced she gave a nervous smile and nodded then once again stared intently at the building willing her Dad to come back and as James looked at the building before them, he nervously swallowed suddenly beginning to feel the same as the little girl.

The Inspector smiled and clapped his hands together, "right Constable, let`s be gettin` ourselves inside eh."

They were met by a uniformed nurse who looked at them sternly. "No visitors allowed!"

Inspector Anderson pulled out his warrant card and showed it to the nurse. "It would appear tae me that I `ave just made a change that wee rule o`yours."

He looked at the card and sniffed. "Wait here please Inspector, I will have to get Doctor Bentham," and he went off down the corridor, the clicking of his brogue heels echoing off the cream painted walls.

Moments later he returned accompanied by, who the Inspector assumed was Doctor Bentham in tow. "Welcome Inspector," and he reached out to shake his hand, "but you must realise this really is unacceptable. We have a strict no visitor rule, due to the.....nature of our patients here, and to be perfectly honest, the families have no interest in visiting anyway so therefore, I really must protest."

The Inspector gripped the Doctor`s hand tightly and

looked him in the eye. "Well ye see doctor, we are investigatin` a potential murda`, so if I`m tae be perfectly `onest with ye, ye protests mean very little tae me at the moment, if ye take ma meanin`," and he winked and released the doctor`s hand.

The doctor looked up at the Inspector and he attempted to stifle a gulp. "Ah, I see, well I still say this is very untoward Inspector, but on this occasion, and only this occasion, we will co-operate. Now please state your business Sir."

"We would like tae speak tae a Mister Henry Billington who we are led tae believe was..... committed here last February or March time."

The Doctor looked at them both then turned to the nurse, "would you fetch the keys to the side ward please nurse. This way gentlemen," and he gestured down the corridor.

As they walked down the shiny passageway James could here grunting and muffled screams from the wards as they passed by. The smell of disinfectant hung in the air and the cream walls and green corridor floor seemed to be closing in on him. He leant in towards the Inspector as they walked. "I don`t like this place at all Sir, and I don`t mind admitting it." James was surprised when the Inspector glanced back at him and grimaced. "Me neither laddie."

The doctor stopped outside a large room with a small window in the door. "Please wait here for a moment gentlemen, the nurse will be here shortly," and the three men stood in an uncomfortable silence.

To James it seemed an eternity for the nurse to arrive, and as he nervously looked down the corridor to see if he was coming he suddenly jumped when someone grabbed his sleeve. "Hello pretty boy, my name is Brenda, and this is my dog. She lives with me."

James turned swiftly and recoiled at the sight of a tiny woman of indeterminate age dressed in an ill-fitting white night gown, her tangled hair pointing in all directions. She was being led by the arm and the nurse gently chided her, "now Dorothy, you know you haven`t to tell lies about a dog or touch the visitors don`t you."

The woman turned to the nurse with an inquisitive look on her face. "Do I know, do I know that?"

"Yes you do, now come along back to your bed."

James watched as they slowly made their way down the corridor, the woman still questioning the nurse. "What about Brenda, does Brenda know?"

His relief was total when the nurse appeared with the keys and began to open the door to the side ward. They stepped inside and before them lay twelve beds neatly laid out in two rows of six. At the very end, a man sat on a pallet bed rocking back and forth in silence, his face blank as he stared at the opposite wall.

The nurse walked over and knelt in front of him, taking his hands gently. "Henry," he whispered kindly, "you have some visitors, would you like to see them?"

After a few moments had passed, he looked at the policeman and shook his head slowly. "Nothing. It`s been like this for weeks. Apparently he doted on his wife and, when she..... well his heart broke and his mind went."

"May I try," and the Inspector moved forward and sat on the bed beside the man. "Good day tae ye Henry. Ma names Robert, and I`d be grateful if ye could try and `elp me. We are thinkin` that the death of ye wife is linked tae a murda`. Now I know ye might not be wantin` tae speak tae anyone at the moment Henry, an` that is understandable, but if ye can remember anythin` that ye wife might `ave `ad any trouble with prior tae ye know, before the sad event took place, I`d be very grateful, if ye take ma meanin`."

James looked at Henry Billington and gave a sigh. There was nothing, no reaction or anything. It was as though he was in another world, a world where nobody else could reach him.

The doctor casually leant against the wall by a nearside bed with his arms folded, "you are completely wasting your time Inspector, the man is devoid of any sense now. Best to leave him be, it's a hopeless case."

The Inspector stood and turned angrily to the doctor. "An` I suppose ye`d be different would ye if the woman ye`d adored all ye married life `ad been taken in such a way?"

The doctor became very uncomfortable as the huge figure towered over him, "well what I mean Inspector is that we have done everything we can, for the moment that is. I mean obviously we will carry on with Mister Billington`s electric shock treatment....."

The Inspector waved his hand dismissively then noticed that James had walked over to the wall and was running his finger along the cream coloured brick work by Billington`s bed. "What`s the matter Constable?"

James bent down and squinted at the wall, "come and take a look Sir."

Anderson walked over and the two men examined the wall. "Tell me doctor," and he spun to face the man, "` as anyone else been stayin` in this bed?"

The doctor shook his head. "No, the wall had been freshly painted before Mister Billington came, he has been the only patient to be held in this bed."

# Four Months Earlier - February 1934

## The Billington Farm – Pendlewick

Henry Billington sat alone in the front room of the farm-house beside the unlit fire as he had done every night since the death of his wife.

He stared at the empty grate, cold and black and a slight chill blew down the chimney and onto his legs. The farm was on its knees but he didn`t care anymore. He had nothing to live for now Maureen had gone and at the thought he felt the pain in his heart once more. She was the only person he trusted. The only person he wanted to be with and now she was gone.

He knocked back the last remnants of the bottle of whis-key and he stumbled slightly as he attempted to stand. Staggering slightly he approached the staircase and stretching his arms out either side of himself, he started to gingerly walk up the stairs that led to the bedroom.

He walked in and once again gazed forlornly at the empty bed and tears began to form in his eyes. He would do any-thing to have her back, even for a minute, just so he could tell her how much he loved her one more time.

He slumped down onto the bed, harder than he expected, and as he tried to steady himself he tumbled onto the floor by the wooden bed side table. Lifting his arm, he began to push himself up but as he did, he peered at some-thing wedged in a small gap under the table. Reaching for it he carefully pulled out a small leather-bound diary. He tried to smile through the tears, *Maureen`s diary,* and he held it warmly to his chest as though it was her he was holding and gently closed his eyes.

Pulling himself up onto the bed, he lay back and started to read his wife`s daily thoughts. As he got part way into the notes, his hands began to tremble, and he could feel his stomach starting to knot. "No, no," he whispered, "it can`t be, he wouldn`t not to my Maureen...." and he dropped the diary onto the floor anger flooding through his veins pushing any sadness away.

# May 1934 – Clitheroe – East Lancashire

On returning to the station, the Inspector was met by Sergeant Entwistle and as he handed a note to him, he smirked at Warburton.

Anderson read the note and nodded. "Right, this way Constable," and they walked into their office leaving the smiling Sergeant behind them.

"I need to make a wee trip to London, and I`ll be back be Friday. In that time I would like ye tae send the revolver and the bullet tae this address," and he scribbled a note on a piece of paper and handed it to the surprised Constable.

"What`s happened Sir?"

"It`s all right laddie, Mister Simpson wants a word, in person ye understand." He clapped his hands together, "now, the package, ye need tae ask fer an examination tae confirm if the bullet belongs tae the revolver, understood?"

"Yes Sir, anything else?"

The Inspector looked around to make sure he couldn`t be overheard. "Aye, an` the scratches on the wall ye found, ye keep that tae ye-self…. fer now."

# Chapter 27

## May 1934 - Security Service Headquarters, Broadway Buildings 54, London

The woman picked up the ringing phone on her desk, "yes Sir, right away," and turning to the man waiting in her office, "Mister Simpson will see you now Inspector."

"Thank ye kindly madam," and he walked towards the door and having knocked purposely, he went inside.

Simpson immediately rose from his desk and shook the Inspector by the hand. "Anderson my man, how the hell are you?"

"I`m well thank ye kindly, and as ye can see, I`m still at ma fightin` weight."

Simpson guffawed and gave him a friendly pat on the back, "you always were first in the Wardroom what?"

Anderson smiled at the memory. "Aye that I was. Now, what is it ye are wantin` fer me to come all the way down `ere?"

Simpson`s face became serious. "Blighters are playing silly buggers with our currency Anderson. Counterfeiting the stuff you know. Had reports from almost every corner of the country and we need to get a firm grip of the situation."

The Inspector sat down in a chair in front of the Rear Admiral`s desk. "An ye`ll be wantin` me tae get involved in some way then?"

Simpson shook his head vigorously, "no no Anderson, we have it in hand. Now we know what to look for, the banks are pulling the currency out and we are destroying it. Top secret you understand, can`t be allowing all and sundry to know. Would cause havoc, already had the *Great Slump* so to devalue the pound would be madness and we shan`t be allowing that Anderson. No, I'm as happy as I could be with that side as the chaps at the Bank of England have come up with a new way of printing the money. Clever chaps indeed these are Anderson. Devised a way of putting some sort of metal strip into the things, helps stop the Bolshies from tampering as easily. Damned if I know how they have done it, but done it they have, just keeping it hush hush if you know what I mean," and he tapped the side of his nose. "Not being announced in public at all, just getting on with the blasted thing."

The Inspector was becoming more frustrated, "aye that`s all well and good Simpson but would ye care tae tell me what ye do want me to be doin` then."

"Ah yes, sorry old boy, got a bit carried away there. I want you to increase the scope of your investigation Anderson. Need you to be a bit more.... far reaching shall we say. Had reports some time ago that we just missed some Communists who had been stirring up some trouble. Scarpered from Salford before we got them they did, up to your neck of the woods actually, so I was led to believe."

Anderson raised his eyebrows," so ye want me tae `ead back up tae Scotland then an` find these people fer ye?"

Simpson shook his head decisively and slid a folder over to the inspector. "No Anderson, I believe they didn't go as far as we thought. Take a look at this, third page in."

The inspector picked up the file and duly flicked the pages until he could read the third one. He scanned his eyes along the page mouthing the words silently then closed the file again. "Interesting, very interesting. Now if ye is lookin` fer me tae expand my investigation, then I`ll be needin` some more men, if ye take ma meanin`."

Simpson stood up and walked over and as he opened the door, "not a problem Anderson. Missus Thomas, tell Cedric Johnson to report to my office immediately."

# Chapter 28

## May 1934 – Clitheroe Police Station

The Inspector walked into the Chief Constable`s office and he was pleased to see Warburton sat at his desk hard at work. "Afternoon Constable, how are we doin` now?"

James looked up and after beaming a welcoming smile, he stood up smartly and saluted the Inspector. "I`m very well thank you Sir, glad to see you back. I got your message and I have made a list of interviews we should have with the locals in Pendlewick."

The Inspector took off his coat and dropped it onto the table, "an` these will be takin` place where might I ask?"

"At their residencies Sir, as instructed."

Anderson sat down with a slight grunt and looked at his watch, "excellent an` when is our first appointment?"

"Three o`clock Sir, with a Missus Porter, the Pendlewick Post Mistress," he added quickly.

The Inspector grinned. "From what I`ve been told, she would be an excellent startin` point young man."


The doorbell tinkled softly as the Post Office door opened and the Inspector smelt a faint waft of perfume mixed with the odour of an old library and he stooped over as he entered. As he straightened up again he was met by a smiling lady stood behind a countertop sorting envelopes.

"Yes Sir, what can I do for you?"

James stepped around the Inspector. "We are here on official police business Missus Porter, this is Inspector Anderson."

"Ah `ello Constable Warburton, how is yer mum doin`? `As she still got that trouble with `er, yeh know `er," and she mouthed some words silently in James`s direction. Anderson was unable to make out what she said but the young Constable appeared to fully understand as he blushed profusely.

"Huh, yes I believe she has but she got some sort of ointment for it Missus Porter."

"Ah good, that`s nice, well tell `er I `ope it clears up soon. Now what can I be `elping you with this afternoon?"

The Inspector pulled out his warrant card and showed it to the Post Mistress. "Can ye be tellin` me what ye know about a Mister Alfred Davenport now Missus Porter."

The smile left her face immediately. "Don`t know nothing about no Alf Davenport. I keeps me self to me self I do," and she turned her back and pretended to be busy checking some paperwork on a shelf behind her.

James gave a, *I told you so* look to the Inspector who nodded back to the Constable.

Driving from the station to Pendlewick, James had explained his endeavours at obtaining information from the locals. "So you see Inspector, no matter what I ask or do, I get nothing. Some I think are genuine, and they have no information, others, well they seem to be hiding something. Sergeant Entwistle told me that he has had numerous complaints about me asking questions and that I need to watch out for myself."

The Inspector had sat quietly listening as they trundled down the country lanes then he suddenly sniffed and shimmied up in his car seat. "Well nay bother Constable, let`s be tryin` one more time eh?"

The Inspector put his arms out and laid his huge hands flat on the countertop. "So let me understand this ma wee hen. Ye say ye know nothin` about anythin`."

"That's right," she replied indignantly without turning around.

"Aye, that`s what I thought. So would it be a wee surprise fer ye tae know that the whole village thinks ye are a nosey busy body then and that ye actually know everythin` that goes on in Pendlewick?"

James`s eyes widened in shock as Missus Porter spun around, her face bright red with anger. "How dare you come in `ere and say nasty things like that!"

The Inspector reached back into his pocket and once again took out his warrant card which he held up to the irate woman before him. "Ye see this wee card madam? Well this says that I can go anywhere I please, say anythin` I want tae and ask anythin` I see fit, so let`s stop ye foolin` around an` get ourselves down tae business now."

James noticed how Missus Porter scowled at the Inspector, but he was totally unperturbed and simply picked up a handful of letters from the countertop and began slowly examining them.

"Them is private them letters, property of the General Post Office.... until they is delivered that is," she snapped.

The Inspector ignored her, and James watched mesmerised. "So Missus Porter," he began absentmindedly whilst still sifting through the envelopes, "this Alfred Davenport, a gentleman ye state ye nothing of but refer tae `im as *Alf* Davenport. Don`t ye find that a wee bit strange?"

After almost thirty minutes of questioning, the two policeman left the Post Office and a furious looking Post Mistress, "thank ye kindly Missus Porter, it was lovely tae meet ye."

As they got into the police car James switched the engine on then paused and turned to the Inspector beside him. "Sir can we speak honestly, off the record I mean."

"Certainly laddie, what would ye like to discuss?"

Warburton took a deep calming breath. "Just now in the post office, I don`t think I will ever be able to think and speak like you do, Sir. I mean...."

The Inspector held his palm up and James stopped talking immediately. "How old are ye laddie?"

James swallowed nervously, "I`m twenty-two, twenty-three in December."

The Inspector twisted and put his arm across the back of Warburton`s car seat. "An` would ye care tae tell me what ye think I was doin` at that age?"

James shifted in his seat, "I don`t know Sir, probably something like....."

"I`ll tell ye what I was doin` young man. I was doin` exactly what ye`re doin` right now and that is I was learnin` ma trade by watchin` and listenin` tae others.

Ye`re a bright laddie Constable Warburton, and I can see that ye have it in ye so take no never mind of what ye think ye limitations are right now. See it as ye`re bein` paid to learn, and one day, ye`ll be havin` this very conversation with another young policeman. Now let`s away to our next appointment and think no more of it."

James nodded, "thank you Sir," and he looked over his shoulder then pulled out onto the road. Less than ten minutes later, they stopped outside a beautiful cottage, it`s sage green door slightly covered by the overgrown clematis around the frame. James walked up to the door and grabbing the brass knocker he rapped it smartly against the door and turned to face the Inspector who was bent over sniffing one of the flowers by the pathway.

He stood up and closed his eyes as he breathed in the heady scent, "ah, reminds me of ma `ome." Just then they heard the creak of the front door opening.

"Yes Constable, how may I be of help."

James removed his helmet and coughed gently into his hand, "good afternoon, Mister Black is it Sir?"

The man looked at him warily, "yes I am Mister Black, what is the reason for your visit Constable?"

James turned to the Inspector, but Anderson merely nodded his encouragement to the young man.

"Well Sir, we are gathering some information regarding a gentleman that you appear to be familiar with. A Mister Alfred Davenport."

The man smiled thinly. "Ah yes, Mister Davenport, he did a few odd jobs for me some time ago. Such a shame about his sad demise."

"And would you please tell me the nature of these odd jobs Mister Black."

"Unfortunately, I cannot go into too much detail as I work for the British Government," and reaching inside his jacket, he confidently pulled out a folded sheet of paper which he passed to the Constable. "I am bound by the *Official Secrets Act*," and on seeing the concern on James`s face, "nothing to be worried about Constable," he quickly reassured him, "but I have been tasked to carry out some surveying work in the area. The subject of the survey is quite an emotive one which is why I cannot divulge too much. I am sure you will understand my situation."

James suddenly realised that he was out of his depth and he turned to the Inspector and held out the document to him.

Anderson read it then nodded, "looks tae be all in order Mister Black," and he handed the document back to him. "Now, and this will no conflict with that wee document ye `ave in ye `and, how would ye describe Mister Davenport`s demeanour the last time ye saw the gentleman?"

Manfred tilted his head slightly and looked upwards as though he was thinking back in time. "Let me see, it was probably six months or more since he carried out some repair work to the front fence there. Seemed a happy kind of chap. Arrived on time, got on with his work, which as you can see, is of a very good standard. So other than that Inspector, to me he was just another of the helpful locals," and he held his hands out. "I realise that is probably not what you wanted to hear, but unfortunately, that is all I have."

The Inspector looked at him then dipped his head, "thank

ye kindly Mister Black. If we `ave any more questions, we`ll be in touch with ye."

"No problem at all Gentlemen," and Manfred turned and once back inside, he quickly made his way to the front window making sure the net curtain hid him from the policemen's view.

As they got to the end of the narrow path that passed through the garden, Anderson stopped and ran his fingers along the top of the fence. "Feel the smooth new wood with ye fingers Constable and tell me what else ye see."

James felt the wood and then bent down and peered at the nails holding the picket fence together. "The nails look recent compared to the ones further along Inspector."

"Aye, so what ye thinkin` Constable?"

"That Mister Black was telling the truth Sir?"

Anderson rubbed his chin in thought. "Aye, ye`re correct Constable, but maybe `e was only tellin` the truth about the fence bein` repaired."


Back at the Station, Inspector Anderson leant back in his chair and gazed out of the window in thought. "Ye father, now he said a Mister Barlow, a gentleman who appears to be an acquaintance of Mister Black by the way, settled Alfred Davenport`s drinks bill at the Sun Inn," and he spun his chair round to face Constable Warburton. "Don`t ye find that a wee bit perplexing Constable?"

"Yes Sir. I spoke to my father and he said Mister Barlow paid the fourteen shillings that was owed and rounded it up to fifteen for his trouble. Paid with a nice crisp pound note as well. He remembers the details well because he was owed so much and is also not used to seeing paper money much round here since the reservoir workers left *Hollins*."

The Inspector leant forward, "a pound note ye say? Well now, I think we need tae have another wee visit to Mister Black but first let`s be havin` a check to see if `e is who he says he is eh?" Anderson stood up and closed the door then picked up the phone and after being put through by the operator, it was answered at the other end.

"Simpson here!"

"Ah good afternoon Simpson, it`s Anderson. I need ye tae check a couple o` names fer me if ye wouldn`t mind."

The Rear Admiral immediately jumped up nearly yanking the phone from his desk. "Excellent, are you on to something?"

"Maybe and maybe not. The two gentlemen are known as Frederick Black and Frank Barlow. Seemingly workin` fer the Government on a secret piece o` work. I`d just like tae know if they`re tellin` the truth, if ye take ma meanin`."

There was a pause as Simpson wrote down the names, "no problem Anderson leave it with me. We`ll find out if they are genuine chaps or not. Give me thirty minutes and I will call you back," and he put the receiver down and quickly opened his office door. "Missus Thomas, a moment of your time please." On seeing she didn't immediately respond, "come along, chop chop."

His secretary snatched a pencil and a note pad and scurried into Simpson`s office where she sat down in front of her boss.

"Now then, I want you to check on a couple of people for

me. Make sure they are who they say they are and all that kind of thing. Here are the names and what they are up to. Need the information in the next thirty minutes so off you go!"

Twenty-five minutes later, there was a tap at Simpson`s office door.

"Enter!" he barked.

The door swung open and his secretary entered carrying a sealed white envelope. "I have got the information you requested Sir, direct from the Home Office. It`s marked Top Secret," and she pointed out the words on the envelope, "so I obviously haven't opened it Sir."

"Excellent, now back to work and close the door on your way out," and he began opening the envelope. He sniffed and scratched the side of his face as he read the letter.

# Top Secret

For the attention of: Rear Admiral Herbert Simpson. May 14th 1934

Please be aware the contents of this document fall under the Official Secrets Act 1911.

Reference: Mister Frederick R. Black and Mister Frank P. Barlow.

The above-named gentlemen are currently carrying out a survey of the land around the village of Pendlewick in Lancashire in order to determine the suitability for a new Royal Airforce base. The work is expected to take approximately two to three years.

I hereby confirm that the facts above are true and abide by the Officials Secrets Act 1911.

This document must be destroyed immediately after reading.

Yours Sincerely,

Keith Shuttleworth

K. Shuttleworth – Home Office.

Simpson grunted with satisfaction, tore up the letter then reached for the phone to contact the Inspector.

In Clitheroe, the phone in the Chief Constable's office rang and after being put through by the operator, Simpson passed on the details of the letter from the Home Office to the Inspector.

"So ye think it`s all above board then Simpson?"

"No problems as far as I`m concerned Anderson!"

"Well all right, thank ye fer checkin` this out fer me," and he placed the receiver back in the cradle, but his hand remained firmly hold of it as he thought the conversation through. Eventually he turned to Warburton, "think we`ll pay one more visit tae Mister Black Constable."

Manfred heard the knock at the front door and immediately closed the suitcase he had just been packing. Lifting it off the bed, he slid it underneath and crept down the staircase and into the living room where he peered through the net curtain. "Damn, those two again!" And went to open the door.

Anderson had his back to the door and as it opened, he spun around and smiled, "ah, Mister Black, apologies fer botherin` ye again, but I`ve a mind tae ask ye a few more questions."

Manfred returned the smile, "no problem at all Inspector, how may I be of help?"

James looked on and tried to pick up on any nuances from the Inspector that he could learn from.

"Well ye`ll be glad tae know that ye wee tale of working fer the Government checks out, not that I did nay trust ye mind, but would ye care tae explain the whereabouts of Mister Barlow now."

Manfred looked down as he stepped over the door threshold, "that is simple to explain Inspector. Mister Barlow had to be reassigned to an urgent piece of work down in Kent, last minute call and all that. You know how it is with Government."

Anderson tilted his head to one side, "well not really but that's by the by Mister Black. Now I know ye canny give me too many details due tae this Secrets Act o`yours but can ye once again confirm the relationship ye had with a Mister Davenport, just so ah` have it clear in ma mind ye understand."

Manfred thought carefully before answering and attempted to give himself some breathing space, "what exactly do you mean Inspector?"

James noticed the Inspector was unfazed and merely shrugged his shoulders, "well exactly as ye just `eard me Mister Black, but if ye `re lookin` fer me tae put it another way, what involvement did ye `ave with Mister Davenport," and he pointed towards the end of the path, "aside from him mending the fence there fer ye."

By now Manfred had gathered his thoughts and went on the front foot. "There is no need to be facetious Inspector, I simply wanted you to explain exactly what information you required from me, that was all. Now," and he rolled his eyes upwards as if he was thinking, "this is as much as I can remember. We employed Mister Davenport on a temporary basis doing odd jobs around the place. You see, his farm like many others around the country are having a hard time and although I admit our work for the Government is of a confidential nature, we thought it only fair to help out some of the locals where we could. As you will appreciate, my mind is on more important matters than Mister Davenport, hence my recollection of his duties and the timings was only an estimate."

Anderson nodded his head slowly, "aye, I can understand

that ye would Mister Black. Now what other of these odd jobs did ye have Mister Davenport doin` fer ye?"

Manfred shook his head, took a deep breath and let it out in an exaggerated sigh. "Is this really necessary Inspector! I don`t want to pull rank in this instance, but if I have to, my Superior will get involved and neither of us wants that do we?"

Anderson ignored the threat with a wave of his hand. "Bein` a farmer now, did Mister Davenport `ave any gardenin` skills that ye know of?"

"Oh I don`t know! This really is becoming tedious Inspector and I am afraid that is all I have time for, now good day gentlemen."

As he turned to walk back into the house he heard the Inspector clear his throat. "One more thing Mister Black. When I checked ye details with the Government, I noticed ye `ad a middle name. Would ye care tae tell me what the letter J stands fer now?"

Manfred stopped dead in his tracks but didn`t turn around and there was a moment of silence and James looked eagerly at the Inspector and then at Mister Black.

"The details you saw must have been incorrect Inspector. My middle name begins with R, for Ralph," and he closed the door behind him.


The following day, Sergeant Entwistle tapped on the cottage door and quickly stepped inside as Manfred opened it.

On seeing the brown leather suitcase in the hallway, the Sergeant frowned and rubbed the back of his head. "Morning to you Mister Black, what`s the problem here?"

"My work here is done, and that interfering Inspector has been around asking questions again. It is time for me to move on, but I should warn you that it is only a matter of time before they link you to the murder of Alfred Davenport."

Entwistle made to speak but stopped and furrowed his brow. "What do you mean linked Sir? I didn`t murder Davenport!"

Manfred smiled, "that`s the way Sergeant…"

Entwistle grabbed Manfred by the shoulder, "no I mean, I didn`t kill him. I thought you had, or you had arranged it!"

Manfred`s face instantly went pale with shock. He felt strange and could hear his pulse pounding in his ears. He realised it was the first time he hadn`t felt in total control, "bu…but I tasked you with dealing with the problem Sergeant."

Entwistle nodded vehemently in agreement, "you did Sir, but as I was arranging it, I heard it had already been, huh, well…. dealt with Sir!"

Manfred started pacing up and down the hallway, his hands firmly gripped behind his back, the different scenarios running through his mind as he tried to focus on the problem. He suddenly stopped and looked Entwistle in the eye. "And why did you not report this to me Sergeant?"

Once again, Entwistle could see the manic look return to Mister Black`s eyes and he swallowed nervously. "I thought…., well I didn`t want to admit that I had failed in my duties Sir, in not sorting the problem fast enough you understand, and it takin` you to solve the problem for me and it not being what...."

Manfred irritably held his palm up to Entwistle. "Stop Sergeant!" he snapped, "you are beginning to babble. I did not kill Davenport, nor did I arrange for this to be carried out on my behalf! That little task was put at your door so the fact that you now tell me you didn`t do it raises a small conundrum."

Entwistle remained silent as he watched the other man begin pacing the floor again. He thought it wise not to ask Mister Black what a conundrum was but pinned his hopes on the fact that it being a small one was a good thing.

Manfred suddenly stopped and swung round. "I will leave within the hour Sergeant and as the net appears to be closing in around me once again, I suggest you do the same."

# Chapter 29

## May 1934 - Clitheroe Police Station

As the two policemen walked back into the station Sergeant Pilkington looked up, "afternoon Inspector," and he also nodded a greeting to James, "Constable Warburton." He leant over and passed a large envelope to Anderson. "This has just arrived for you Sir, oh and there is a gentlemen waitin` for you in your office. He seems to be gettin` the once over from the Chief Constable."

Anderson took the envelope and passed it to Warburton then began removing his coat as he made his way into the office. "Johnson, nice to see ye again."

Cedric Johnson immediately spun round," ah Inspector Anderson, and pleased to meet *you* again Sir."

James followed and looked at the small bespectacled man before him and took him to be either a scientist or a librarian. The Inspector turned to James and he was surprised when he introduced the man and to find out that he was a Secret Service officer.

The Chief Constable closed a file on his desk and rose from his seat. "Well, I will leave you three gentlemen to it," and he left the room.

"No problem at all Sir," and gesturing Johnson and the Constable to take a seat, "ye see, Johnson `ere has been on tae some.... well let`s just say on tae some gentlemen we would like tae speak tae, in person ye understand."

Johnson reached out to Warburton and shook him by the hand as they walked to the chairs, "nice to meet you Constable, the Inspector speaks highly of you."

"Well sit ye`selves down and let`s take a wee look at the contents of this envelope shall we," and Anderson proceeded to open the packet. "Just tae get ye up tae speed Johnson, the Constable here sent a bullet and revolver found at the scene of a suicide fer analysis tae see if they match each other. The gentleman in question was a Mister Alfred Davenport."

Johnson excitedly pulled up a chair, "excellent right up my street this you know."

"Well, I`m glad tae `ear that because we have a feelin` and it`s only a feelin` mind, there is more tae it than that and we `ave two cases that are linked and `ere`s why. After a wee visit tae see a Mister Henry Billington whose wife, God rest `er soul, took `er own life last year, the Constable `ere noticed initials scratched in the wall of Mister Billington's room at the `ospital. Now these initials were AD and had been scratched intae the paint on the wall several times mind. Now maybe I`m wrong, but I`ve a feelin` that they stood fer Alfred Davenport.....but as yet, I`m no certain of it."

The Inspector carefully read the report and slowly nodded at the contents whilst the other two men looked on with anticipation. "Well gentlemen, looks like we `ave ourselves a wee problem. The two don`t match, meaning Mister Davenport was shot be something else."

Johnson and Warburton both leant forward but James

managed to speak first. "Does the report say what type of gun the bullet came from Sir and do you think Mister Billington shot him?"

The Inspector turned and walked towards the window in thought. "Aye it does Constable, an` it`s possible that Mister Billington, maybe in anger at somethin`, shot Mister Davenport as the timeline certainly fits," and under his breath, "but how would Mister Billington manage tae get himself a Government issue weapon?" Turning back to the two men, "I think we need tae make a quick journey back to Mister Black`s cottage."

The three men quickly made their way out of the station and jumped into the Wolsey parked opposite on the street.

"Put ye foot down laddie, I`m thinkin` there`s more tae our Mister Black than meets the eye."

James looked over his shoulder, then with a chirp from the rear tyres they set off down King Street and turned right at the Railway Station towards Pendlewick.

Johnson leant forward between the two front seats, "what`s your thinking Inspector?"

Anderson maintained his view firmly on the road ahead, "keep your eyes on the road laddie, not me."

James jerked his head back to look at the road and gripped the steering wheel tightly. "Sorry Sir, just wondering what your answer is."

Anderson sniffed, "well it would appear the gun is a Government issue weapon. Unlikely tae be in the `ands of anyone `cept Government employees, which gentlemen, is what our Mister Black portrays tae be."

Cedric Johnson quickly looked left then right at the two men in the front seats, "phew that`s a turn up, and we are on our way to apprehend the chap are we Inspector?"

"Aye, that we are gentlemen."

Johnson sank back into the soft leather seat and he felt his mouth go dry and his hands tremble imperceptibly.

James eventually came to a halt on the lane about one hundred paces from Mister Black`s cottage. "Do you want me to get any closer Inspector?"

Anderson gazed at the cottage through the car windscreen. "Nay laddie, `ere is just fine. Johnson, there`s a wee path `round the back that leads tae the rear of the cottage. I`ll give ye two minutes tae get in tae position, then me an` the Constable `ere, will go an` pay a visit tae the front door."

Johnson gulped and he hoped a sound would come out when he spoke. "Am I...am I not better waiting here Inspector, in case he makes a run for it down the lane? Wouldn't want that would we?"

Anderson turned and looked at him for a moment...., "ye watch the back door of the cottage now, there's a good man."

Johnson got out of the car with great trepidation, *come on Cedric, come on man*, he thought to himself.

As they got to a small gate, Anderson pointed into the field at a hedge that ran along the side of the cottage. "Keep ye head down Johnson and stay outa` sight along be the hedgerow there and that`ll lead ye tae the back of the cottage, in case he makes a run fer it."

Johnson looked at the two policemen and tried to muster

as much bravery as he could and just as he was about to make his way towards the gate, he heard Anderson`s voice whisper in his left ear.

"Ye come with a wee reputation Cedric. Now kindly show me that they`re all wrong, if ye take ma meanin`."

Johnson turned and gave a nervous smile, "I...I will do my best Inspector," and he opened the gate and headed for the hedgerow.

James saw the interaction between the two men and how the Secret Service Officer had slunk away towards the hedge and as they made their way down the garden path to the cottage, "is everything all right with Mister Johnson Sir?"

The Inspector stopped at the front door and turned to the young Constable. "Everythin's fine laddie," and he knocked sharply.


Manfred pulled the strap on his suitcase tightly then put on his coat and hat. Taking one last look around the cottage dining room he smiled and whispered, "you served a purpose."

Just then he heard a knock at the door and instinctively reached for his gun underneath his coat. Making his way to the window, he peered through the curtain and then made his way to the front door. Smoothing down his coat and removing his hat, he opened the door in one smooth movement.

"Hello Sir, I believe you ordered a cab to the railway station."

"I did indeed, please take my bag," and he pointed to the brown leather case in the hallway.

"Right you are Sir," and the cabbie heaved the case up onto his shoulder and made his way to the car at the bottom of the garden path.

Pulling the door closed, Manfred walked down the pathway nonchalantly running the fingers of his left hand through the fading daffodils and as the cab drove away he had one last glance at the cottage in Pendlewick.

Anderson knocked again with a little more force.

"Maybe he is out Sir," offered Warburton.

At the back, Cedric Johnson paced back and forth in the grass by the rear gate. *Got a reputation have I? I`ll wager it`s one for being an excellent agent,* but his shoulders sagged with despair. *For once in your life man, be honest with yourself. You live a lie every day. You hide from any danger, that`s the reputation you have, and you damn well know it is!* He shook his head angrily. *I`ll show them,* and he made his way down the path to the back door.

"Take a wee look through the window and tell me what ye see Constable."

James pushed some plant stems to one side and cupped his hands to the window and peered inside and after a moment he concluded, "can`t see anything Sir. In fact, looks as though the place has been almost emptied!"

Anderson cursed under his breath and reached for the brass doorknob which surprisingly opened the unlocked door. He looked warily at Warburton then pulled out a small revolver from the inside of his coat and stepped cautiously inside.

James`s heart skipped a beat at the sight of the gun but he wasn`t going to miss this for the World and he followed the inspector into the cottage, his mouth dry but his heart pounding with excitement.

As they got halfway down the hallway they heard an almighty crash and the sound of shattering wood.

The two policemen quickly looked at each other then ran towards the noise, Anderson`s arm outstretched leading with his gun. They burst into the kitchen and found Cedric Johnson in a heap on the floor, nursing his right shoulder, the remnants of the door hanging from its broken hinges.

Anderson put his gun back into his coat. "You all right Johnson?"

He looked sheepish and he winced as he rubbed his shoulder again. "The chaps make it look so easy when they do it Inspector. Thought, I would give it a try and prove them wrong, and all that."

The Inspector smiled and reaching down and taking Johnson firmly by the hand, he heaved him up to his feet. "Ye did fine Johnson, just fine. Ye just need a wee bit more practice eh. Now let`s away an` take a look around. See if we canny find somethin` incriminatin` left behind."

The three men started to search through the rooms and soon came upon the *Koenig & Bauer* printing press and the Inspector ran his hand along the metal frame. "An` what have we got `ere then?"

Cedric Johnson joined him. "It is a printing press Inspector, a heavily modified *Frankonia* by the looks of things. My brother-in-law runs a small printing business in *Redditch*, and I am certain I have seen one of these in his workshop.

James bent down and squinted at the machine. "Looks like you push sheets of paper in here and," twisting his neck a little further, "the roller thing up there prints on the paper."

Johnson eagerly leant over and took out his magnifier, "excellent deduction Constable and if we look carefully, we will be able to see what the machine was printing," but he sighed disappointingly. "No good gentlemen looks as though they removed any evidence."

The Inspector`s eyes narrowed. "Would the thing they removed be of a cylindrical shape or of a flat shape?"

Johnson turned and he raised an eyebrow. "A good question Inspector. It would be a flat rectangular sheet that is bent around the roller."

Anderson nodded, "aye that`s what I thought."

Warburton felt the adrenaline race through his veins as he realised where this was going. "Do you think it may be buried in the garden Sir, is that why you asked Mister Black if Alfred Davenport had done any gardening work?"

Anderson looked at the young man and gave him an appreciative smile. "Well done Constable, shows me ye taken in what ye `ear now. There`s a patch of ground be the side of the cottage that does nay match the rest of the garden. I took tae noticing it on one of our visits to question Mister Black. Now I would say we take a wee look and see what we can find eh."

James followed the two men out of the back door and immediately spotted a small wooden shed. "I will see if I can get some tools Sir."

Within minutes James joined the others who were stood

looking down at a patch of ground. Taking off his jacket he rolled up the sleeves of his shirt and adjusted the straps of his braces to make sure they didn`t slip off his shoulders, then set to work with a spade.

In no time at all, they heard a *ching* and no more than six inches below the surface, they found a metallic sheet. Anderson took out his handkerchief and knelt down. Dabbing the cloth against his tongue, he started to wipe at a small area of the metal sheet and after a few seconds he stopped. "Think we `ave found what we were lookin` fer gentlemen."

The others also knelt down and James`s mouth opened in amazement when he saw the imprint of what looked to be money.

Johnson quickly wiped a little more with the palm of his hand then turned to the Inspector. "Counterfeit. This must have been where the money was being printed. How long do you think it is since Black left, I mean do you think there is still a chance we can catch him?"

Anderson shook his head and grimaced slightly as he stood up." Britain is large place Johnson, he could have set off in any direction ye know. Let`s away and take a look at the rest of the cottage, see if we can`t find a wee clue to where `e may be `eaded."

But there was very little left apart from a small table with a black telephone in the front room, the wires roughly frayed where they had been cut and the odd picture here and there on the walls.

The Inspector forlornly held up one end of the telephone wire. "Well I dare say it`s goin` tae be a bit difficult tae find Mister Black, what do ye think Johnson?" But there was no reply.

Anderson cleared his throat as he looked at the Secret Service Officer. "Ahem. I dare say it`s goin` tae be a bit difficult tae find Mister Black, what do ye think Johnson?" But he just stood there and continued to stare at the wall.

James walked over and tapped Johnson lightly on the arm who jerked round at the touch as though he had just been given an electric shock.

"The picture on the wall with the women working in the fields....."

"Aye we can see that Johnson, now what the `ell is wrong with ye man?"

Johnson`s gaze remained transfixed on the picture and his face lost all colour. "It.... it`s the exact same picture that is on the wall in Doreen`s office."

"Aye and Doreen would be who may I ask....?"

Johnson turned around slowly, and his eyes began to turn glassy as tears formed. "She is Rear Admiral Simpson`s secretary," and he put his head down in a mixture of embarrassment and anger.

Anderson slapped him on the back, "well this gets better and better Johnson. We find the counterfeiter and Simpson`s wee mole all in one fell swoop. Ye should be proud o` yerself man."

Johnson tried to show his appreciation but deep down his stomach turned over and he could feel himself getting hotter. "Yes Inspector a fine day indeed."

"Sir," James interrupted, "I believe Mister Black had the use of a motor car while he was in the area. A black Morris Minor was parked halfway into the ditch down the lane when we drove here. Could it be possible that he left the car there and hasn't made his escape by motor car but somehow got to the train station at Clitheroe?" He put his head down when he realised the others were looking intensely at him.

"Sounds good tae me Constable, let`s away tae the Station, we may be able to grab Mister Black after all."

The three men rushed out and jumped into the car. James turned the Wolsey around and after momentarily getting stuck when the rear wheels went onto some soft earth by the roadside, they were soon hurtling down the country lanes towards Clitheroe train station.

The police Wolsey careered around *Waddington Road* then onto *Railway View* and James glanced nervously as he saw the locomotive pulling into the platform, the smoke billowing up and over the covered footbridge that spanned the tracks. Honking his horn repeatedly at an unsuspecting cyclist, who steadfastly refused to get out of the way, Warburton eventually pulled up onto the kerb and swerved around the cyclist then roared forward and finally screeched to a halt outside the station. All three men jumped out leaving the car doors wide open and ran towards a bustling crowd leaving the station platform. A uniformed guard stood at a wooden gate checking tickets whilst smiling and nodding at the passengers and well-wishers. As he ran, Anderson reached into his coat and pulled out his warrant card just as the guard stepped into their way and held his hand up. "Whoa, `old yer horses gents, where`s yer tickets then?"

Anderson flashed the warrant card in his face, "out the way man, this is police business," and he barged past the shocked guard and on to the platform where he dodged in and out of the slender canopy support columns looking for their target.

Manfred leant against one of the cast iron columns on the platform and looked up the line, then once more at his pocket watch. *The train should be here by now*, he thought. Other passengers had started to congregate, and the chatter and laughter began to irritate him. Reaching into his pocket he pulled out his silver cigarette case and after lightly tapping the end against the case he lit one. It always seemed to calm his mind and he took another deep draw and tilted his head back slightly and blew a jet of smoke into the air. Things hadn`t gone perfectly, but they had gone well enough and Joseph was pleased with his efforts in Britain but more so with the interference in the US political system. All was going well and as he dropped his cigarette end on the platform and twisted his foot back and forth he heard the cheery whistle of an approaching steam locomotive. Manfred stepped back from the platform edge as the train puffed, hissed and clanked to a halt in the station. Reaching down for his case he approached the carriage door but as he reached for it, he felt a firm hand on his right shoulder. He surreptitiously reached into his coat and as his fingers wrapped around the handle of his revolver, he turned around.

"Is this the train to Preston fella?"

Manfred slowly let out his breath. "That is correct Sir, this train goes all the way to Preston."

"Right you are, after you fella," and he gestured for Manfred to get on the train then after waving to someone in the throng of people on the platform, the man followed him onto the train.

Manfred found his seat and after placing his suitcase in the overhead compartment he sat down and leant back in his seat with a relaxing sigh.

"Don`t mind if I join you do ya fella?" And the man slumped down beside him.

Manfred slowly closed his eyes and opened them again, "I am afraid I will not be very good company Sir so maybe it would be wise for you to sit elsewhere. Afterall, Preston is but a short time away."

The man slapped him on the shoulder which made Manfred wince irritably. "Don`t ya worry `bout bein` good company fella, I can talk th`hind leg off a donkey I can so I can talk for both of us. Now, did I tell ya `bout when I was in the trenches….."

Anderson panted heavily and his disappointment fell heavy on him as he saw the train slowly pulling out of the station. He shook his head in dismay but then squinted in an attempt to focus on the back of the train. *Wh…who`s that runnin` along the tracks?*

The guard came running past him, "hey you two you can`t be on them tracks! It's against the law it is, get off right now!"

Anderson laughed heartily and he slapped his thigh with his hand. "Well I`ll be damned," as he watched Warburton reach down from the guard`s van and pull Johnson up by the arm.

"Come on Cedric, come on you can make it!" Screamed Warburton, his hand outstretched towards the sweating man sprinting along the tracks behind the train.

It had almost been telepathic. The two of them had the

same idea as they reached the platform and saw the back of the departing train draw level with the end of the sloping platform and they had set off running with Johnson showing an amazing turn of speed for his age.

As the concrete platform ended they ran down onto the tracks timing their run to land on the railway sleepers with every stride. They could hear the locomotive cadence getting faster as it began to haul the heavy carriages forward and each of them encouraged the other as they ran.

"Run Constable run. Is that as fast as you can go? You should be ashamed a man of your age," gasped Johnson, and in turn James shouted back, "yer past it old man, leave it to us young lads!"

Eventually James's superior speed meant he could take hold of the railing at the back of the guard`s van and pull himself up where he immediately turned and held out his hand to Johnson. "Come on Cedric, come on you can make it!"

Sweat was streaming from Johnson`s face and he was just about to give up when the smirking face of Doreen came into his mind. *I lied all along, you are not as good as you think you are little man.*

James unexpectedly saw Johnson`s face snarl and he roared with anger and threw himself towards Warburton`s outstretched hand who gripped it firmly and dragged him onto the standing plate.

The two men couldn`t speak as they both gasped for air and it took a moment to recover from their exertion. Finally Warburton slapped the other man on the back. "Knew you could do it Sir!"

Johnson carried on taking deep calming breaths, "well I`m glad you thought I could Constable," and he attempted a smile of appreciation. "Come on, let`s make sure our efforts are not wasted young man."

"Would you like me to go first Sir, it might be dangerous?"

Johnson looked at him. "Ah good point, huh, yes you...." but the words of the Inspector drifted into his mind. *Ye come with a wee reputation Cedric. Now kindly show me that they`re all wrong, if ye take ma meanin`*, and he hesitated. "No Constable, as the Senior officer here, it is my duty to go first," and taking a deep breath, he wiped his sweating brow with his handkerchief and opened the guard van door.

The two men walked inside, and a uniformed man jumped up, "what the...."

Johnson quickly raised his hand, "nothing to worry about my man, me and the Constable here are on Government work," and the guard physically relaxed on seeing the dishevelled uniform of the policeman stood behind him. "Now quickly, how can we get to the passenger carriages?"

The surprised guard looked flustered then gathered his thoughts, "huh well you can..."

Warburton stepped in, "Sir, can`t we just pull the communication cord and stop the train?"

Johnson nodded. "Nice idea Constable, but Black will know something`s afoot and will jump from the train as soon as it stops and will be gone by the time we get there. No, we need to get in close then make our move." He turned back to the bemused guard, "well man, come on I haven`t got all day!"

The guard shrugged his shoulders, "well as I was about to say gents, yeh can go through that there door an` jump across to the rear passenger carriage and make yeh way through."

"Ah, well, that's better, why didn't you say that in the first place," and Johnson spun around and marched over to the wood panelled door. As he opened it the clatter and noise of the wheels on the tracks increased. "Come on Constable," he shouted, "let`s get our man!"

"Make sure you jumps right across when you..." but the guard gave up as the two men disappeared through the door.

Manfred had closed his eyes in an attempt to ignore the bore sat beside him, but it appeared he had thick skin and chattered on regardless.

"So ya see, when me and me mate built that garden shed, we never got enough wood so by the time..." but he was interrupted as a man and a young Constable sat down opposite.

"Good afternoon Mister Black, nice to finally meet you."

Manfred heard the incessant talking suddenly stop then a strange voice greet him by name. He slowly opened his eyes and he quelled his anger when he saw a skinny older man smirking and the Constable sat before him.

Warburton placed his hands on his knees, a triumphant smile on his face. "I take it your assignment is over then Mister Black, as you seemed to leave in a little bit of a hurry?"

Manfred smiled, "yes, I have been reassigned you know. Here I will show you my orders from the Home Office," and he reached inside to pull out the forged document.

Johnson leant forward, "now would that be a genuine document Mister Black, or has it been printed on your *Koenig & Bauer* printing press?"

Manfred froze and instead of reaching for the paper, he slowly grasped his revolver from his inside pocket and in one smooth movement he pointed it at the men before him. "Now gentlemen, unless each of you want a bullet in your foreheads, I suggest you both sit quietly whilst I take my leave," and he began to stand and reach for the communication cord.

As he did so the man beside him suddenly lunged up and gripped the revolver with both hands and pushed it harmlessly towards the window where a deafening bang saw the window shatter and the roaring wind came rushing into the carriage.

James dived at the two men and grappled the fugitive to the floor then knelt on the man`s arms to prevent him causing further trouble. "It`s okay Sir, I will take it from here, thank you for your assistance."

Johnson smiled. "Yes, well done Smith, just like the old days eh."

"Right you are Guv," and the two men shook hands.

James looked non plussed.

"It`s all right Constable Warburton. Mister Smith here was a member of my Salford team a few years back. Bit of a misunderstanding went on and I`m afraid he got accused of something he didn`t do. Not something I`m very proud of you know so thought it would be the right thing to do to get him involved again in solving the case once and for all."

Smith smirked, "looks like you aint bothered no more about it being saf…..secure before going in now Guv."

"Well, one learns from one's mistakes Smith so let`s leave it at that. Now what is the next station Constable?"

James grimaced as he tightened his hold on the struggling Mister Black on the carriage floor. "Whalley Sir, in about two or three minutes."

"Excellent, we will disembark and," pointing down at the prostrate figure, "take this bounder with us gentlemen."

# Chapter 30

## May 1934 - Security Service Headquarters, Broadway Buildings 54, London

Rear Admiral Simpson`s face was like thunder as he listened to the phone call from Cedric Johnson.

"You certain of this Johnson, I mean you were sure it was this Smith fellow not long ago!"

"I am certain this time Sir. The picture on the cottage wall is identical to the one in your secretary`s office." He was in a fix as he was now well aware that he was the one passing on the confidential information to her, but there was no way he could admit to it. "They must have been using it as some sort of reference or code."

Simpson harrumphed, "could be one of many pictures man! They do reproduce these things in great numbers you know, and as for Doreen, well she`s been with me for years. I can`t see it Johnson, I just can`t."

"Well how about a watch is put on her Sir, just to be on the safe side?"

"What! I`ll be damned if I start putting a watch on one of my most trusted employees Johnson," and as he made to put the phone receiver down he immediately put it back to his mouth again. "Your barking up the wrong tree man.... now get on with your assignment!"

The Rear Admiral sighed and leant back in his chair to think. *Could the pictures be a coincidence? I mean, some bugger is giving our information away, but surely not Doreen! Besides, the woman is nice enough, but not bright enough to be doing this kind of thing. All a lot of nonsense!*

Meanwhile, at Clitheroe Police Station, Johnson was pacing back and forth. "It has to be her," he whispered, "it has to be, and she is not going to get away with it!" Sitting down at a nearby desk he put his head in his hands, *think man, think!* Moments later, he looked up and smiled. *The letter from the Home Office. Anderson said Doreen had been asked to get the information on Black and Barlow!*

"Simpson here....., what you again! I thought we had......."

But Johnson interrupted, "Sir, please just listen to me. Check with the Home Office. Ask Shuttleworth to confirm the authenticity of the letter about Black and Barlow. Please Sir I beg you!"

The Rear Admiral held the phone receiver at arm`s length and frowned at it as though he was appraising the man on the other end of the line. In all the years he had known Johnson, he had never heard him be so animated, or this emotional. He paused for a moment then, "very well Johnson, but if you are wrong again and you are wasting my time, it`s the end for you, understand?"

"Yes Sir, just check please, we need to find the mole and stop them."

Simpson hung up then immediately dialled the Operator who put him through to the Home Office.

"Rear Admiral Simpson here, put Shuttleworth on," he snapped abruptly.

"Sorry Sir, Mister Shuttleworth is not in the office at the moment."

"Well find him damned you and get him to call me in the next five minutes!" And he slammed the phone down.

No more than two minutes had passed when the phone on his desk rang.

"Simpson here."

"Rear Admiral, this is Shuttleworth from the Home Office. You wanted to speak to me Sir," he panted.

Simpson smirked to himself, *had the buggers running round by the looks of things, that's the ticket.* "Now then Shuttleworth. I believe you had a request from my department recently from a Missus Doreen Thomas."

"Yes Sir, I remember that request."

Simpson harrumphed to himself. *Knew she would be in the clear. I`ll string that bugger Johnson up by his....*

"She asked if there was an update on *Sinn Fein* for you Sir," he added.

The Rear Admiral`s eyes narrowed, and he absent-mindedly hung up the phone. *Well I`ll be...*Jumping to his feet he marched to his office door and swung it open and as he strode past his Secretary, "I won`t be long Missus Thomas, stay were you are please."

As she watched Simpson leaving the office she noticed him glance at the picture on the wall and her heart skipped a beat. Snatching up her things she ran over to the coat rack and grabbed her jacket. Slowly opening the door, she looked left and right down the corridor, then content it was clear, she quickly walked to the stairs and descended as fast as she could without trying to draw any attention.

Simpson swung the office door open and marched in closely followed by two agents, "Right then ...," but the office was empty. "Damn where is she?" He quickly went into his own office and seeing the same result he went to the window and looked out scanning the crowds and street below. Then he saw her.

"Smithson, Williams, get after her, she is heading towards the Underground! Black jacket with a brown fur collar, you know the rest," he shouted as the two men ran for the staircase.

Sprinting down the stairs they burst out of the main entrance doors and onto the street narrowly missing an old lady pushing a battered pram. Scanning the area Williams pointed, "there she`s just entering the station!"

The two men dodged their way through the crowd and much to the chagrin of the underground employees, vaulted over the barriers and ran down the steps taking them two at a time. They knew time was short as they could hear the approaching train and feel the breeze building as it pushed the air from the tunnel into the surrounding platforms and passageways.

"`Scuse me, `scuse me," they shouted as they pushed past surprised and in some cases, angry travellers. Finally they came on to the platform and looked right and left trying to see Thomas in amongst the masses gathered waiting for the train.

"Can you see her Tom?" Shouted Williams over the hub bub of the waiting commuters.

Smithson nodded and pointed over to their target who was standing behind two men with her back to them.

"You walk past her slightly then we will grab her from both sides."

Williams casually walked along the platform then as he passed Thomas, he turned back and signalled to Smithson and they each put a firm hand on the woman`s shoulders. "We would like to have a word please Missus Thomas."

The woman turned and screamed and as the train pulled out of the tunnel and slowed to the platform, one of the bystanders turned on the two agents and he shoved Williams in the chest. "Hey what you up to harassing the poor lady like that!"

Smithson took a step back and held his hands out in apology. "It`s okay, we are Secret Service agents, we mistook this lady for someone we need to speak to that`s all."

The other man stepped up to Smithson and grabbed him by the shirt collar. "Leave it out! Secret Service my backside! Probably tryin` to rob folk that`s what you`re up to more like."

Watching from the side passage, Doreen Thomas took her chance and slipping quickly in beside a businessman walking to the open train doors, she linked her arm with his and stepped onto the train.

"Oops sorry dearie, thought you were someone else I did," and she left the bemused man with his mouth open as he stared at the strange woman nonchalantly taking her seat by the window.

As the doors closed and the train pulled out of the station, Doreen took a small mirror out of her handbag and re-applied her lipstick then smiled when she saw the four men still arguing and tussling on the platform. *It had been close, but it would take more than that to catch me*, she mused as the train entered the dark tunnel.

Two days later she was in a small hotel in Southampton awaiting the departure of the RMS Empress of Britain to Canada.

# Chapter 31

## May 1934 – Clitheroe Police Station

The following day, Anderson and Warburton were discussing the Davenport evidence they had collected so far when Cedric Johnson popped his head around the door.

"Sorry to interrupt gentlemen, but I will be leaving with my prisoner this afternoon. It would also appear we have located our mole, but unfortunately she has made her escape although I believe the Service is hot on her trail. On a separate note, I would like to thank you for your assistance, and I do hope you solve the Davenport case. Let me know if you need anything," and he waved his hand and disappeared back into the station reception area.

James turned to the Inspector, "It`s strange, I think I will miss him."

"Aye, I think the wee man had a bit more about him than he or most people thought. Shame his lady friend managed tae make her escape."

Warburton looked shocked. "His lady friend, do you mean...."

"Aye laddie but let`s cut Johnson a wee bit o` slack and keep it tae ourselves, if ye take ma meanin`." He stood and clapped his hands together. "Now I'd like tae take another look at Mister Black`s cottage. I `ave a feelin` there`s more tae that place than meets the eye Constable."

On their way-out Anderson tapped on the countertop as he walked past. "We`re away fer a couple o` hours Sergeant Pilkington, in case anyone cares tae know our whereabouts," and as they left the police station, a bearded man wearing a large over coat stood to the side and gestured for them to go first as they passed him in the doorway.

As Warburton drove towards Pendlewick the Inspector took out his notebook and pencil, "right Constable where do ye think we should start?"

"Well, the printing thing was buried in the garden, so if it was me leading this investigation Sir, I would take another look to see if there is anything else there. Also, see if the cottage has an attic or cellar maybe?"

Anderson nodded, "sounds like a good plan Constable, lead the way laddie."

Sergeant Pilkington watched as the Inspector and Constable left and smiled as a man in a large overcoat walked in. "Yes Sir, how can I help you?"

"Ah good morning Sergeant, I am here to collect a prisoner, I believe agent Johnson is my contact here."

Pilkington put down his pen, "ah you are a little early Sir, I got told you`d be here this afternoon."

The man reached into the inside of his coat, "I took the earlier train just in case. Here are my documents Sergeant. I think you will find them all in order."

Pilkington flicked through the paperwork then nodded.

"All appears correct Sir."

The man took the paperwork back and slipped it into his pocket. "Now if you would prepare the prisoner we will be on our way."

"Right you are Sir, I will go and get Mister Johnson and let him know you are here to collect the prisoner."

Moments later, the Sergeant returned closely followed by the Secret Service agent who held a welcoming hand out to the man. "Morning, Cedric Johnson and you are?"

The man gripped his hand firmly, "what *the* Cedric Johnson! When I got told my contact would be a Mister Johnson it never clicked. You`re the talk of the operators Mister Johnson and it`s an honour to meet you and by the looks of it, I`ll be working with you as well. Wait while the lads hear about this!"

Johnson puffed his chest out with pride, "well you are a little early but yes, I am Cedric Johnson and although I am a modest man by nature, it is welcoming news that my exploits are known by the lower services. Now then, what is your name and may I see your papers please."

The man once again handed over the paperwork, "the name is Edwards, George Edwards Sir."

Johnson put on his spectacles and examined the documents. "Mm, all seems in order Edwards, now I believe the next train to Preston leaves in," and he pulled out his pocket watch, "about fifty minutes. Sergeant Pilkington, would you please bring the prisoner out and I would also like to avail you of a pair of handcuffs and the keys."

"Right you are Sir," and the Sergeant spun on his heel and marched to the holding cell at the back of the station.

Edwards gently cleared his throat. "Begging your pardon Mister Johnson, but the Rear Admiral would like us to meet him personally in Manchester this afternoon. So he could thank you in person like. He is on his way to some big meeting somewhere and he said we had to be there by three this afternoon sharp. Which means we will have to drive as the trains won`t get us there in time. That`s why I arrived early Mister Johnson, the Rear Admiral was very strict on this point he was."

Johnson shrugged, "ah well, I suppose this is what happens when you are famous hey Edwards? Top Brass wanting to thank me all the time. I`m afraid it`s part and parcel with me you know."

Edwards smiled, "it must be remarkable Sir, and hopefully one day, I might be as good as you."

Johnson sniffed casually, "well, one day maybe Edwards."

Just then they heard a commotion and Sergeant Pilkington pushed the prisoner into the reception area. "Now wait there if you know what`s good for you!"

Edwards walked over and looked the prisoner up and down with contempt. "Not so clever now are we Black," and he grabbed him roughly by the chin and tilted his head back. "Thought you could outwit the British Secret Service didn`t you. Well you didn`t and I wouldn`t be surprised if you don`t get an appointment with the hangman for what you did," and he pushed the prisoner hard up against the countertop then pushed his snarling face into the prisoner's.

Johnson put his hand on Edward`s shoulder, "now now Edwards, we don`t lower ourselves down to their level, especially in front of the common constabulary."

Edwards remained where he was, and spittle flew into the prisoner's face as he spoke. "I lost two good men because of this piece of filth!" And he pushed the prisoners face to the side once more then stood back and turned to Johnson. "My apologies sir, it's just that...."

"No need to apologise Edwards, we have all been there. Now Sergeant, the handcuffs if you please."

Johnson made one final check of the handcuffs that linked the wrists of Edwards and the prisoner and satisfied, he bid farewell to Pilkington and then walked out to Edward`s car parked outside the station. Having secured the two men in the back, he jumped into the driver's seat and set off towards Manchester. As the car made its way up King Street, he looked in the rear-view mirror, *Simpson wants to thank me personally* and he smirked, *and Doreen will see what it means to take advantage of Cedric Johnson.*

As Anderson and Warburton pulled up to a halt outside the cottage, they could see Constable Jones standing outside the front door. He and Constable Balmforth had taken it in turns to stand guard until the Inspector was sure all evidence had been found.

"Good mornin` tae ye Constable Jones, how are ye doin`?"

Jones stood to attention. "Very well Sir, an` glad I can be of a-ssistance Sir." He winked and gave a friendly smile to Warburton as he passed and James patted him on the back, "well done Jonesy".

"Now Constable Warburton, where would ye like tae start?"

"The garden Sir, I`ll go and get the spade again," and a few minutes later, Warburton was digging in the same spot where they had found the counterfeit printing sheet.

Only a few inches below where they had found the first metal sheet, they found another, and James held it up to the Inspector. "Looks a strange one this Sir," and he rotated it back and forth as they looked at it. "Never seen any money like this before Sir."

"Me neither Constable, but I do know what it is. American Dollars laddie. Looks like our Mister Black was expanding his operation elsewhere. Now get ye spade in again and see what else we can find."

James put the spade into the soil again then pushed it down with his boot. The spade went halfway in then suddenly stopped. He grunted as he pushed harder, but the spade wouldn't go any further. "Feels springy Sir and look there`s some cloth or somethin`."

"Stand back Constable," and Anderson knelt down and pulled at the material with his fingers then he froze. "Go an` tell Constable Jones tae fetch the Coroner laddie."

At one in the afternoon, the door to the Clitheroe Police Station swung open and a tall well-built man walked in and removed his leather gloves before addressing Sergeant Pilkington.

"Agent Barwick`s the name. I'm here to pick up a prisoner of yours by the name of Frederick Black," and he offered a piece of paper to the man before him. "Well! What`s the matter with you man, cat got your tongue!"

The Coroner arrived within the hour and he was met

by Anderson on the garden path. "What have we got Inspector?"

Anderson gestured towards the side of the cottage and the Coroner followed him. "This way Mister Mitchell. Looks tae be very decomposed be the look of the body."

The Coroner placed his bag by the newly dug hole and grimaced slightly at the sight before him. He lifted the remnants of a limb, "she has been here a while by the looks of it Inspector."

"She! It's a lady ye say?"

"Yes, the body is badly decomposed, but the nails are still intact, and one can see the pink nail polish on the tips. This is certainly the body of a lady, Inspector."

Anderson stood up and rubbed the back of his head. "Well, there's a wee surprise now."

Mitchell half turned and looked up at the Inspector, "were you expecting to find the body of a man Inspector?"

"Truth be told, I was no expecting tae find the body of anyone, but if ye now askin`, maybe the evidence we have uncovered over the last few months would point tae a Mister Barlow, not a lady."

Mitchell stood up and rubbed his hands together briskly. "Well be that as it may Inspector, I need to get the body to my laboratory and see if I can identify her. I will advise you of the time and date if you wish to attend."

Anderson nodded, "aye, we`ll be there Mister Mitchell, don`t worri` about that now."


As the motor car reached the crossroads, Agent Edwards lent forward slightly. "Would you please take the road towards Lancaster Sir, we have a rendezvous with another agent before heading to Manchester."

Johnson half turned his head over his left shoulder but was still able to keep his eyes on the road ahead. "Isn`t that going to take even longer than going by train?"

"They have a faster car waiting Sir, it will get us there in plenty of time."

"Oh, all right then. Tell me, how long have you been with the agency Edwards?"

"About one and a half years Sir. Thought I was going to join the police then saw an article in *The Times* newspaper and thought I would have a go at joining the Secret Service instead."

Johnson slowed the car down for a tight bend, then accelerated off up the steep hill and he glanced in the rear-view mirror. "What was your last case?"

"Huh…., we were looking for some damned Irish, causing trouble near the Welsh border."

Johnsons eyes narrowed slightly. "Never heard of that one and I like to think I know what`s going on you know. Who did you work with?" But no answer came so Johnson turned his head a little further and raised his voice over the chugging of the car engine. "I said who did you work with Edwards?" Johnson felt something wasn`t quite right and adrenaline suddenly started to course through his veins but before he could react, he heard a click and felt the barrel of a gun against the back of his neck.

Edwards leant forward and hissed, "pull over to the side, now!"

Johnson took a deep calming breath, slowed the car down

and bumped it up on to a grass verge by the roadside and pulled on the handbrake. "What`s this all about Edwards?"

"The name is Blacklock, not Edwards," and he pulled the trigger.

The Inspector was discussing the find at the cottage with Warburton as he pushed the Police Station door open and they both walked in only to be met by a solemn looking Chief Constable.

"Ah Inspector, glad you are back. Got some bad news I`m afraid."

Anderson started to remove his coat, "bad news about what Sir?"

"Black has escaped. An accomplice imitating one of the secret service agents took him out from right under our noses! Forged papers you see. Problem only came to light when the real person turned up two hours later.

The Inspector banged his fist on the table. "Damn! What does Johnson make of it?"

The Chief Constable bit the bottom corner of his lip, "Johnson went with them. Not sure who is who at the moment so not even sure if Johnson is in on the whole show. Can`t trust anyone at the moment Inspector!"

"Aye it`s beginnin` tae look that way Sir. Do we know if they escaped be train or be motor car?"

Sergeant Pilkington stepped from behind the countertop. "It was a black Austin 10 Sir. I`m afraid I didn`t get the licence plate number," and he looked down at the floor, "I didn`t think it was important at the time Sir."

"Nay bother Sergeant, these are cunning men and I don`t doubt the paperwork looked in order even though it will `ave been a forgery. `Ave ye set any roadblocks in the vicinity?"

The Chief Constable unfolded a map and laid it on the countertop, and he began pointing to locations on the map. "We have roadblocks here, here, at these bridges and finally here at these crossroads. They are the only routes they could have taken, and we started at a twenty-mile radius from the Station and are now moving inwards."

The Inspector raised an eyebrow, "would ye care tae explain why ye chose a twenty-mile radius Sir."

"Certainly Inspector, Sergeant Pilkington would you explain your reasoning."

Pilkington saw his chance to redeem himself. "When we realised we had been duped Sir, no more than one hour had passed. Now since the maximum speed of an Austin 10 is fifty-five miles per hour, even with a tail wind Sir, and also taking into account the car was carrying three men, then I calculated that as most of the surrounding area is hilly, the furthest they could possibly have got would be twenty miles. At most Sir."

Anderson smiled broadly. "Excellent work Sergeant, excellent work."

Pilkington proudly stuck out his chest, "thank your greatly Sir."

"Unfortunately, we have no reports back yet, but we will be the first to know if anything or anyone is found Inspector, so it is now a waiting game gentlemen," and the Chief Constable walked into his office closely followed by Anderson.

"Got ye self a busy wee place here at the moment Sir, what with counterfeitin`, suicides and potential murda`s."

The Chief Constable sighed, "I am told Clitheroe and the surrounding area is normally very quiet Inspector. The worst case we have had in years was linked to violence when poaching deer and even that did not involve any deaths. Seems everything has arrived at once, and not in a good way."

Anderson sat down opposite, "aye ye right there Sir. Do ye mind if I ask what ye know of the Alfred Davenport and the Maureen Billington cases Sir."

The Chief Constable shrugged his shoulders, "suicides Inspector, or so I was told by Sergeant Entwistle. Don`t tend to let myself get embroiled in things of that nature. As sad as they are, I leave that to the Sergeants to deal with," and he opened a drawer by his leg and pulled out a file. "Now if you don`t mind Inspector, I have some work to do. I will be sure to let you know as soon as we hear anything about our missing fugitive."

# Chapter 32

## May 1934 - Clitheroe Coroner's Office

The two policemen stood reverently beside a raised table in the Coroner`s laboratory. The pungent smell of disinfectant hung in the air. "Ever been tae an autopsy before Constable?"

Warburton swallowed deeply, and he tried in vain to form a smile. "No Sir, I haven`t. They tend not to do them for bicycle thefts and stolen chickens."

"Well nay bother laddie. If yer feelin a wee bit queasy, just step outside, ye`ll not be the first no the last tae faint at one."

"Right gentlemen," and the Coroner began rolling up his sleeves and as he walked over to the table, he put a rubber apron on and tied the strings at the back., "Let's see if we can find out who this poor lady is or was should I say."

The Inspector smiled politely but James felt like he was going to be sick and no sooner had the Coroner pulled back the stained sheet covering the body, he fled clutching his hand to his mouth.

Thirty-five minutes later, the Inspector found Warburton sat on a wooden bench in the corridor with his head between his knees breathing deeply.

"Well Constable, `ow did ye enjoy ye first Autopsy then?"

And he placed his hand gently on Warburton`s back.

James looked up his face still ghostly white, "I really must apologise Sir...,"

But Anderson just held his hand up. "It`s nay bother Constable really it isn`t. And besides, ye lasted longer than I did when I went tae ma first Autopsy!"

"You're not just saying that are you Sir, I mean I tried my best to stay."

"It`s over laddie, and although they`re never goin` tae be ye favourite thing, ye do get used tae them with time. Now, wouldn't ye like tae know who the lady is then?"

James sat bolt upright. "You know who it is?"

"Aye, Mister Mitchell knew the poor lady unfortunately. Appears tae be the previous owner of the cottage where Mister Black resided.

James shook his head sadly. "Missus Snook! We were told that she had gone to live with relatives to look after a sick cousin and that is why the cottage was up for sale. She used to bake cakes for us when we were at Sunday School!"

The Inspector sat down on the bench beside him. "Well I`m sorry tae have tae tell ye that Missus Snook met a violent end tae her life, most probably be the hands of Mister Black no doubt."

The young constable clenched his fists with anger. "This area is nice and quiet. There is never trouble in Pendlewick Sir, and now we have murders coming out of our ears!"

"It would appear so laddie, and it's up tae us tae bring the perpetrators tae justice," and he stood up and stretched his arms in the air. "Oh by the way, do you be any chance remember who told ye the tale about Missus Snook`s cousin?"

James paused for a moment then his eyes widened, "it was Sergeant Entwistle Sir!"

"Right then, on yer feet, time we made an appointment with a certain Sergeant Entwistle don`t ye think."

Later that day, the two men sat in silence and James wondered if it was his imagination or if the tick from the large clock on the Police Station wall was actually getting louder as the time passed by. After waiting in their temporary office, they heard the Station front door open and a faint greeting. "Afternoon Bill, couple of gents waiting to see you in the Chief Constable`s office." James swallowed nervously but when he glanced at the Inspector, he was calmness personified.

Sergeant Entwistle walked in, and he bristled with suppressed anger when he saw Anderson and Warburton awaiting him. The inspector merely looked at him without any emotion, "sit ye self down Sergeant," and he gestured to a chair opposite them.

Entwistle began to sit down, "what`s all this about? I have some important work I need to be getting on with.... Sir," he added quickly.

The Inspector leant back and clasped his hands behind his head, "ye see Sergeant, I `ave some wee concerns, and I am a man who does nay like tae `ave concerns, large or small, if ye take ma meanin."

The Sergeant shifted in his seat, "not sure how that would be anything to do with me Sir. I mean, I `m a good policeman, you can check my record Sir."

The Inspector looked at Entwistle but said nothing, and the silence grew making both James and the Sergeant uncomfortable. Eventually Anderson smiled, "would ye no like to `ear what ma concerns are before ye comment Sergeant Entwistle?"

The Sergeants cheeks flushed slightly, and he nodded, "huh, yes Sir, my apologies."

The inspector leant forward and opened a worn beige cardboard file that was on the desk in front of him. "Right then, let`s be doin` this in some sort of order," and he proceeded to lay out the papers onto the desk. "Now I`m led tae believe a lady be the name of Maureen Billington committed suicide in July of last year. I`m also led tae believe a gentleman be the name of Alfred Davenport then committed suicide in February of this year. Are ye aware of this information Sergeant?"

Entwistle nodded his head in agreement. "Yes Sir, I heard something about that, unfortunate cases...so I`m told."

The Inspector tapped his fingers lightly on the desk as he stared at the Sergeant. "It would be advantageous Sergeant, `specially fer ye self mind, if ye did nae treat me as a foolish person."

Entwistle sat up indignantly, "I don`t know what you....."

The Inspector lurched up and leant over the desk, his face no more than an inch from the Sergeant's. "A simple check tells me ye know these cases intimately! Now the sooner ye start bein` truthful with me, the better it will be fer all of us Sergeant!"

After almost three hours of questioning, Inspector Anderson finally concluded the proceedings and came to his decision.

"Well now Sergeant Entwistle, I `ave come tae the conclusion that ye`r not a stupid man," at which the Sergeant smiled smugly, "but then again, ye`r not an intelligent man either. Not intelligent enough tae `ave come up with a complicated plan such as this," at which point it was James` turn to look smug.

"Now, I know that ye`r involved in this in some way but we canny quite prove it and Rear Admiral Simpson, would like me tae become involved in more pressing matters and waste no more time on these incidents. Now, ye`r alibies appear, appear I might add, tae put yerself in the clear and it looks most likely that our Mister Black had some involvement in the murda` of Mister Davenport but yer incident reports `ave clouded the situation and fall well short of what is tae be expected of a professional policeman. So, tae be perfectly `onest with ye, I no trust ye as far as I canny throw ye, if ye take ma meanin`! Now mine and Constable Warburton`s report on these two cases will recommend that ye are dishonourably discharged from the police with immediate effect and with nay recompense. Do ye understand me Entwistle?"

The Sergeant stood and made to speak but Anderson also stood and snarled at him, "ye`r a disgrace tae the uniform Entwistle, now get outa ma sight before I throw ye from this station ma self!"

Entwistle blustered and tried to speak again then thought otherwise and marched out of the room. As he strode past the countertop he grabbed his coat and nearly took the front door off its hinges as he rammed his palm against it.

Constable Warburton sat in an uncomfortable silence as the Inspector placed the documents neatly into a folder. "Makes ma blood boil it does Constable," he muttered as he finally stood up. "We ar` `ere tae serve an` protect the people, not undermine them! At some point, it`ll come out, an Entwistle will get his comeuppance, mark my word laddie! Now, we will close the case, fer now mind, but make it very clear that it`s pending further investigatin` at some point. Do ye agree Constable?"

James stood to attention and once again put on his best voice. "Yes Sir, I agree, and I would like to very much thank you for all the help and guidance you have given me during our investigations Sir."

Anderson looked at the young man and smiled, "aye laddie, it was nay bother but would ye promise me one thing?"

Warburton nodded vigorously, "anything Sir, it would be my pleasure."

"Be yerself laddie, no need to go changing yer accent. Be proud of who ye ar` and where ye come from."

Warburton blushed profusely. "Sorry Inspector, `as it been so obvious?"

Anderson slapped him on the back and laughed, "aye just a wee bit, but nay bother. Just make sure ye true tae yerself and yer roots. If ye pretend tae be somethin` ye `re not, then how can ye be truthful tae others? Policin` work is all about trust laddie and don`t ye ever forget it. Now let`s away an` get this paperwork in order an` filed away. Who knows, ye may solve it in years tae come, if ye take ma meanin."

Later that evening Bill Entwistle sat in his armchair by the hearth and nursed a small glass of ale he had just warmed by thrusting a red-hot poker into it from the fire.

The day`s events ran through his mind and anger once again began to rise within him. "Who the hell did they think they were dismissing him like that!" He exclaimed as he looked towards the flames. "Well I`ll show them," and standing he strode over to the sideboard and opening a drawer he took out an old leather-bound book. Placing it on top of the sideboard he opened it at page one hundred to reveal a roughly cut out pocket that contained a large wad of pound notes bound together with string and some folded paperwork. As he took the money from the book and began to unfasten the string, he heard a knock at his cottage door. Quickly replacing it into the cavity of the book and closing it he went to answer the door.

"Ah, it`s you, come to offer me my job back have you.... Sir," he added quickly.

# Chapter 33

## May 1934 - Trough of Bowland, Lancashire

The two Constables had been cautiously driving down the valley towards *Dunsop Bridge* and every so often, they would stop and one of them would get out and check outhouses and shepherd`s huts whilst the other maintained a watch on the road ahead.

Constable Walters gazed out of the car window at the sparkling *Langden Brook* as it too made its way down the valley. "What do yeh think will `appen if we come across `em Jack."

The other Constable briefly turned to him, "don`t know what to expect Tommy. They is supposed to be dangerous folk, very dangerous the Sarge said."

Tommy looked straight ahead at the road. "I`m not scared Jack, `onest I`m not."

Jack also looked straight ahead, and he gripped the steering wheel tighter. "Me neither Tommy," he lied.

As the police car approached *St Huberts Roman Catholic Church*, Constable Walters spotted a black car on the verge by the roadside. "Look Jack, a black motor car! We are lookin` fer a black motor car aren`t we?"

Constable Saunders slowed down and pulled up to a halt about two hundred paces from the black car. "Can you tell what type of motor car it is Tommy? They all look the same to me they does."

Tommy squinted his eyes in an attempt to identify the car. "Nope, need to get closer Jack, I can`t see it clear enough."

Jack released the handbrake and slowly crept along at walking pace. "Let me know when you can tell what it is Tommy."

"Stop!" And Tommy grabbed the other Constable by the arm. "It`s an Austin 10 Jack. I remembers seeing one in one of them there advertisements in the newspaper. `Undred and forty-seven quid! Can you believe that Jack!"

Jack looked at him angrily, "for gawds sake Tommy! We needs to know if anyone's in it not `ow much it bloody well costs!"

Tommy looked crestfallen. "Sorry Jack just thought yeh might like to know that`s all," and as the police car came to a stop, the two Constables warily got out. They looked at each other briefly then they pulled out their truncheons and started to walk the short distance to the car.

"Do yeh reckon they got shooters Jack?"

Jack turned and hissed, "if I hear you say another stupid thing Tommy Walters, I swear you will be in more danger from me than them, now shut it and let`s see what `appens when we get there."

The two Constables separated and each of them walked slowly either side of the black car that was tilted at a slight angle on the grassy verge.

Tommy made a pointing motion towards the car and whispered, "what`s that stuff on the front window Jack?"

Constable Smithson held his finger to his lips and then reached for the handle on the drivers' door. As he was about to pull it, he glanced inside and immediately turned away and slammed his hand to his mouth.

"You all right Jack?" And he peered cautiously into the car and sniffed. "`E don`t look well does `e."

Jack quickly gathered himself together. "You stay here and stand guard Tommy. I`ll drive into Dunsop Bridge and call the station."

No more than fifty minutes had passed, and Warburton slowed down and the Inspector slid the side window of the Wolsey open and offered his warrant card to the Constable stood by the roadblock. The policeman saluted and allowed the car to pass and James steered it around a temporary barrier and stopped by the Austin 10.

"Right Constable let`s take a look eh."

They walked over to the car and were met by a large muscular man who by comparison, made Anderson actually look normal size. Holding his hand out to the Inspector, "agent Barwick and you would be Inspector Anderson Sir?"

"Ay, that I am, pleased tae meet ye Barwick. What `ave we got `ere then?"

Barwick, followed by the two policemen, walked over to the open driver's door of the Austin, "we have a dead body Sir that I am pretty certain is Agent Johnson. Looks to be the right size, but unfortunately the face is…. unrecognisable. Wondered if you could take a look and see if you remember the clothes he was wearing."

James leant round to take a look, but the Inspector quickly

put his arm across his chest. "Not now laddie, ye `ave seen enough dead bodies fer one day don`t ye think."

He knelt down on one knee by the car and looked at the clothing, then he reached in and felt inside the small waistcoat pocket and pulled out a watch on a chain and examined it. Satisfied he stood up and nodded to Agent Barwick. "Aye it`s Johnson all right."

As they made their way back to the car Warburton could see three Constables in the middle of an animated conversation each one waving their hands one way then the next. On reaching them James stopped, "what`s goin` on boys, yeh look like three bookies at racecourse," and he gave them a friendly smile.

Tommy Walters turned, a grim look on his face, "your Sarge, `e`s been murdered `e has. Got found this mornin`. `E`d bin stabbed right enough, in`t belly. We was all wonderin` if one of us is next! These lot are bad buggers by t` looks of it, nowt ner sure."

Warburton swallowed and looked at the Inspector, but Anderson just carried on walking. James shook his head then trotted after him and on catching up, "did you `ear that Sir? Sergeant Entwistle dead. Murdered by the sounds of it Sir."

The Inspector carried on walking then as they reached the cordon, "in the car laddie, let`s be away and pay a wee visit tae the murder scene, just you an` me eh."

The two men drove and the silence was making Warburton extremely uncomfortable. He racked his brains trying to think of something sensible he could say that would instigate a conversation with the Inspector and eventually, "shame about Mister Johnson isn`t it Sir. Do yeh think `e was in on it or a victim of these men?"

There was no reply and glancing at the Inspector, James swallowed nervously and tried to concentrate on the winding lanes leading to Pendlewick. After twenty minutes, the car stopped outside the small terraced cottage of Bill Entwistle and no sooner had the car pulled to a halt, the Inspector jumped out, walked to the front door and stepped inside.

James hurried after him then as he got to the door he suddenly felt a chill and stopped abruptly. Cautiously leaning into the vestibule, "Inspector, is everythin` all right?" But no reply came. The young Constable`s mind was now racing, and confusion, logic and doubt vied for dominance and suddenly, the Inspector`s final words came rushing into his head.

*Let`s be away and pay a wee visit tae the murder scene, just you an` me eh.*

Warburton took a step back to gather his thoughts. *Surely th` Inspector isn`t involved in this? Don`t go in Jimmy, wait fer back up!*

*But it`s th` Inspector, e`s all reet is th` Inspector!*

*Jump back in t` car and get thi`self sum `elp!*

James glanced at the half open front door then the safety of the police car and just as he was about to make a decision, "Constable! What ar` ye waitin` fer? In ye come laddie."

James spun and looked warily at the man before him. A man, who thirty minutes ago, he would have trusted with his life.

"Well come on Constable, we `ave nay got all day," and he

disappeared back into the house.

James pulled out his truncheon and as he walked in he held it behind his back, just in case.

"In `ere laddie."

Warburton took a deep breath and brought his weapon from behind him and cagily stepped into the small living room.

"You`ll no be needin` that laddie, no danger `ere."

James peered into the gloomy room and Inspector Anderson sat in a chair, his huge hands resting on the arms at the side.

"Put ye truncheon away and tell me what ye see Constable."

Warburton, by now, was thoroughly confused and he held his truncheon tightly and stared at the man before him. "I don`t know what`s goin` on `ere Sir. Can yeh explain why we travelled `ere in silence and yeh rushed inside afore me?"

The Inspector waved his hand in the air dismissively. "Och, ye need tae accept ma apologies Constable. Once I`m in serious thought, ma mind blocks off anythin` else and I wanted tae get `ere before there was anyone goin` disturbin` anythin`. Tell me what ye see young man."

James relaxed slightly but maintained a firm grip on the stick by his side. Looking round he found it difficult to see anything as the curtains were still drawn across the window.

"Can I open t`curtains Sir?"

Anderson had steepled his fingers together on his chest.

"Aye Constable."

James walked over and as he pulled back the curtains with a swish, a flood of light illuminated the room and the body slumped on the carpet surrounded by a pool of blood. Walking to the middle of the room, he slowly turned full circle taking in as much information as he could. He then did the same but in the opposite direction.

The Inspector smiled, "excellent laddie. Keep goin`."

Finally, James stopped, and Anderson raised an eyebrow in expectation. "Well Constable, what are ye thinkin` now?"

"Well, Sir, room`s very tidy, no signs of any struggle, and t`front door or window shows no sign of bein` broken into," and with that, he immediately went out of the room and a minute later, returned. "An` neither does t` back door or windows."

The Inspector nodded sagely, "aye and what could that be sayin` tae ye Constable Warburton?"

James gently bit the corner of his bottom lip, "that t`person who did this was known t`Sergeant.... t`Mister Entwistle Sir."

The Inspector slapped himself on the knee and stood up with a grunt. "Excellent laddie, just as ah thought ma` self. Now come an` take a wee look at this," and he walked over to the sideboard. "`Ere, we find ourselves a book, a very thick book with a large number o` pages I might add. Now would ye take Mister Entwistle tae be a readin` or a religious man?"

James looked at the Inspector and shook his head. "No Sir, I wouldn`t. In fact earlier this year when Jonesy said `e

wanted to learn more about readin ` an ` writin `, Serg....
Mister Entwistle had laughed at ` im and told ` im to forget it and what a waste of time books are. Said books are
fer scholars not policemen and religion is fer weak men."

The Inspector looked at the sideboard and lightly stroking the book he whispered, "so what would a man who
` as no likin ` fer books or religion, be in possession of
such a lovely thick book?"

James leant over, "what ` s the title Sir?"

"See fer yerself laddie," and he spun the book to face the
astonished Constable.

"A Bible!"

"Aye, a Bible Constable Warburton," and picking it up he
began to open it to see if there were any clues or hand-
written notes. But within seconds, he stopped, closed the
book and handed it to James. "Tell me yer first thoughts
on takin ` the book from me laddie."

Warburton took the Bible and rotated it in his hands looking at the front and back covers. "It looks old," and running his finger along the edge, "an ` a bit worn on t ` spine
but other than that, it's a Bible Sir."

"Think laddie, don ` t just use yer eyes when lookin ` fer
evidence now."

James gently cleared his throat and once again appraised
the book. As he was just about to open it, he smiled and
looked up at Inspector Anderson. "It ` s light sir, very light
for such a thick book."

"My thoughts exactly Constable, now put it on the sideboard and let ` s take a wee look inside shall we."

Anderson licked the tip of his finger and slowly started

to turn the pages and in no time, "ah what `ave we `ere Constable?"

James looked on excitedly as the other man lifted a wad of tightly packed Pound and Dollar notes bound with string. He placed the money on the sideboard then removed a folded sheet of paper and began to read it. Content with what he had just seen, he put the money and paper back in the book cavity and slammed it shut. "It would appear Constable, that we `ave all the evidence we need tae link our deceased Mister Entwistle with Mister Black and his associates. Didn`t ah say Entwistle would get his come-uppance?"

Warburton smiled, "you did Sir, I remember it well. We just need to capture the ones who did this to `im."

The Inspector twisted his mouth slightly and rubbed his chin, "aye we do, which won`t be an` easy task, I might add."

One-week later James stood on his doorstep in Duck Street and as Inspector Anderson roared off on his motor-cycle he felt a real pang of sadness as he waved farewell to the enigmatic Scotsman.

The Inspector had been seconded to the Secret Service in order to stay on the Spy Ring case and as the two police-men had parted ways, Anderson had shook Warburton firmly by the hand. "Ye `ve the makin` of a great police-man James, and don`t ye forget that ye `elped me as well in all this."

It felt strange to Warburton when the Inspector had re-ferred to him by his first name and he looked at the older man and smiled, his words echoing through his mind. *Be* *yerself laddie, no need to change yer accent. Be proud of who ye ar` and where ye come from.*

"Aye Sir, it weren`t no trouble at all, but would yeh promise me one thing like?"

Anderson had smirked and bowed theatrically, "anythin` Constable, it would be ma pleasure."

"I like it best when yeh call me laddie, not James."

"Well laddie, how `bout ye try an` find who made an effort tae kidnap ye sister then? Would be a grand feather in ye cap. Use what ye `ave learnt but also `ave a mind tae think differently, if ye take ma meanin Constable."

# Chapter 34

## July 1935 – Pendlewick – East Lancashire

It was a late balmy evening as the young man applied his lipstick and pulled on his blonde wig.

"I feels a reet idiot I does Jimmy. You sure this`ll work!"

Constable Warburton got up from the chair and walked over and tugged and tucked as he adjusted the man`s dress. "Course it`ll work Jonesy, nowt ner sure, now come on and spray a bit o`me mam`s perfume on," and as he squirted the liquid onto the back of Constable Jones's neck, the other man spluttered and laughed.

"Bloody hell Jimmy, du we need tu go tu this much trouble? An` look, I can`t even walk straight in these `ere `igh `eels!"

Warburton stared at him seriously. "Aye we does Jonesy, we`ll get that bastard whose bin tryin` tu grab our women off`t streets, nowt ner sure."

Constable Jones had left the cottage first and as James peered from behind the slightly open front door, he noticed how his tottering colleague, who was doing his level best to remain upright in his mother`s high heel shoes, actually added to the ruse and made it look as though she was intoxicated.

Having let Jonesy get about twenty yards up the lane,

he slipped out and kept to the shadows as he followed. They had tried numerous methods of trying to find the perpetrator since more and more reports were coming in of ladies being followed late at night, and some unfortunate enough to be assaulted. There had been a lull in the attacks then suddenly, they started again, and Sally Tomlinson was still missing. The Inspector`s words had come into his mind, *use what ye `ave learnt but also `ave a mind tae think differently, if ye take ma meanin."*

And think differently he had. "Yeh wot, yeh wants me tu dress up as a woman! Yeh must be mad Jimmy!" It had taken a bit of persuading but eventually, Jonesy had agreed to the plan and late that night, they had put it into action.

Warburton could just see Jonesy semi-stumble around the corner near the *Buck i` th Vine* pub and could hear him attempting to put on a false high-pitched voice. Keeping his back firmly against the metal railings by the brook, he made his way up towards him, making sure he kept out of site of the area where his sister had been attacked.

In the dark ginnel, the man could hear his own breathing and he tried to stop himself panting with excitement as he heard the clicking of high heels on the lane. *Another harlot.... and drunk by the sounds of it. Even worse. She has no excuses.*

He moved towards the alley way entrance being careful to stay in the shadows and slipped his gloves on. He could feel the adrenaline coursing through his veins as another helpless victim wandered towards him. Then she came into view. *Look at her, disgusting tramp. No way for a lady to be. She needs getting rid of.* He ran the same message through his mind each time. To him it was a warped justification for his actions. Having been laughed at by the girls when he was at school, as he got older, he had tried to court ladies but always with the same and miserable outcome. He had taken to religion and reading the Bible every day and deciding the failure was down to them and not himself, he had started to despise them, all of them. They were nothing like the scriptures in the Bible. He had taken the advice and had lain low for several months until his leg had healed. The dog bite had become infected and it was only by luck that he survived, but he had put his survival down to the word of God which he had read every day of his illness. The women were to blame for his predicament, everyone could see that, which only solidified his belief that they were all filth and as soon as he was fit again, he started his crusade to rid the world of women.

Jonesy felt ridiculous and he winced as he went over again on his ankle. As he was about to bend over to try and adjust the shoe straps, he felt someone grab him roughly around the throat and attempt to pull him towards the ginnel.

Unfortunately for the attacker, he had seriously underestimated his prey and he panicked as he felt the power in the arms and shoulders of his victim. He tried in vain to swivel her around so he could get a better hold of her throat, but all this seem to do was make her angrier. Just as he was about to try and let go and make his escape, he felt a thump in his kidneys and as he collapsed to the floor in agony he felt a huge weight fall on him and pin him to the ground.

"Got yeh, yeh bastard!" Snarled Warburton as he grabbed the man`s arms and held him down in the darkness of the alley. Jonesy quickly pushed his high heels off and joined in trying to aim repeated kicks at the man`s face but James shielded the captive with his arm allowing only one blow to land on its target.

"Stop it Jonesy, now!"

James had seen this overtly aggressive behaviour before when they had tackled the poachers and seeing that the man was semi-conscious, he jumped up and grabbed him, "stop it Jonesy, enough, he`s done, no need fer no more now stop it we`re policemen, not thugs!"

Constable Jones took a step back and began to take deep calming breaths. Snatching his wig off and throwing it to the floor he continued to stare at the prostrate figure. "I`m all reet Jimmy, I`m all reet, leave me be."

James hauled the attacker to his feet, and he dragged the groggy figure towards the streetlamp to examine him.

"Bloody hell!" Exclaimed Warburton as he held him at arm's length under the light. "Father Swarbrick! But why?"

One month later, Samuel Swarbrick had been brought before the magistrates court in Lancaster and after a lengthy trial, had been deemed to be mentally stable and was found guilty. Only the intervention from the Vatican who requested clemency due to Father Swarbrick`s previous charitable work prevented him from being sent to the gallows and amid public outcry in certain areas of Lancashire, his sentence was committed to life in prison.

Rumours were rife that the Church knew about the crimes even before he had been captured and had squirrelled Father Swarbrick away for six months to try and heal him of his ways which was why the attacks had stopped then suddenly started again. Unfortunately for the victims, this was never proven, and the Church remained steadfast with their story of events.

Swarbrick never saw the light of day again and unfortunately neither did his final victim whose body was never found.

As for Warburton and Jones, they each received commendations and there was a huge celebration at the *Sun Inn* where the residents of Pendlewick had offered their thanks, although Jonesy had been teased endlessly by the regulars with Old Walter even asking him if he would be applying for a bar maid`s job.

"Tek no notice Jonesy, there only ribbin` yeh," James had said as they both leant against the end of the bar each nursing a pint of ale.

Jonesy had returned a lopsided smile, his eyes glazing over slightly due to having drunk too much. "Aye a` knows that Jimmy, a` knows that. Wi did a grand job dint we lad," and as he went to pat his friend on the back, his supporting arm gave way and he fell on the floor in a heap closely followed by his glass of beer.

Everyone in the pub turned on hearing the smash of glass and all conversation stopped. On seeing the source, there was a loud cheer then everyone returned to their conversations as though nothing had happened.

James bent down and hauled him to his feet. "Come on Jonesy, time wi` wer` gettin` yeh `ome."

# Chapter 35

## May 1937 - Security Service Headquarters, Broadway Buildings 54, London

It had been a frustrating time for Inspector Robert Anderson, and he had started to feel the pressure due to the lack of progress in finding Black and his accomplices.

The pressure was all of his own making and the Rear Admiral, whose health now seemed to be failing had reassured him on several occasions that these things took time.

There had been leads here and the odd report of suspicious activity there but nothing concrete and he was beginning to think that Black and his collaborators had slunk away into the woodwork either in Britain or abroad.

He sighed, and as he sat at his desk, he looked out of the window in thought. Suddenly he smiled at the memory two years ago when the news had reached him regarding the capture of the criminal who had been attacking women in the Clitheroe area. He had sent a telegram straight away to Constable Warburton with the simple message, *knew ye could do it, well done laddie.*

Turning back to his desk he clapped his hands together, "right then Anderson, `bout time ye did it as well," and he started once again to sift through records, files and bits of information spread out on his desk and pinned to a cork board on the wall.

"There must be some link tae this," and he concentrated on a forged American dollar bill pinned to the wall."

"Must be some link to what Sir?"

Anderson spun around, "ah Barwick good mornin` tae ye. Just musing tae ma`self, as I do," and he scratched his chin thoughtfully as he gazed at the forgery. "This `ere note. Now our Mister Black and his many associates would appear tae have been able tae produce all manner of things from their wee printin` presses such as money, papers an` the like. Now it would nay be beyond the realms of possibility fer them tae forge travel documents ye know."

"That is correct Sir," and Barwick walked over and started looking at the information pinned to the wall. "What`s on your mind?"

The Inspector kept his eyes firmly on the board and reached up and rubbed his head. "Well, I`ve been thinkin` could we get a `old of the records of people travelin` to and fro across the Atlantic now? Passenger names and the like, see if there`s any sorta pattern, if ye take ma meanin`."

Barwick raised an eyebrow and then nodded. "All shipping lines have to keep manifestos of cargo as well as passenger numbers and names. Shouldn't be too hard to get the information Sir. It will take some time to go through the details when we receive them but I`ll start on it straight away."

Anderson still didn`t take his gaze from the board, "aye an` be sure tae check ships goin` tae Canada an` Mexico not just America, if ye please."

Two weeks later, Anderson and Barwick were still poring through the shipping logs checking the minute details looking for any sort of pattern.

Eventually the other man sighed and leaning back he stretched his arms in the air and groaned. "Nothing Sir. I`ve been through the manifestos of all the ships sailing to the East coast of America and also Mexico for the last seven years." He leant over and handed the Inspector a sheet of paper. "Here is a list of passengers who have had repeated trips and they all check out as legitimate."

Anderson nodded his thanks. "This may seem a thankless task Barwick, but I just get a wee feelin` in ma water that this is where the answer lies. I`m nearly finished checking the Canada shipping lines, now you get yerself `ome, it`s gettin` late, I'll finish off `ere fer tonight."

The tired agent stood and after putting on his hat and coat he made for the door. As he was about to leave he turned, "we will catch them Sir."

Anderson didn`t look up, "aye that we will Barwick. Goodnight now."

# Chapter 36

## June 1937 – RMS Empress of Britain – North Atlantic Ocean

The sleek three funnelled liner slid effortlessly through the ocean, its white hull reflecting in the water it pushed easily aside as it steamed its way from Southampton to Quebec.

Manfred leant on the railing of the promenade deck casually smoking his cigarette, the Ocean breeze blowing his blonde hair back across his forehead. He took a deep breath of the salty air, the vast expanse of grey water surrounding him made him feel small and insignificant, but he soon shook off the feeling. He was part of the new *Third Reich*, how could he feel small!

Over the last two years, Isaac Ventnor in the United States had worked tirelessly to cultivate and influence several anti-war figures and politicians and now was the time for Manfred to speak to the main ones in person.

Canada had been chosen as a more suitable meeting place and he had chosen a small rural hotel outside of Quebec where the Americans would not be easily recognised. Here he would set the expectations and the rewards for those who supported the cause. He would also explain the consequences of failure.

The ship was only half full. The expected business for the owners had not materialised and Manfred failed to see how it made any money. The opulence of the first-class cabin they occupied was second to none as was the service from the many attendants, but this all cost money that couldn`t be justified by the passenger numbers. The cost for the trips was high and he smiled at the thought of paying for them with counterfeit currency.

It had been so easy to dupe the British. What had started as an experiment in Pendlewick with one-pound notes, soon became a widespread operation in other locations around the country and soon the money was spreading throughout the banks and changing hands without problems. They had set the limit to one pound and ten-shilling notes as anything more than this value would raise suspicions as to the average Briton, one pound was a great deal of money, a five pound note a fortune. Manfred took a long drag on his cigarette and flicked the stub into the Ocean and watched as it slowly disappeared. The counterfeit currency would still have the impact we are looking for, he thought, which was to hit Britain economically and reduce their capability to wage war. In two or three years, the British pound would be worthless, any confidence in it shattered and sooner or later, that warmonger Winston Churchill would be disposed of. His second task was more difficult. He took a deep breath and stuck out his chest with pride. He would succeed and Joseph, who was now rapidly rising through the ranks of the Nazi party, would be most pleased.


The two American Senators sat in the wood panelled lounge of the *Rapids View Hotel* on the outskirts of Quebec with two other men, listening to *Harbor Lights* playing on the radiogram that sat by the fireplace.

The two politicians looked nervously across at the two other men sat opposite who they had been told to meet at this location at precisely two thirty in the afternoon. "Not before, and not after," they had been politely advised. The time wasn`t critical but Manfred liked to keep the men focused at all times.

A portly man in his late forties held a thick stubby cigar clenched between his teeth and amongst this company, he looked uncouth and dressed as though he had just come from his workplace but for all these visual attributes, he had an unerring confidence about him.

The other man sat casually smoking a cigarette, his jet-black hair slicked back from his forehead and his dark blue suit immaculately cut. All of them turned and made to rise as Manfred walked in with his senior operator Isaac Ventnor.

Manfred held his hand up and waved it in a gentle downward motion. "Please gentlemen, remain seated, we are all friends here are we not?"

Senator Jim Henson smiled, "we sure are Sir, we sure are."

Manfred sat down on a soft leather chair and removed his hat placing it carefully on the low table that separated the four men and let the silence grow. As expected, Henson became a little uncomfortable and looked furtively at his colleague beside him.

"So Mister Black, what`s the deal?"

Manfred didn`t speak but looked at the fidgeting Senators, his glittering eyes boring into them.

Eventually he closed his eyes slowly then opened them

again. "The *deal* as you put it gentlemen is that I require your aid in keeping the United States from needlessly spending millions of dollars on a foreign policy that will be of no use in the development of your great country.

The German people have no quarrel with you, so we only see it to be beneficial for us both that you do not become embroiled in petty arguments amongst countries thousands of miles from your shores. Afterall, look at the problems the people of you country have faced recently. Dust bowls, famine, thousands unemployed and social unrest everywhere! You are still recovering from an economic recession, the last thing you need is to waste any money you may generate."

Senator Henson sat up. "As you will understand, we are both patriots and only want what is best for our country, therefore we are open to discussions.....and any rewards that may come our way."

Manfred smiled thinly. "It goes without saying that anyone who helps me, will be richly rewarded," and he calmly gestured towards the other two men with the palm of his hand, "wouldn`t you agree?"

The man with the cigar leant forward and placing the stub into a metal ashtray, he wiped his mouth with the back of his hand, but the suited man spoke first. "You may now recognise me Senators, if not me, then you will be very familiar with my oil company *JessOil*."

The two Senators nodded knowingly, everyone in the United States knew of *JessOil* and its power base in Texas. "So," continued the man, "it would be in all our interests should President Roosevelt become unelectable."

At this point the faces of the two politicians became pensive and they looked at each other then back again at the man.

Unperturbed by their reaction, "we have identified and have been cultivating a lawyer who we are grooming to become our next President of these United States. A man who will be wise enough to keep us out of any foreign conflicts, but we need your help. Help that has it`s rewards."

The two Senators looked at each other and one of them, a large balding man in an ill-fitting plaid suit, leant forward. "I am assuming boy, that this help you want aint exactly above board."

Manfred stifled his anger at the obvious disrespect, but as always, he remained calm and interjected the conversation. "An excellent deduction Senator. As you will be aware, there are self-interests at stake within your political system. Self-interests that would gain value from the potential manufacture and sale of arms and munitions. My Government see this as a waste of your resources and potentially the lives of young American men and we would therefore like to encourage you to refrain from entering any conflict that may arise in Europe. With this in mind, we have been engaging with…. intelligent politicians who have their country and the lives of their young men at heart. Men who would rather see an American Government elected that seeks peace not war, prosperity, not another descent into poverty brought about by military spending for no return. Which is why gentlemen, we are here today speaking to your good selves."

Manfred`s American operator Ventnor had done well, he could almost feel the greed oozing from them. Here were two men easily manipulated by wealth, patriotic to a degree, which was important, but critically, they had influence in Washington and the propaganda techniques being perfected by his leader Joseph in Germany would help turn the American people away from war mongering.

The Texan oil baron and the New York teamsters Union leader had been easily swayed to his cause and now the two politicians were the final pieces in the jigsaw.

After finalising the expectation and rewards, Manfred sat back. "You appear pleased with my proposed deal gentlemen, but remember, the price for failure is high, for all of you."

The Senator in the plaid suit leant forward angrily. "Hey, wait a minute buddy, don`t you go starting with no threats. You do realise who you are dealing with here? We are no fools and we both of us said we agreed to your terms."

Manfred remained calm and also leant forward speaking in a low tone. "I am merely pointing out gentlemen, that now that you have agreed to my terms, they are set in stone. Do not think to undermine me or there will be severe consequences, no matter who you are or how powerful you think you may be."

Just then, a crackling voice could be heard from the radiogram speaker, "And yes folks, the darling of America, our own brave Emilia Earhart is on her magnificent journeys again. This time all the way round the world in her flying machine and today, she has landed in Darwin, Australia! Wadda gal folks!"

The two senators leant back and both smirked. The balding man nodded proudly. "Ya see Mister Black, we will help you, but only because it's the right thing to do for our country you understand, but," and he pointed to the radiogram, "that gal there is what Americans are all about. We got technology and power you can only dream of and we aint scared of nobody so don`t you start getting all high and mighty with us boy!"

Manfred stood up, put on his hat and stared at the four men. "Our business here is concluded gentlemen. My colleague here will be your main contact and paymaster. It would be wise not to disappoint me." He clicked his heels together, nodded his head curtly and left the room.

# Chapter 37

## July 1937 - Security Service Headquarters, Broadway Buildings 54, London

Agent Barwick bobbed his head around the office door. "You called for me Sir."

"Aye Barwick get ye-self in and sit ye-self down," and he pulled out a folder and removed a sheet of paper. "Now then, `avin` found some information, I took it upon ma self tae dig a wee bit deeper. It would appear that we `ave some repeat passenger trips on a ship be the name of *Empress of Britain*."

Barwick leant forward in anticipation, "yes Sir and....?"

"Well now, it would appear a gentlemen travels on a regular basis to and fro tae Canada, a place called Quebec tae be exact. Also would appear the very same gentlemen frequently travels with a lady."

Barwick grimaced slightly, "yes but I found quite a few of those Inspector and the passenger names checked out as all above board."

Anderson looked him in the eye, "aye that's what I thought, but ye see, the passenger names that I took a fancy tae gave me a strange feelin`."

"What are the names Inspector, I can check them out for you."

"Their names are Lord and Lady Turner Hope and there is no need fer ye tae go checkin` now."

Barwick looked perplexed, "oh how come Sir?"

"Well it appears Lord Turner Hope died in 1928, never took tae bein` married and had no `eirs. Now wouldn't ye say that`s a wee bit intriguing Barwick?"

# Chapter 38

## July 4th 1937 – RMS Empress of Britain – North Atlantic Ocean

The ship lifted in the swell as it headed back to Southampton and the two violinists expertly adjusted their feet and played on seamlessly. Manfred smiled at Doreen Thomas as he reached for his wine glass as it slid towards the edge of the table. After having a sip he placed the glass back in position and returned his attention to his lunch being served in the *Jacques Cartier* dining room.

As the waiter came and began to top up their glasses with a fine vintage claret, he overheard two American couples frantically chatting at the next table. Manfred tutted at the interruption and looked up at the waiter. "They appear rather animated today."

The waiter nodded and bowed his head slightly. "Please accept my apologies for the disturbance Lord and Lady Turner-Hope." He looked across at the two couples and rolled his eyes with disappointment. "It would appear that a mishap has occurred to a lady pilot which has caused somewhat of a stir with the Americans. Apparently she was attempting an aeroplane flight around the world."

Manfred nodded, "very well, thank you," and the waiter

bowed his head slightly and walked away.

Manfred moved his fork to his mouth and paused. *The Senators were not foolish men. The message was clear, he could reach anyone, anywhere and was not a man to disappoint,* and he continued with his lunch.

# Chapter 39

## July 8th – 1937 Southampton Docks, England

The majestic liner eased its way towards the *Ocean Dock*, a myriad of tiny tugboats puffing and panting as they aided the manoeuvre.

Manfred stood on the balcony of their suite, his arm linked with Doreen`s as they viewed the ships arrival into Southampton. They were dressed immaculately as befitting a Lord and Lady and confidence oozed from the couple.

It was a usual check and one that had become quite tedious but nevertheless, Manfred scanned the skyline looking for the signal on the pier. Shutters open meant all clear, shutters closed meant a problem.

The day was particularly smokey as other ships were arriving and leaving which when combined with the multitude of coal fired boilers in nearby factories meant visibility was at best poor. Manfred tutted, he could normally see the signal by now and he walked further along the balcony attempting to get a better view.

Doreen was oblivious and she checked her makeup once more with the compact mirror from her handbag. She had enjoyed the trip again and felt the luxury lifestyle was worth the physical sacrifices she had to make for Manfred. She paused and lipstick in hand, glanced at him. *He at least was interesting, and the rewards were many.* Even though the touch of any man was now becoming obnoxious to her, she had cleverly worked her way into his mind, and he adored her.

The night before they had laid in bed luxuriating in the first-class suite and Doreen had snuggled up to Manfred`s side.

"Will we be a real Lord and Lady one day Manfred?" She had whispered.

He had gently stroked her hair with his fingers, "of course we will my dear, you mean everything to me and one day when the might of the German people spreads throughout the world, you will become my official Lady."

She smiled to herself as she dozed off to sleep, *how easy it was to control men.*


Inspector Anderson leant against the wall of a nearby warehouse and admired the ship as it gradually became larger as it neared the port. He smiled at the crowds on the dock cheering as the horns blared out announcing the ship`s arrival. Easing himself from the wall he made his way along the quay and linked up with agent Barwick and Salford Smithy, as he was now known.

"Right we are gentlemen, I believe our Mister Black and a Missus Thomas are due tae arrive at any moment. Is everythin` in place Smithy?"

"All set Guv. Two men on the gates and two at either end of the pier. All of `em `ave shooters, just in case. We`ll get `im this time, no problems."

Anderson frowned slightly, "I must say, I do admire an optimist but let`s be on our guard eh. Over the years, our Mister Black has shown `imself tae be a worthy adversary."

As the ship moved closer to the dock and thick ropes began to be flung out in all directions like a huge spider`s web, Manfred got a clear view of the pier...., and the closed shutters. Quickly pushing past Doreen he stepped back into their cabin.

"What`s the matter Manfred, is everything all right?"

Manfred ignored her and started loading his revolver and pushing bits and pieces into a small leather bag.

Doreen stepped inside and tugged on his shoulder to get his attention, "whatever`s the matter Manfred?"

He turned and smiled, "nothing dear, just need to be ready, in case of any mishaps. Always be on our guard, that`s our motto," and he winked at her.

As the ship gently bumped into the buffers on the dock wall and more ropes began to be thrown to and from the ship, Manfred went out onto the balcony and scanned the waiting throng of people below. Made up of a mixture of dock workers, well-wishers and people just generally interested in such a magnificent ship, it was difficult for him to make out individuals...., apart from the very large person stood talking to two men. *Damn that man*, thought Manfred.

Turning to Doreen, "come out here my dear, you are missing all the entertainment and excitement," and he guided her out onto the balcony and they both leant on the polished wooden rail looking at the people below. "I need to inform you that there is a small problem my dear in that we appear to have a welcoming committee. Therefore we need some sort of diversion."

Doreen looked at him, a worried look on her face. "A welcoming committee Manfred, are we in danger?"

Manfred put a comforting arm around her shoulder. "No my dear, no danger at all. We just need to divert their attention from our arrival that is all."

Doreen smiled, "I trust you will get us out of this Manfred," and she kissed him gently on the cheek. "Tell me, how do you plan to divert their attention?"

"Like this," and grabbing her behind the knees and shoulders he lifted her and threw her over the rail where she crashed to the dock amid screams and panic on the quay.

Barwick, on seeing the melee, strained to see what was happening. "What the...Inspector, something's happened on the quay."

Anderson climbed a nearby Porter`s barrow and resting one hand against the wall he balanced on one of the wheel tops. Moving his head one way then the other, "looks like a fight `as broken out or somethin`. Get yerself o`er there Smithy and find out what`s `appenin`."

"Righto Guv," and Smith began pushing his way towards the ever-increasing crowd around the incident.

Barwick shouted over the noise, "shall I go and take a look as well Sir?" But Anderson wasn`t interested and was looking elsewhere. "Sir, shall I go with Smith?"

The Inspector turned and curled a finger at him, "nay laddie, you come wi` me," and he set off pushing through the crowds towards the rear of the ship.

Barwick saw how the Inspector was pulling his revolver out from the inside of his coat and did likewise with his own weapon. "Out the way, out the way, Secret Service comin` through!" Screamed Anderson as they tried to get through the crowds.

Suddenly Barwick saw the subject of the Inspectors efforts. Working his way hand over hand down a rope was Black! "I see him Inspector, it was a diversion!

"Aye Barwick, let`s away and get `im."

Manfred could see the agents pushing and shoving to get towards him and his breathing became heavier as he gritted his teeth at the strain of climbing down the rope. But his hopes rose when he saw how close he was to the quay and how far they were away. There was no way they could get to him in time. Then he heard a gunshot, then another and he snatched his head back towards the agents and saw one of them with a revolver pointing up to the sky and firing it into the air.

The dockside was already in panic and confusion, now it was bedlam.

In an attempt to get away from the new threat, people ran in all directions and children were whisked up off their feet or dragged to anywhere that was perceived as safe.

On seeing the crowd suddenly parting, the two agents ran through the gaps towards their quarry.

Manfred dropped onto the quay side and ignoring the rope burns searing into the palms of his hands, he unstrapped his bag from his shoulders and set off running towards the exit gates. After no more than ten yards, he suddenly stopped and swung round raising his revolver in one smooth movement and fired three shots at the two agents.

"Watch it man!" Bellowed the Inspector and both men dived to the floor as the bullets whistled overhead. Looking back over his shoulder, Anderson quickly checked if any innocent by-standers had been hit and on seeing that the bullets appeared to have harmlessly hit the brick wall nearby, "get after him Barwick!" And as the younger agent set off in pursuit yet again, the inspector grunted to himself, "it may take me a wee while tae get ma`self up from this position ye know!"

Manfred snarled on seeing that he had missed his enemies and he began sprinting once more towards the exit gates whilst all the while, constantly scanning the area in front and to the sides with his revolver held in his outstretched hand. On reaching the gates and just as he thought he was free, a short stocky man in a flat cap stepped out and raised a gun at him.

"Stop or I`ll shoot yeh!" Bellowed the man.

Manfred sneered and without hesitation, fired his gun at the man who just managed to spin out of the way as shards of metal and paint erupted from the gate where he had been standing only a split second before. Smoothly stepping back again he raised his revolver and fired.

Manfred laughed manically as he ran through the gate and to freedom only to feel a powerful pain in his right kneecap and the ground rushing up towards him as he tumbled head long to the floor. He made to move, *I can still escape, come on Manfred, you can do it!* But the pain was excruciating and as he tried to get up he fell back clutching his leg. He could hear muffled screams and shouting, and he gasped again at the pain. *If I am to be captured it will be as a dead man. No one will take me alive. The Reich must succeed!* Scrabbling into his pocket he pulled out a capsule and thrust it towards his mouth but without warning, he felt a booted foot pin his hand to the floor. "Ye`ll no be needing that just yet Mister Black."

As the limping prisoner was taken away, Anderson stood and discussed the day`s events with the team of agents. "An excellent piece o` work boys. And as fer ye shootin` skills Stan, well I have tae take ma hat off tae ye, that was a remarkable shot tae just disable the man in the knee. Enables us tae interrogate the man a wee bit further. Very difficult tae interrogate a dead man I might add."

"Thanks Guv, but in all `onesty I was aimin` fer `is `ead!"

The Inspector smiled, "ah well...., we`ll keep that tae ourselves eh, if ye take ma meanin."

# Chapter 40

## August 1937 - Security Service Headquarters, Broadway Buildings 54, London

Inspector Anderson and the Rear Admiral sat in his office and as Simpson stood to make his way to the window, he grimaced and held his lower chest.

"You all right there Simpson? I`ve seen ye do that a number o`times recently."

"Fine, I`m fine man stop your fussing!" And he peered out of the window on the scene below. "Finally got the blighter to talk then did we?"

Anderson nodded, "aye that we did, and everythin`s been passed on tae the Americans. I believe they are currently gatherin` as much information as they can then they`ll make their move. Want tae catch the big Salmon Simpson, not just the wee fry."

The Rear Admiral turned from the window, "and rightly so Anderson, rightly so. Who would have thought the Germans would try and interfere with the Presidential elections!" He returned to his desk and sat down. "Still no news on the other fellow though. Expect we will catch the bugger at some point."

Anderson nodded in agreement. "Will ye be lookin` fer me tae get involved with that then? It`s just that it`s

been a wee while since I was `ome and Ma will be gettin`
tae worryin` again."

Simpson shook his head. "No, no Anderson, no need to
worry about that. Got it all in hand. Sure he`ll surface at
some point, they always do. You get yourself back to Scotland, you deserve it man."

# Chapter 41

## September 1939 – Pendlewick, East Lancashire

The first golden leaves had started to fall from the trees as William Blacklock carefully drove into Pendlewick. It had been five years since he had last been here, but nothing had changed, and the apathy of the British made him despise them even more.

Drizzle started to fall and as he got out of his car, he pulled his hat down to partially cover his face and turned up his trench coat collar. The risk he would now be recognised in the village was low, and this was the reason he had waited so long to close down the operation once and for all.

Walking over to the Old Smithy Cottage, he knocked on the door and waited.

Eventually, the door opened a fraction, and someone peered out through the gap. "Yes, how can I help you?"

"It`s me," hissed Blacklock as he pulled his collar down and removed his hat to reveal his face.

"William, good to see you again," and as the door opened fully, he caught a glimpse of the Chief Constable putting his revolver back inside his jacket. He beckoned Blacklock inside closing the door quickly behind him, "please sit and I will make us a cup of tea."

Blacklock remained standing. "Yes it is also good to see you again, but I am afraid I cannot stay long my friend. Joseph is unhappy regarding our work on the US Presidential elections," and reaching into his coat pocket and pulling out his black leather gloves, "I am only here to sort out some loose ends in the village."

"There are no loose ends William, it has been dealt with and as you know, our work together will always remain a secret."

The other man put on the first glove, "but can you keep a secret?" And he slipped on his second glove.

"You know I can, it is what we have based all our work on over the years."

"Unfortunately I cannot allow anything to impact my future standing within the party," and after reaching into his pocket once more, he smiled and walked over putting his arm around the other man`s shoulder. As he moved to thrust the cyanide capsule into the Chief Constable's mouth he was surprised to find a revolver barrel thrust under his chin. He tried to swallow but the tip of the cold gun prevented him.

"You thought to kill me!" Hissed the Chief Constable through clenched teeth as he slowly eased the pressure on Blacklock`s throat.

"No, no, I.... I just wanted to discuss a new plan, that`s all!"

The other man looked at him with contempt. "You have outgrown your usefulness," and Blacklock felt a cold knife blade slide into his ribcage and up into his heart.

With the body slumped on the floor, the Chief Constable

calmly walked over to the telephone that sat on the small table by the window and after a series of clicks and short conversations with the operator, he was put through.

"Simpson, it`s Burke, Pendlewick is secure. I will leave at dawn and await my next assignment."

It had been a gamble not to chase the last remnant of the German spy ring around the World and Simpson had put his neck on the line by leaving the agent in Pendlewick and eventually, he had come to them.

The Rear Admiral put down the phone and whispered to himself. "Damn and blast, I was right."

The following day, Britain declared war on Germany.

# *Epilogue*

## September 1939 - Scotland

The salty breeze washed over Robert Anderson`s face as he angled his motorcycle around a sweeping bend on his way to the tiny Scottish fishing village of *Auchmithie*.

Pulling up to a halt outside a whitewashed stone cottage, he removed his helmet, closed his eyes and took a deep breath of the sea air. *It`s grand tae be back!*

After turning off the engine he leaned the motorcycle against the dry-stone wall that marked the boundary to the small dwelling by the coast and tapped gently on the wooden door. Within a few moments, the door swung open and he smiled. "Well good mornin` tae ye Miss McGregor and `ow are we doin` on this fine day may I ask?"

The attractive middle-aged woman smiled, the laughter lines appearing by her pale blue eyes softening her face. "I am very well Inspector Anderson and it just so happens that I have not five minutes ago taken some of ye favourite Oat cakes out the oven, fresh and warm I might add."

"Och ma wee hen, ye certainly know the way tae ma heart," and he stepped towards her.

"Aye and I also know another way big man," and she

stepped into his embrace and kissed him tenderly.

# 55 Years Later, February 1994

## Pendlewick, East Lancashire

The old man lay in his bed and stared up at the ceiling of his bedroom and tried to give a wry smile to himself. It had been a good life and ideally he would like a little longer but, things were now out of his hands.

The young man tapped lightly then opened the door to his Grandad`s bedroom.

Peering through the gloom, he walked over and opened the curtains a fraction of an inch to let a sliver of light in which prompted a grunt and snort from the older man tucked up in the single bed. Walking over he gently stroked the dying man`s forehead and wiped a tear that was forming in his own eye.

"Grandad, it`s Tony, can yeh `ear me Grandad?"

The older man groaned with pain. "Ah Anthony, it`s grand tu see ya lad," and he pulled his trembling hand out from under the bed covers and held it towards his Grandson. "Did yer Mam tell yeh I was near th`end?"

"Aye, but yeh can fight it Grandad! Ye`ve fought all yer life, yeh can beat this as well", he pleaded.

The old man took a deep breath that crackled deep in his

lungs. "No lad, not this time. I`m buggered, an` I know it." He sighed and just managed to turn on his side to face his Grandson. "Come `ere lad, I needs tu tell yeh summat."

His Grandson knelt down by the bed and took hold of his Grandad`s hand. "What is it?"

"Can yeh keep a secret lad `cus there`s somethin` I need to tell yeh afore I leave this world, somethin` I`m not proud of."

"Yeh know I can keep a secret and we`ll always be proud of ya Grandad. Yeh`r a war `ero an` a decorated policeman, yeh `ave the medals tu prove it."

The older man slowly closed his eyes as if in thought. "Aye a war `ero," he whispered. "Lost many of me best mates on that beach `ead I did. If it weren't fer all them little boats rescuing us, there`d o`bin a lot more lad. Cut down like they weren`t never there. If only I `ad…….." But his voice trailed away to nothing.

His Grandson grabbed at his arm. "Grandad, don`t die, Grandad!"

The old man chuckled, the sound dry and rasping, "I`m not goin` anywhere yet lad. Now listen careful, I `as tu tell ya this. Did yeh know ah killed a man back in thirty-four, stone cold dead."

"Grandad, yeh don`t need tu tell me nothin`, it don`t matter now, it really don`t."

"Matters tu me lad now `ush, I `asn`t got long left. Man was called Davenport, Alf Davenport. Turns out `e was forcin` him sen on a lady friend o`mine be the name of Maureen Billington. Not proud tu say it, but I fancied her rotten, but she was married yeh see. She was a proper lady. Nice an` kind an` always had a smile fer me but in me youth, I took it wrong way and thought she was in love wi` me as well, an` love meks men do daft things. So, when ah found out `bout Davenport and it leadin` tu Maureen tekin` `er own life, well, I just lost it an` `ad tu do somat."

His Grandson bowed his head not wanting to leave but also not wanting to hear his Grandad`s confession.

"So ah follas him, an` every neet, seems `e follas t`same route `ome. Like clockwork. So one neet, ah borrows the Chief Constable`s gun from `is desk an` just `as `e gets on top o`t`gate, I shoots him right in t` back an` tu mek sure, I then walks o`er tu check an` `e is stone dead. Finished `im I `ad then I shoves an old pistol next tu `is hand tu mek it look like suicide, an` it wer` gud riddance tu the bastard. Day after we went up from t` station to look at body. Four of us there were, all policemen. Thought Jimmy Warburton might be on tu somat what wi `im talkin` `bout footprints an all, so I goes over an` steps about round body so me footprints were there, just i`case mind." His breath shuddered and his voice almost faded away, "ya still proud o` me now lad?"

The young man sniffed, and he wiped tears from his eyes but as he was about to speak, he realised the man had took his last breath, and after stroking his wrinkled face, he laid his head on his Grandad`s chest and wept.

Donald Herbert Jones was laid to rest in Saint Augustine`s Churchyard in Pendlewick two weeks later. His Grandson thought it ironic, that his Grandad`s and Alf Davenport`s graves were only feet apart, but he didn`t say anything to anyone, after all, he could keep a secret.

# End

If you enjoyed this book, why not try my first novel , Insurrection.

What would you do if someone asked you to take over a European country? What would you do if the person asking was a ghost?

Whilst exploring the beautiful countryside near his East Lancashire home, Thomas hears a voice in an ancient dialect.

Surprised to discover that he is intrinsically linked to the ancient Roman empire, he and his wife must join forces with a ghost and a mystic with supernatural powers in order to make the Roman Eagle rise again.

Embarking on a journey where they face adventure and danger at every turn, Thomas strives to throw off his self-doubts and develop his leadership skills in order to achieve the ancient prophecy.

Can he fulfil his destiny and emerge as the new uncompromising Caesar of modern-day Italy, a destiny that if successful, will prevent a disaster of Atlantean proportions and reverberate around the globe changing his life forever?

*Insurrection: An act or instance of revolting against civil authority or an established government.*

*I am prepared to resort to anything, to submit to anything, for the sake of the commonwealth.*

*Julius Caesar.*

## Prologue
### AD93 – Gallia Narbonensis - Gaul

"I am Gnaeus Julius Agricola, yet it is strange you choose my fifty third year to write of my life and achievements?" He looked suspiciously at the younger man. "Or is it because you sense my enemies are closing in?"

The two men had met in the darkened room, the cloying smell of burning incense sticks hung in the air as the older man rolled the black knife handle between his fingers. Taking a sip from his pewter goblet, he returned it gently to the table beside his low wooden bed.

"When I am free of this accursed and unexpected illness, Rome will rise once more and under my leadership, we will be the pinnacle that all civilisations admire and aspire to be. Our people will prosper like never before, but know this young man, the wheels are already set in motion."

"But father...."

"Do not call me father," hissed Gnaeus wiping the spittle from his mouth with the back of his trembling hand. "You are family only by marriage and I care not for the lies you put to paper."

Tacitus walked over and picked up the pewter goblet offering it to the older man. "You are not well, please take some more of the potion I had made, it will make you well again."

Gnaeus reached for the goblet and tried to take another drink but his grip was weak, and it slipped from his grasp and fell to the floor with a clang. "It has already been foretold and in this darkened room, I can sense my future here is coming to an end, but the plans are already in place and my spirit will live on to see Rome great again. It is my spirit`s destiny to seek out the Grandfather of Luca in Britannia, for only he can make the Eagle rise again." Gnaeus took a final long shuddering breath. "So much to do, so much I can offe..."

"Father...." Tacitus realised that Gnaeus Julius Agricola was no longer of this world.

He calmly walked over and gazed down at the body of the once powerful Roman Governor of Britannia and smiled as he put his hand into his pocket. Pulling out two small objects, he carefully placed a coin over each of the dead man`s eyes, then walked thoughtfully back towards the door.

"I hope the ferryman likes you more than I did...... father," he said bitterly without turning around.

"Ubi est avo De Luca," came the ethereal reply.

Tacitus paused at the door, half turned his head on hearing the sound, then quickly hastened from the room. Moments later, the manservant entered and on seeing his master`s body, duly collected the knife as instructed.

October 1914 – Dinkley, East Lancashire.

Annie Braithwaite was an adventurous twelve-year-old, but oh how she hated Sunday school.

Why should she sit listening to boring stories told by a man who must be at least two hundred years old when she could watch the red squirrels in her favourite wood by the river? Here, Annie had become obsessed by the little creatures after she had read a book about one called Squirrel Nutkin.

It was written by a lady called Betty Potter or something like that, Annie couldn`t remember, she was not good at remembering names and to her, it didn`t matter. She could remember what a beautiful red squirrel looked like though and she liked nothing more than slowly creeping in between the brambles and bushes to get as close as she could to them.

Each Sunday morning, she would put on her best tunic, hooded black shawl and her riding boots that had been passed down to her from her older sister Hannah, on the pretext of attending Sunday school. Of course she had no intention of actually attending, but the outfit was snug and warm against the Autumn chill and her riding boots protected her legs from the needle-sharp thorns in the woods.

Her school friends had told her not to go into Dinkley Woods as it was haunted. This had also been confirmed by her sister Hannah who constantly berated her for her repeated visits. According to Annie this was absolute

piffle and was only a made-up tale to keep children from
missing Sunday School.

It was only about four in the afternoon as she made her
way through the damp and prickly bushes towards the
riverbank, but the sun was already getting low in the sky
casting long shadows across the muddy ground. Annie
shrugged to herself knowing full well her mother would
now be well aware that she had skipped Sunday School,
again.

Then she spotted him sitting on a fallen log by the riverbank, eating an old acorn he had just dug up.

Annie was fascinated how the little fellow could sit on
his haunches and hold the food between his paws nib-
bling away until he had finished. Suddenly the squirrel
became anxious, his bushy auburn tale flicking from side
to side, his eyes darting right, left, then upwards. Within
a flash, he had deftly shot off up a large nearby oak tree
and was gone.

"Ubi est avo De Luca," came a faint whisper that drifted
away on the breeze.

Annie, gently biting the corner of her bottom lip, looked
around nervously but could see nothing.

"Ubi est avo De Luca," came the plaintive cry again,
almost drowned out by the noise of the wind rustling the
Autumn leaves above her.

Annie peered through the dappled light to a large flat
rock by the flowing river and there, no more than ten
feet from her she saw a man dressed in a strange uniform
holding an outstretched arm to her as he sat on the rock.
At first, she thought she couldn`t see him clearly because
of the late afternoon mist forming like a blanket over the
cold river, but then she realised the figure wasn`t clear at
all; his image seemed to shift and swirl as though he was

made of the mist himself.

"Ubi est avo De Luca," he cried one more time as he rose from the rock and walked towards Annie.

With her heart pounding as though it was going to burst from her chest, Annie could not stand it any longer and she turned on her heel and ran towards the small country lane that led back to her house and as she did, she slipped and slid in the damp mud and tripped head long over an exposed tree root.

Covered in mud and woodland debris all down the front of her shawl and tunic, she scrambled to get back to her feet whilst all the time, desperately looking behind her at the oncoming figure.

Back on her feet she finally reached the stile in the old dry-stone wall. She was so terrified she almost leapt through in one go and smashed straight into a tall figure who grabbed her tightly around the shoulders.

"Now, now little Annie, what`s all the rush about and look at you, you are filthy girl?"

Annie looked up into the kind eyes of Harold Radcliffe, the local farmer, and started to shake and cry. Half turning, she pointed a trembling finger towards the wood.

"A ghost chased me Mister Radcliffe, a ghost talking all funny and chasing me, Mister Radcliffe."

"Ah, a ghost is it, well lucky your mother sent me along to look for you then isn`t it?" He peered into the darkening wood for several seconds looking one way then the other with squinted eyes as a way of showing Annie that he did believe her tale about the ghost. "Well," he said bending down and smiling to the young girl, "looks like that ghost of yours has gone back to bed, which is where I believe your mother is going to send you as soon as we get you back home."

The pair set off down the lane, Annie`s small mud-covered fingers gripping the farmer`s huge hand for comfort whilst taking furtive looks behind her to make sure nobody was following them.

Harold waved goodbye at Annie`s front door. "Take it easy on her Mavis, she doesn`t mean any harm, and to be honest, I hated Sunday School as well."

"Get yourself back to your farm Harold Radcliffe and don`t you be encouraging my daughters into mischief," scolded Mavis as she slammed the front door shut. Realising she had taken her annoyance with Annie out on the farmer, she quickly pulled the front door open again and shouted, "thank you Harold, pop round for some apple pie in the morning......, if you want to, that is."

Harold gave a nonchalant wave of his hand and disappeared behind the hedge and down the lane back to his farm. Mavis could hear his happy whistling get quieter and quieter till eventually he was out of sight.

She shut the door, tutted and shook her head. "Silly Mavis Braithwaite, what would a fine gentleman like Harold Radcliffe be doing getting all interested in a widow like you?"

In the days and months that followed, Annie`s insistence on seeing the ghost gave her constant nightmares where she would wake up screaming in the middle of the night drenched in sweat. The fact that nobody believed her only compounded the situation.

She felt particularly let down by her sister who, instead of trying to understand Annie`s feelings, told her how she was silly and how the other girls where making fun of her. They would ask every day, "how is mad Annie today?" She then took out her frustration and embarrassment on her younger sister.

The cruelty of young children who teased and bullied her at school meant that Annie stayed in her bedroom day after day rocking back and forth on her tiny bed. Her Mother often found her gazing out of the window and blamed the new Roman museum being built in Ribchester for the silly fantasies her daughter was having every day.

Annie`s only comfort, was a toy red squirrel that Harold Radcliffe had made for her using some old straw, ebony beads and some dye made from left-over elderberry juice. She loved the way the small beads Harold had stitched into the straw face gleamed at her when she held it.

Now, the little toy squirrel was the only thing she trusted in her young life and two years later Annie, clutching her tattered little squirrel, entered the recently built Sixth Lancashire County Asylum near Whalley and never left again.

## Chapter 1 -
### AD79 - Bremetennacum Veteranorum, Britannia.

The Decurion took one last look at his men assembled outside the timber fort and swallowed nervously as the entourage approached.

He stood to attention and took a deep breath then bellowed. "We welcome you Governor Agricola."

Gnaeus Julius Agricola ran his trained eye over the Decurion before him. The waiting cavalry stationed here had Spanish origins which were unmistakable, as was the discipline and attention to detail.

Their mounts fidgeted nervously in the soft mud. The creaking of the immaculate, freshly oiled leather traces and the snorting breath from the horse`s nostrils were the only sounds punctuating the silence. The mounted men were stern, battle-hardened veterans and they stared straight ahead awaiting a review by the Roman Governor of Britannia.

The Decurion had the swarthy looks of a Cypriot, with short cropped black hair and olive coloured eyes it was clear he was not a true Roman but the many scars on his muscular forearms clearly demonstrated his undying devotion to Rome.

Removing his polished ceremonial helmet and nodding in the direction of the waiting cavalrymen, Gnaeus smiled contentedly. "I shall inspect your cavalry now Decurion Cyprian."

Gnaeus always went against tradition by removing his helmet when inspecting the legions. He had done so ever since an earlier experience during the civil war where a lack of pay and poor conditions had caused a distinct feeling of mutiny to hang in the air. Gnaeus had bravely walked into the centre of the restless legionnaires with his battle-damaged helmet under his arm and resolved the situation. He felt it displayed he trusted them implicitly, and more importantly, that he feared nothing.

"If your men perform as well as you did in Mona young man, then Rome is in good hands. Lead the way Decurion."

Cyprian quickly replaced his own helmet and fastened the chin strap. He swelled with pride and led the way to the waiting cavalry assembled outside the fort gates. The Governor of Britannia knew of my actions…. my name, he thought to himself as he marched towards his men. Father would be so proud.

As Gnaeus approached the line of mounted cavalry, his

voice rang with authority. "Ah, I see we have the legendary Silver Eagle amongst us gentlemen."

The cavalry men fought back smiles of appreciation, iron Roman discipline still on show.

As far as Gnaeus was concerned, the Decurion and the other men were just soldiers of Rome. People from a myriad of lands around the Mediterranean, Gaul, Iberia.... the list went on. These were soldiers from lands and provinces Rome had had either conquered or peaceably occupied, but he had found over the years it did no harm to ask the names of the soldiers he would meet or learn some of their exploits beforehand. This as always, he had done. High morale in the legions was a trait Gnaeus actively encouraged and in most cases, it was easy to obtain by using simple techniques.

"Names and achievements," he whispered to his Centurion as they dismounted and strode towards the waiting men outside the fort.

"Decurion Cyprian, Sire, an excellent soldier and cavalryman, fought well in Mona by all accounts. The one on the grey horse is nicknamed the Silver Eagle and is well respected by his fellow Alaris."

"We welcome you Governor Agricola."

"I shall inspect your cavalry now Decurion Cyprian.........."

Concluding the inspection, Gnaeus retired to his quarters and slumped into a chair awaiting the news as to when his bath was ready. It had been a long journey from the South, and he took immense pleasure in a hot bath, even if it was just a temporary arrangement that had been organised by Lucius his man servant.

"One of the truly great inventions of Rome," he had once told his friends whilst entertaining in the Atrium of his villa in Tuscany. "It is my humble opinion gentlemen, that the great Roman Empire invented roads only so we can get ourselves to the bath houses with more haste." Gnaeus smiled at the memory and at last, Lucius came, bowed as low as his elderly frame would allow, and informed his master that the bath was now ready.

Bremetennacum Veteranorum had developed well since his last visit and was becoming an important mechanism for controlling the unruly hoards in the surrounding areas. A small town was developing around the Fort and it was now an important Roman settlement. The outpost was also a logical stopover on his way to evaluate his strategy for conquering the savages in the very north of this misty island. Having seen how the area had developed, Gnaeus was pleased that the influence of his beloved Rome reached this far into Britannia.

More importantly though, they planned to build bath houses there.

Stripping off his white wool toga and tunic, he lay back in the warm water, the scented oils relaxing his tired muscles and he dreamed of his estates back in Tuscany. He must have dozed as he didn`t hear the footsteps of the woman, nor even notice her, until she was standing right next to him. He momentarily tensed but then relaxed; if she was a danger to him, he would already be leaking his life blood into the bath water.

He gazed up at the old woman who, from the look and smell of her, needed the bath much more than he did and as she opened her mouth to speak, he noticed only one crooked brown tooth.

She looked down at him and drool began to seep from the side of her mouth. "As much as it pains me, I must give you this message as I am in debt to the spirit who sent it."

On the plus side, thought Gnaeus, she spoke Latin perfectly, which proved that looks are often deceptive. "You are a brave woman to enter a Roman fort just to give me a message, hag, especially since no doubt the guards could smell you well before you arrived."

The old woman cackled, the sound like the burning of dry bracken. "They said you were a.... nice man," she said sarcastically, "but I will give you the message anyway as I am sworn in death to do so."

Gnaeus sighed. "You have two more heartbeats to give me your message, then you will be dragged out of here by my guards." A group he would deal with afterwards for allowing the hag to get so close to him in the first place.

"Your spirit must seek out the Grandfather of Luca for he is the only one to make the Eagle rise again."

"I must seek out the what? Guards, guards, to me!"

Within seconds, five legionnaires sprinted into the tented bath house their Gladii already hissing from the leather scabbards.

"Take the ha.... hag," ordered Gnaeus, as he circled in the water looking for the woman, but the bath house was empty apart from himself and the five guards.

After a thorough search of the area to ensure there was no danger, one of the guards approached Gnaeus. "Is all well Sire?"

Gnaeus looked at the guard thoughtfully. "All....is well, return to your posts and say nothing of this."

The guards returned their Gladii to their scabbards, slammed their fisted arms across their chests in salute and marched from the improvised bath house.

Chapter 2.
October 2019 – Dinkley Woods, East Lancashire.

Thomas had parked up near some bushes and as he passed by, he nodded to a man who was busily trying to round up his children.

The young man clapped his hands and then waved them to the nearby car. "Okay it`s late, now let`s be getting home, you don`t want the ghost to catch us do you?" The fearful look on his face was enough to make them squeal and they pushed and shoved each other into the car, buckling up their seat belts without any hesitation. Their anxious looks as they scanned the bushes and pathways as they drove from the car park made Thomas smile.

A ghost in Dinkley Woods, it was a local legend happily promoted by the locals.

Sitting on a rock or up in a tree, on a fence, over eight feet tall, the size of a child, surrounded by mist, only seen at twilight.... the tales went on and on and only differed depending on who told the story or claimed to have seen the ghost.

The only consistent thing with all the tales was that the ghost spoke in a strange language.

Channel 6 had even aired a programme to try and prove or disprove the legend. A group of so-called celebrities had spent the night in the wood by the River Ribble scaring the life out of each other with Blair Witch style filming but in the end, concluded there was no mysterious apparition.

To be honest, Thomas sat on the fence when it came to the existence of anything paranormal.

He was open minded on the subject and didn`t really lose sleep over it one way or the other. In fact, in his early teenage years he had visited the local corner shop and had seen Mickey Johnson, a young boy who he vaguely

knew, wandering around between the grocery shelves.
On returning home, his mother was washing dirty pots
in the kitchen sink as Thomas walked in and poured himself a glass of cold milk from the refrigerator.

"Such a shame about that little Mickey Johnson. Did you
know he was killed in a car accident last week?"
Thomas stopped in mid-swallow and had mused over
his mother`s question. He was positive he had just seen
Mickey but then he had shrugged and thought he was
probably mistaken. He had never seen another ghost
since then.

Now forty years later, Thomas was going on his favourite
walk by the River Ribble. He was new to the area having moved into a small cottage with his wife eighteen
months earlier and had heard about the ghost stories in
the local pub, the Brown Cow.

The barflies had told him the story so many times. They
were real characters and that is why this pub was one of
his favourite haunts. "You like walkin down by the River
do ya? Watch out fer them ghosts then big lad, they will
av ya."

They liked nothing better than to tell the tale to the naïve
holiday makers from the caravan site next door who descended on the area each Spring.

"Buy me a pint and I`ll tell ya a guaranteed spot to see
that ghost," they would promise. "Ah you must not av
been lookin properly," was the standard reply when the
disappointed holiday makers returned from yet another
ghost free zone.

For years, many local people had avoided the Dinkley
woods. Not because they were afraid of a ghost, oh no,
only because there were... well, other areas they could
walk instead weren`t there?

As he sauntered down the tree-covered winding path that descended to the river, Thomas realised he wasn`t afraid of much. At over six feet tall and well built, he didn`t really need to be. Well, not exactly true, he wasn't afraid of anyone physically. He knew he could look after himself and had done so very competently in the past, so a ghost story didn`t bother him at all. His uncle even reckoned Thomas could pull up tree stumps with his bare hands and over the years, he had been casually questioned in bar conversations about fights and scrapes in earlier life.

 "You haven't got a mark on that pretty face of yours so looks like you managed to keep out the way of trouble." Which wasn`t totally correct. He didn`t have a mark on his face because he had always been able to anticipate trouble and was able to get away the first punch, after which, the assailants were in no position to get anywhere near his face.

Thomas fondly remembered his Dad`s advice when first going to school. "If any of the boys tries anything, tries to push you around or bully you, don`t ask questions, just hit 'em as hard as you can on their nose, they`ll not do it again lad."

And his Dad had been right. At both Junior school and Secondary school, they had tried it on, but only ever the one time. After that, he was left alone by the bully boys who went for easier pickings. Unless of course Thomas was on hand to do the right thing and have a quiet word with them.

Thomas wasn`t religious in any way but he knew what was right and wrong. His parents had strong 'Christian' values, and these had rubbed off on him, though he didn`t need any number of commandments to advise him on how to behave. He knew picking up a stranded worm in the middle of the road and putting it into some soft damp soil was the right thing to do. And he didn`t need to be told that being courteous to people was the right thing to do either.

He was an accomplished manufacturing engineer and had decided to retire early due to a stroke. His wife, who had a very well-paid job in finance was happy to be the bread winner and had encouraged Thomas to take it easy. But he found it difficult to take it easy.

He had come to terms with the fact that there was a very good health reason why he had to give up smoking his favourite Cuban cigars, but what really irked and frustrated him was that in his opinion, the country`s political system was wrong.

Thomas failed to see how many members of Parliament could ignore the will of the very people who voted them into that position.

Thomas would also despair at the media. Where had all the excellent journalists gone? He was all in favour of a free press and freedom of speech, but he felt that many went against the good of the country with their sensationalist headlines in order to gain profit. This would be one of the first areas he would deal with if he ever ruled the country.

He had pondered the subject many times. It was his view that only during times of conflict could a country make a step change in how it was governed when the populace was seeking inspiration and hope. He had said many times that dictators such as Adolf Hitler would have been laughed out of Germany had he tried to come to power with his thoughts and visions in the 1980s when most of the German population was happy and prosperous. It had been the right place and time.

I could lead a country; I would be a good leader. He had once thought to himself. No, you wouldn`t, you can`t even stand up in front of your own family and do a speech without falling to pieces, never mind stand up in Parliament for Prime Minister`s question time.

So, Thomas gained solace by walking in the beautiful countryside near their home.

He had travelled the world over, but here, his heart lifted at the beauty of the British landscape. Only one other place in the world gave him such elation, and that was Italy. Whenever he visited, Thomas felt as though he belonged there, almost an unconscious affinity with the country. He had travelled there many times, both with work and for holidays.

It was now dusk and the ideal time for Thomas to spot wildlife down by the river. This was another of his favourite pastimes and he made his way down the path then turned right along the riverbank towards the fields. The setting sun was playing through the tree branches making it difficult to see clearly so he shaded his eyes with the palm of his hand and as he looked towards the nearside riverbank a strange localised mist appeared, clinging and swirling like grey smoke to a large flat granite rock.

"Ubi est avo De Luca," came a sibilant voice. "Ubi est avo De Luca".

Thomas turned around slowly trying to see where the sound was coming from. The lads at the Brown Cow knew he walked here around this time of day and no doubt Billy Rogerson would find it hilarious to tell everyone how he had duped the big lad.

The voice came again. "Ubi est avo De Luca," this time

more pained.

Thomas had attended a Grammar school and to this day had never understood why they taught the kids Latin, but he could just make out from the sound that this seemed to be Latin.

One more time came the now desperate cry. "Ubi est avo De Luca," then all was quiet.

Thomas listened again but could hear nothing except for the soft babbling of the river as it tumbled over the smooth rocks on its way to the sea. The swirling mist had gone, and the river was clear again. Ubi est avo De Luca, something about where or why is Luca, mused Thomas. So he set off with the words Ubi est avo De Luca still running through his mind.

Back home and after taking off his jacket and muddy boots, he looked at the dog-eared notes from his childhood, shook his head and decided to boot up his laptop where he started to research the phrase on the internet. It didn`t take him long. He put the phrase into an online translator and pressed go. It took a few spelling variations, his Latin was understandably rusty, but eventually he got the translation he was looking for. He typed, Ubi est avo De Luca, pressed go, and was immediately presented with - Where is the Grandfather of Luca.

Mm, that doesn't make a lot of sense, he thought to himself as he stretched his arms in the air and yawned.

Just then his wife returned home from work and bustled into the small living room. "Good news luv," and she quickly slipped her trench coat off and put her brown leather briefcase on the dining table beside Thomas`s laptop. "Livvy just messaged me, her and Richard have chosen the baby`s name, let`s give them a ring and find out what they have gone for."

Excitedly, they called their daughter, after all, the first grandchild for any parent is a big moment in life.

"Livvy, it`s Mum and Dad. Well go on, what`s his name going to be?"

"Well, we know how much you both love Italy, so we are going to call him Luca."

Thomas`s stomach turned over, his blood ran cold and for the first time in his life, he was scared..........

Insurrection is available on Amazon
https://www.amazon.co.uk/dp/B08L3NRTY7

Printed in Great Britain
by Amazon